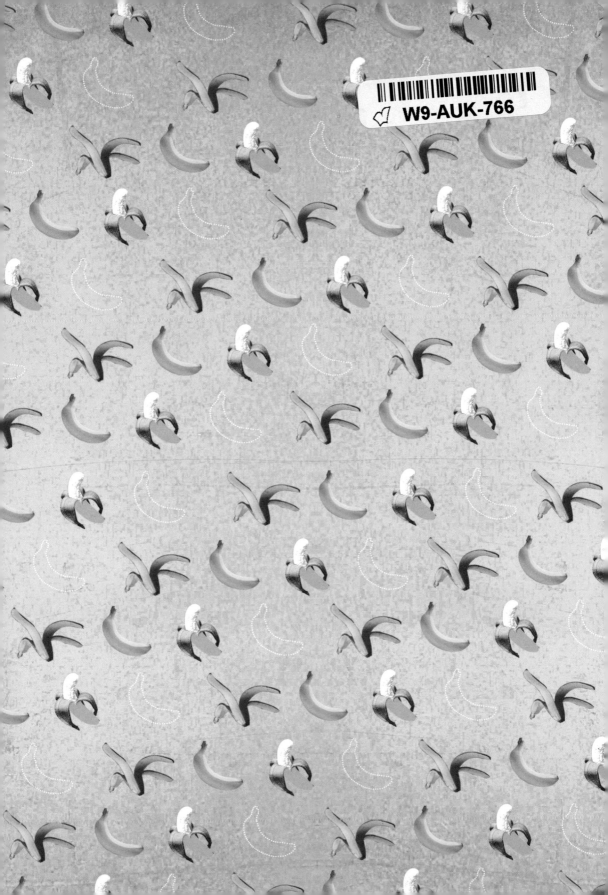

CAPTAIN COCONUT

& THE CASE OF THE MISSING BANANAS

A Number Mystery by
Anushka Ravishankar

Illustrated by
Priya Sundram

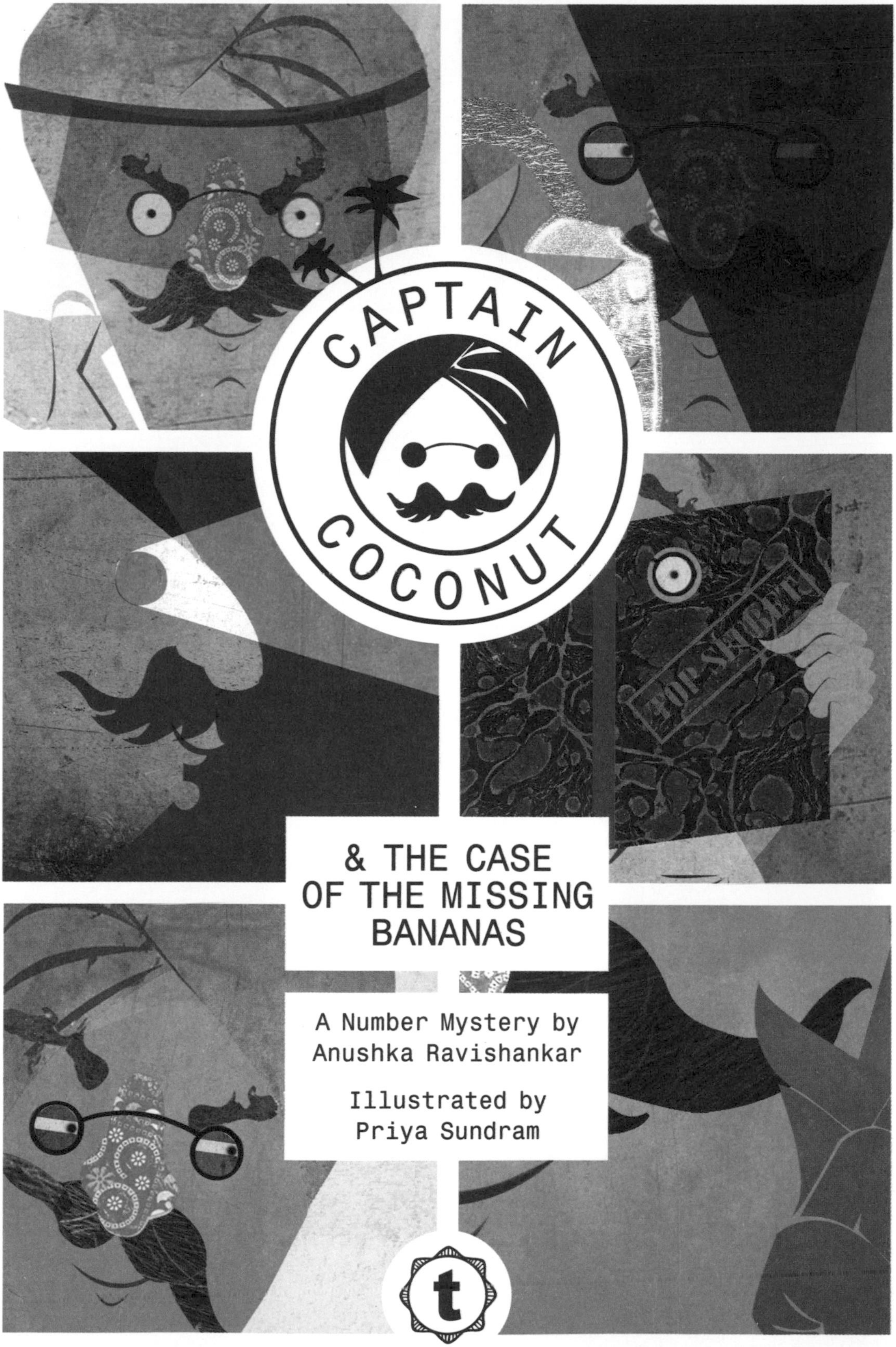

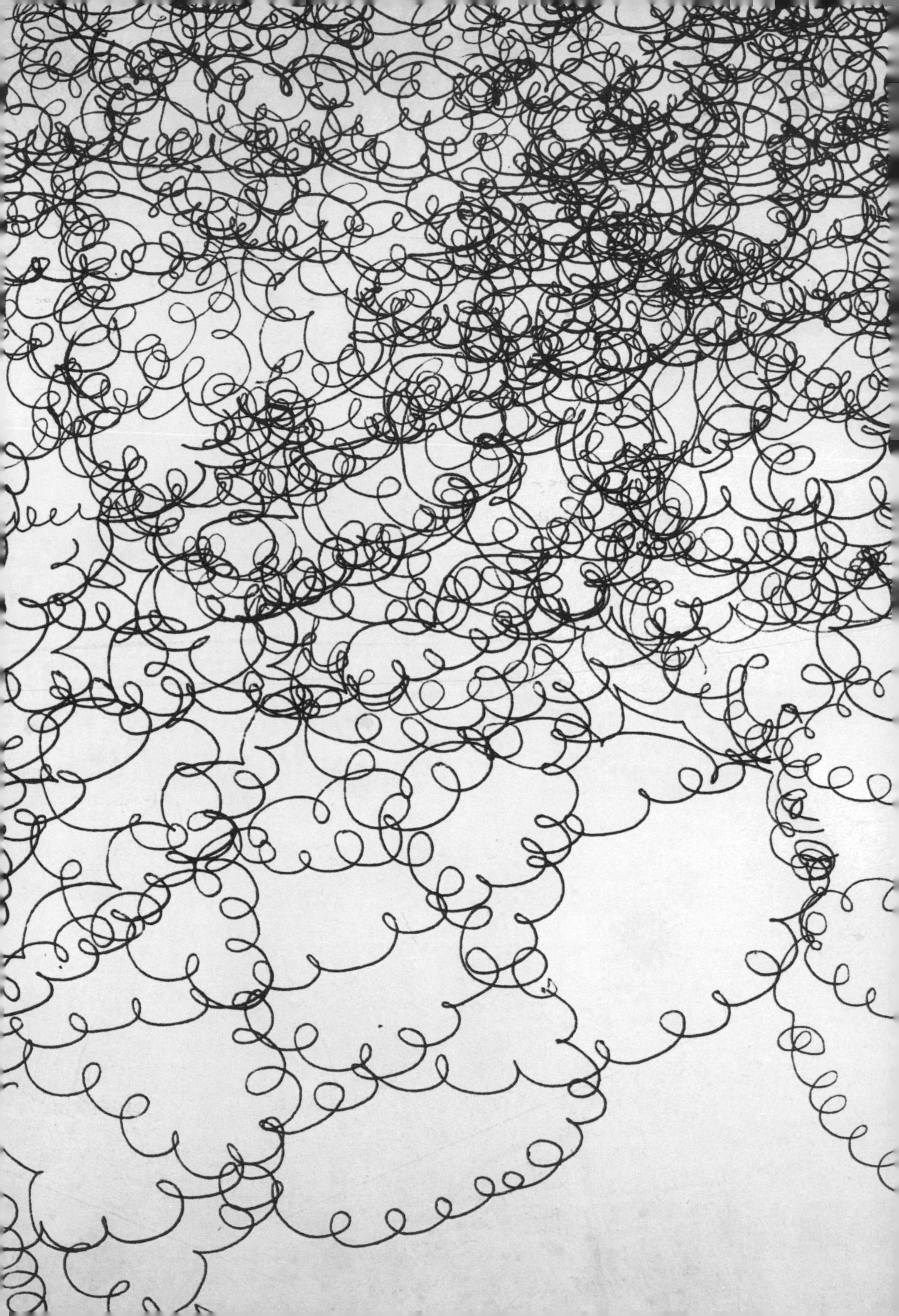

1

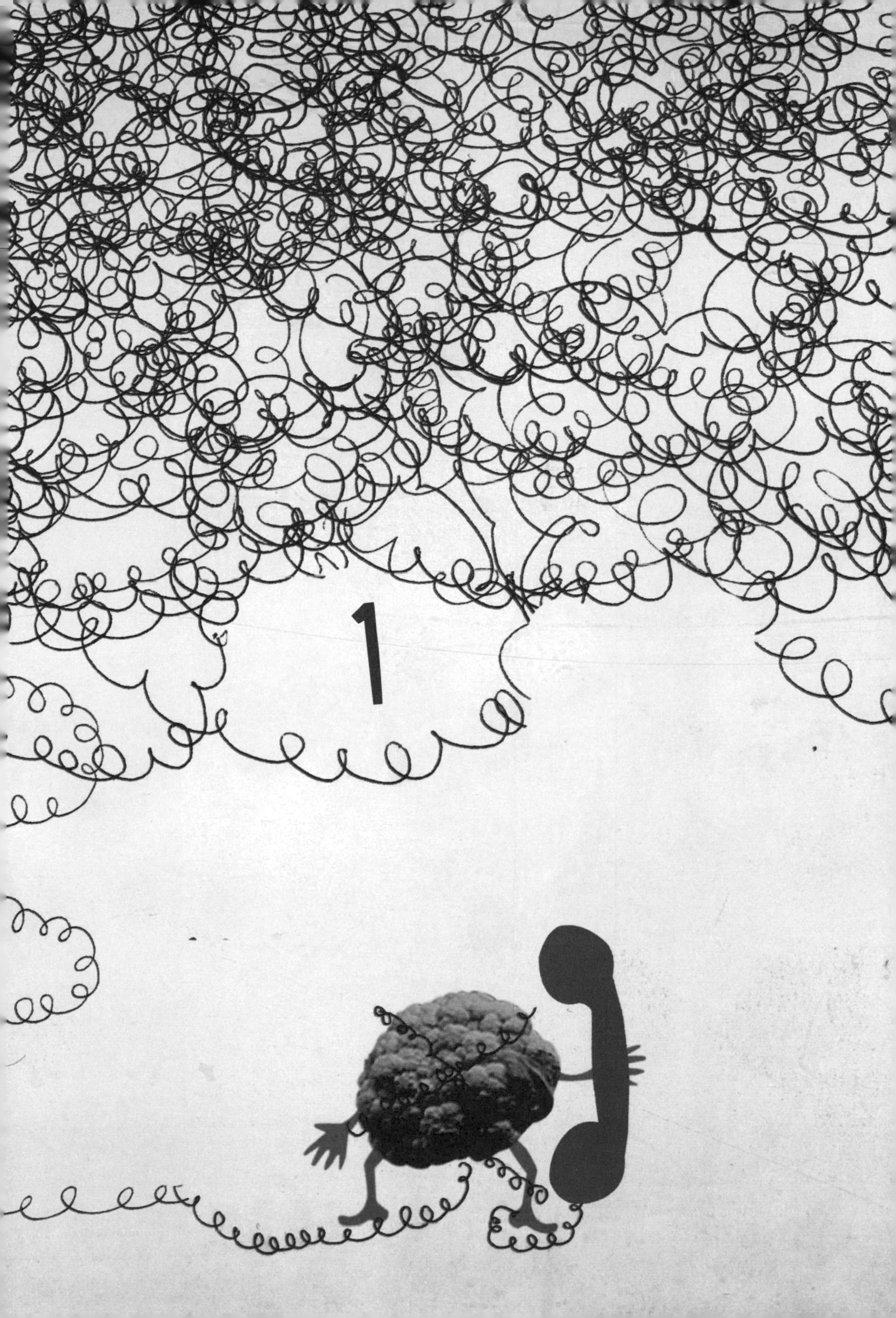

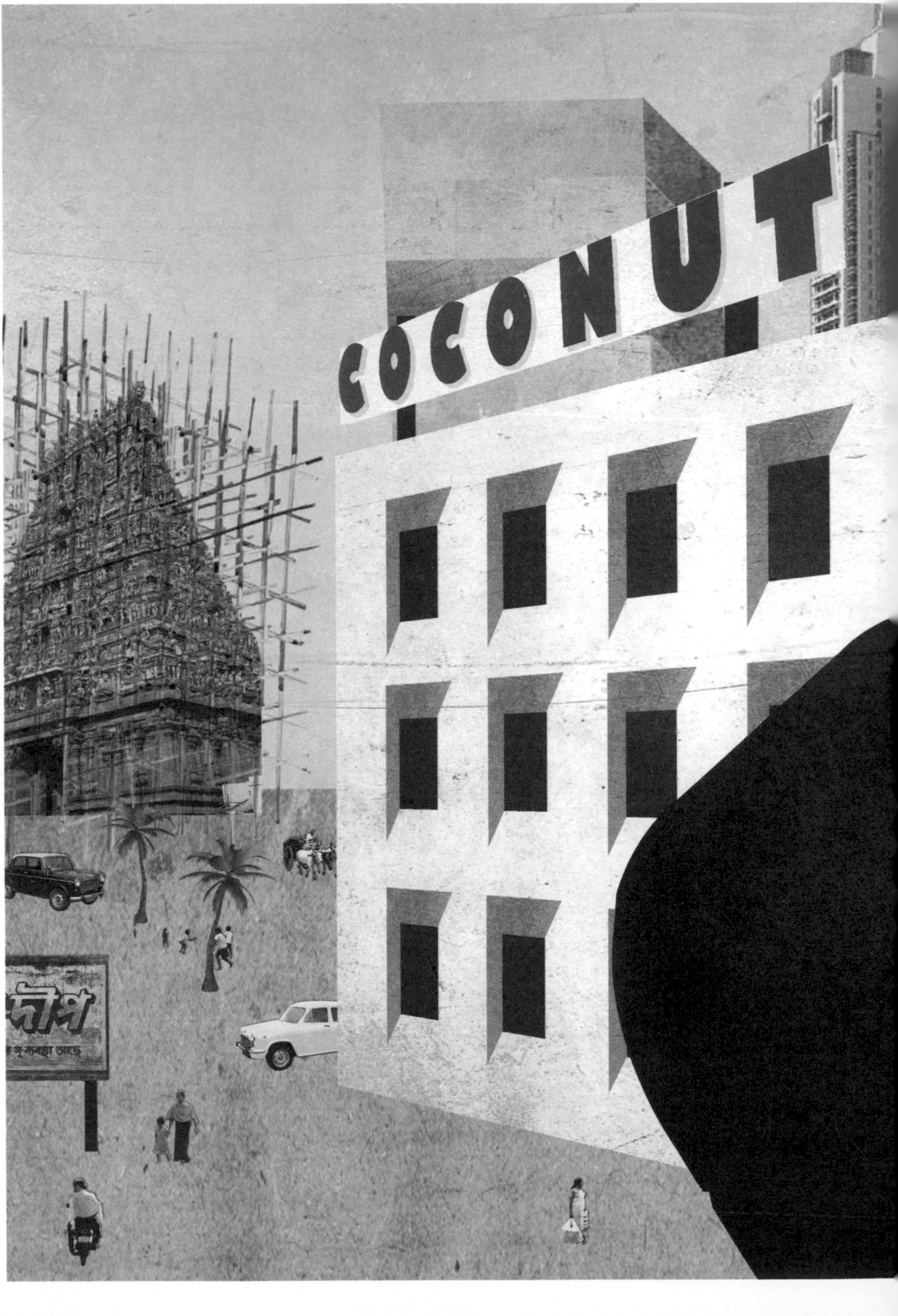
COCONUT

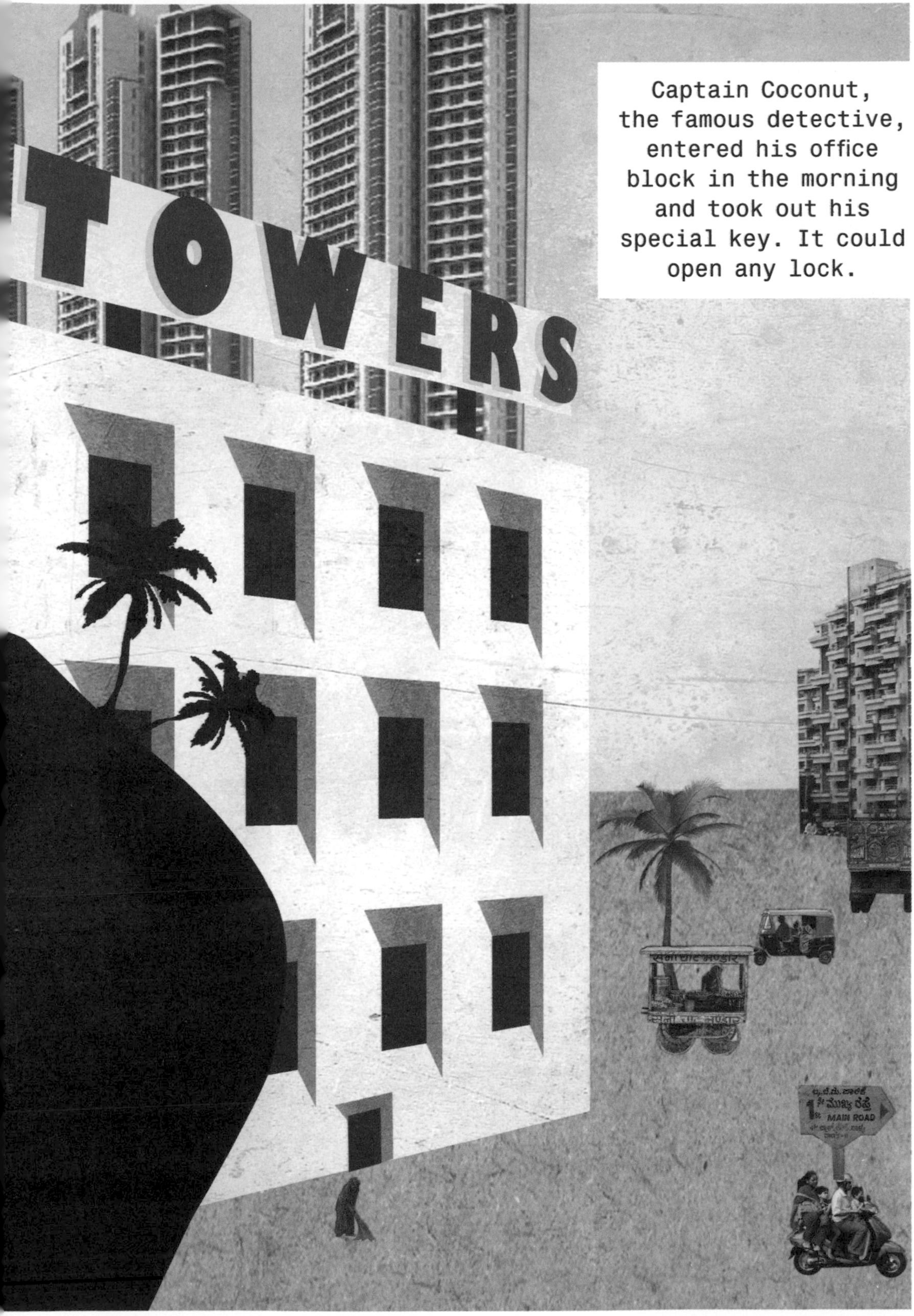
TOWERS
Captain Coconut, the famous detective, entered his office block in the morning and took out his special key. It could open any lock.
MAIN ROAD

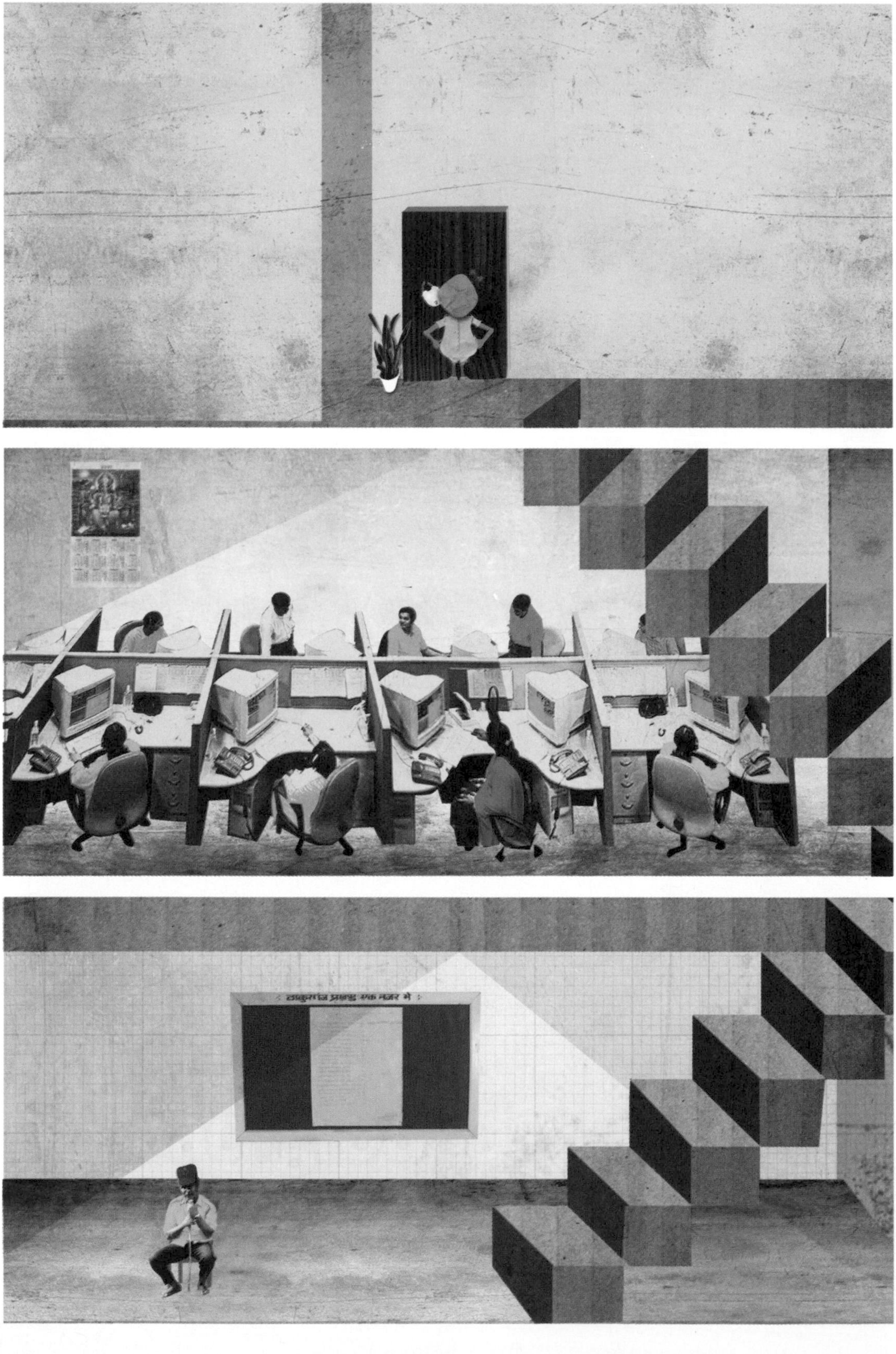

But it could not open the door to his office.

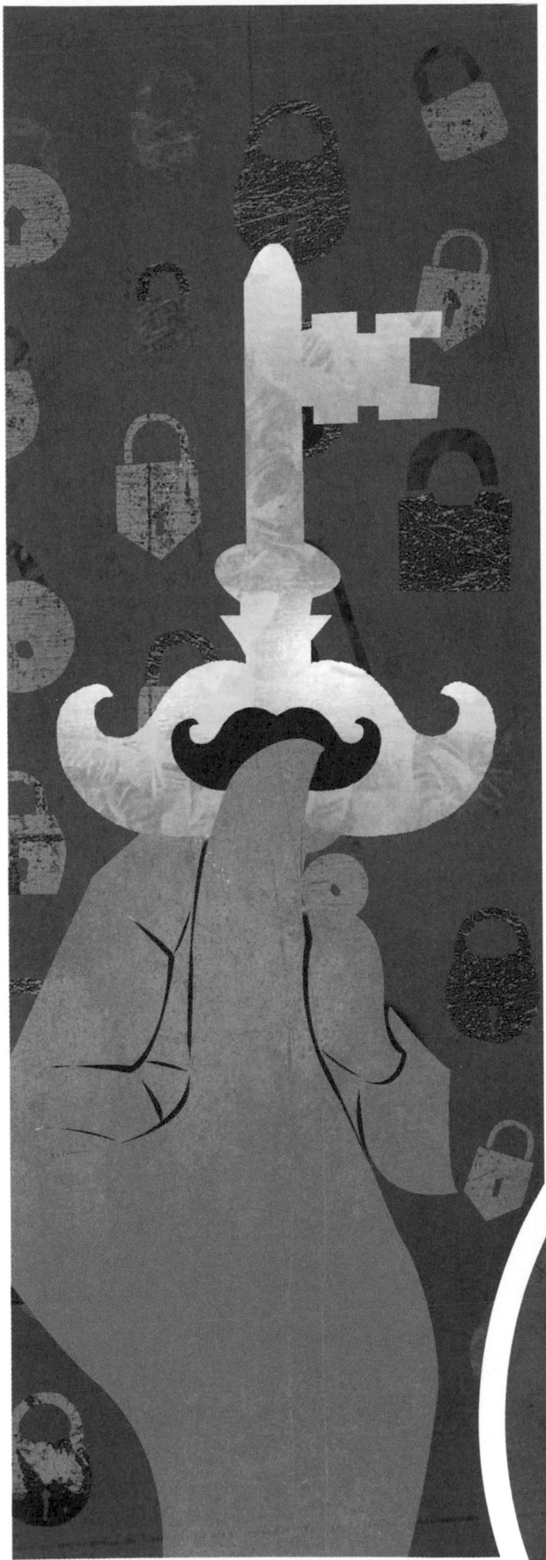

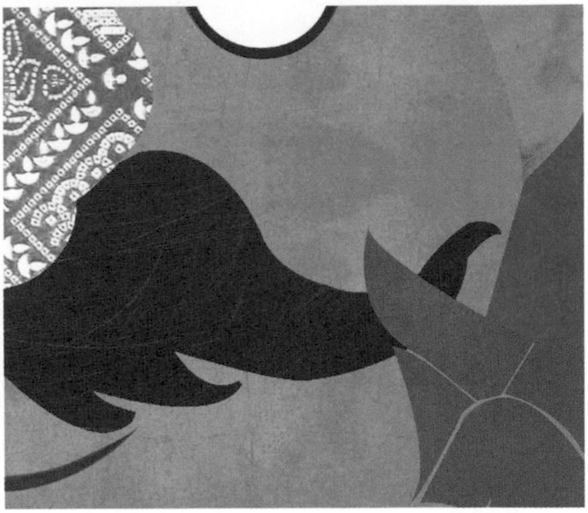

Captain Coconut smiled at his cleverness. He had put a special lock on the door only last night.

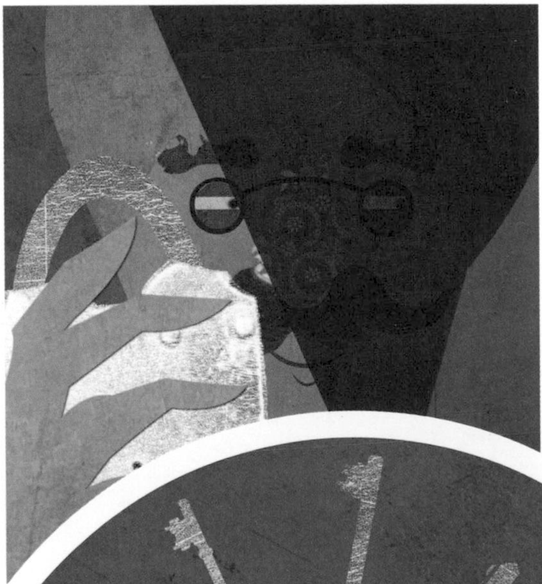

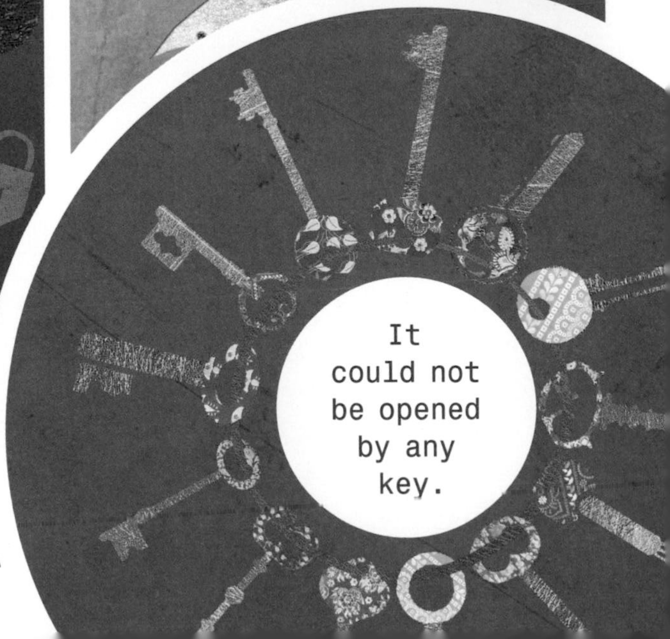
It could not be opened by any key.

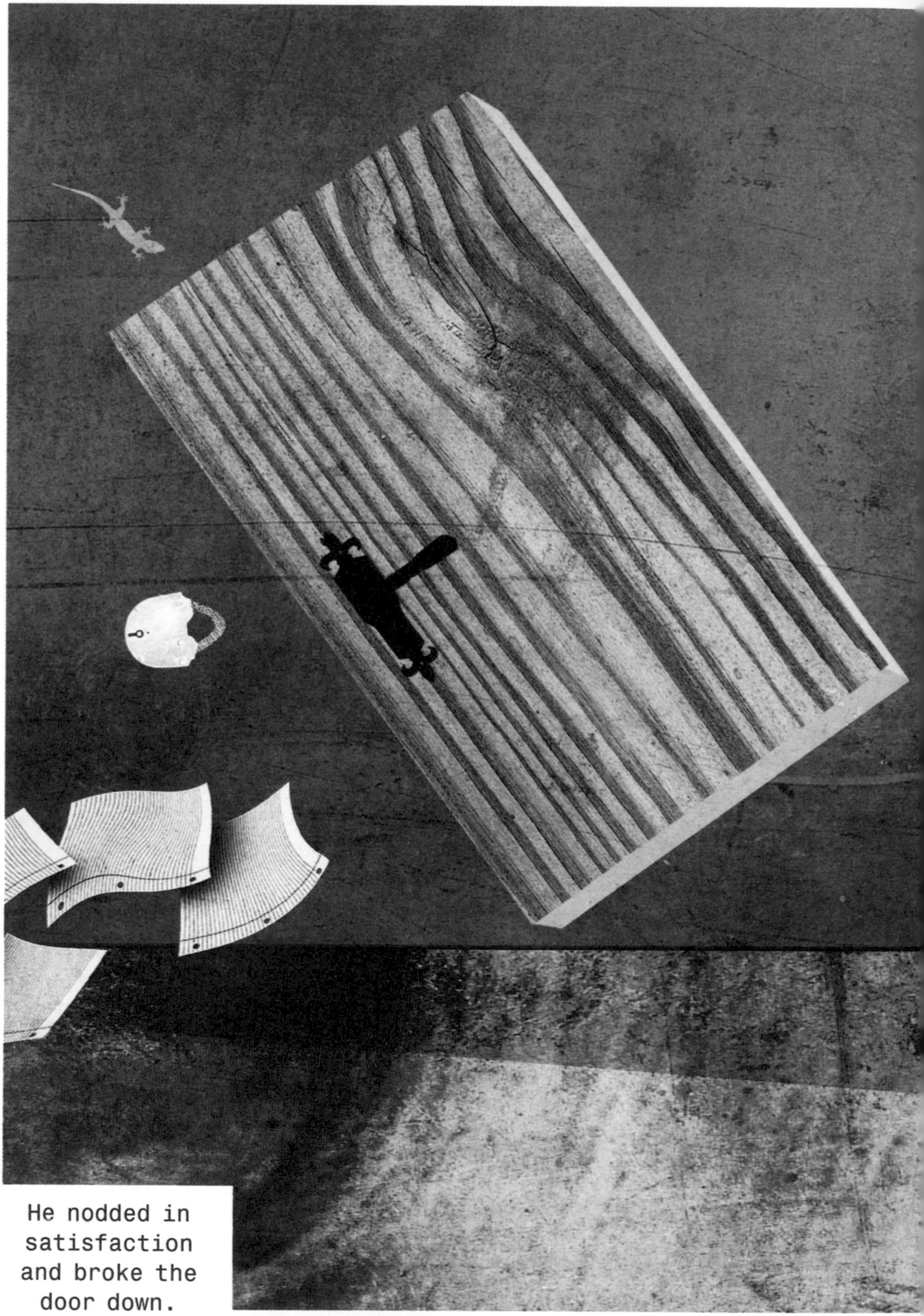

He nodded in
satisfaction
and broke the
door down.

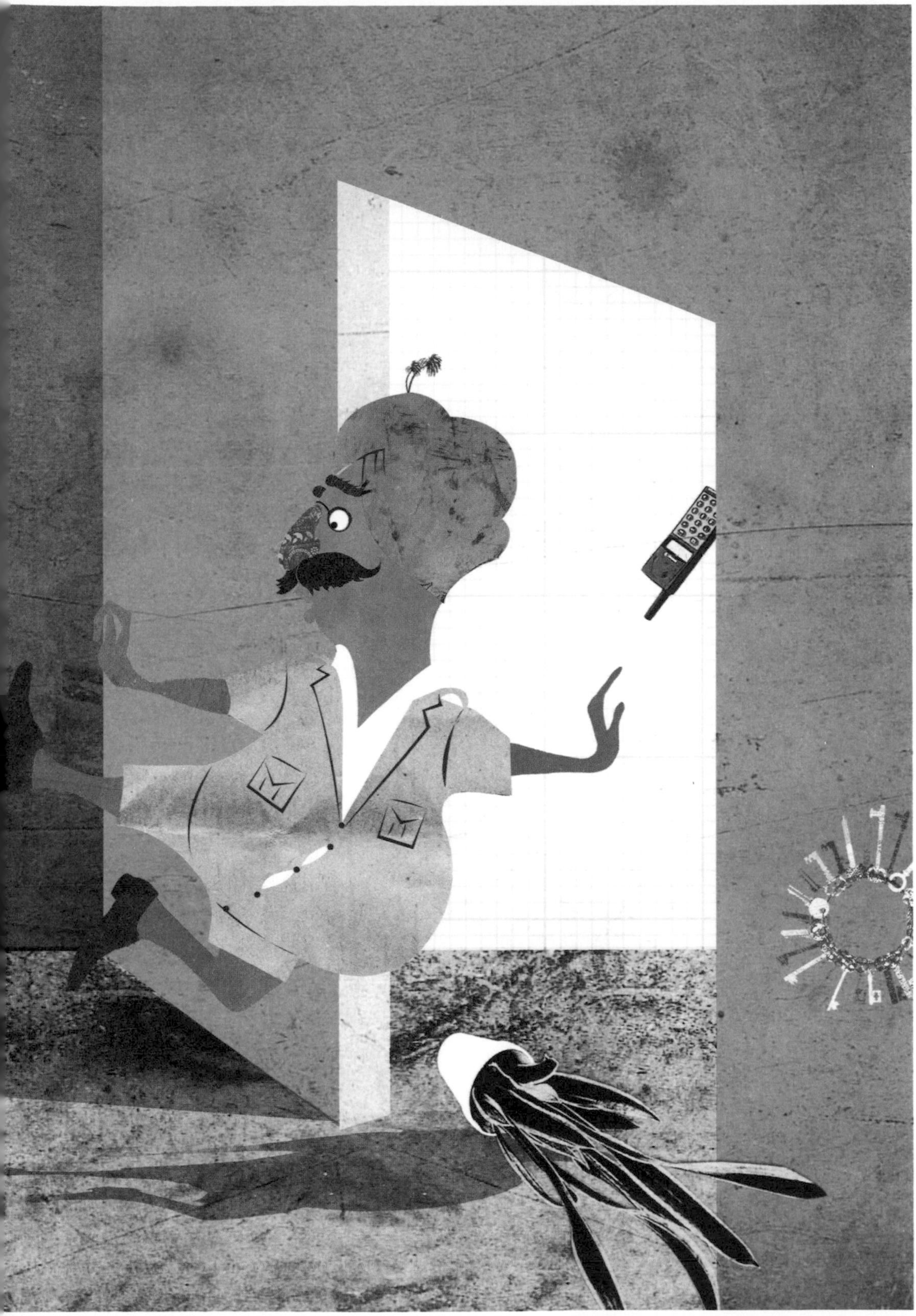

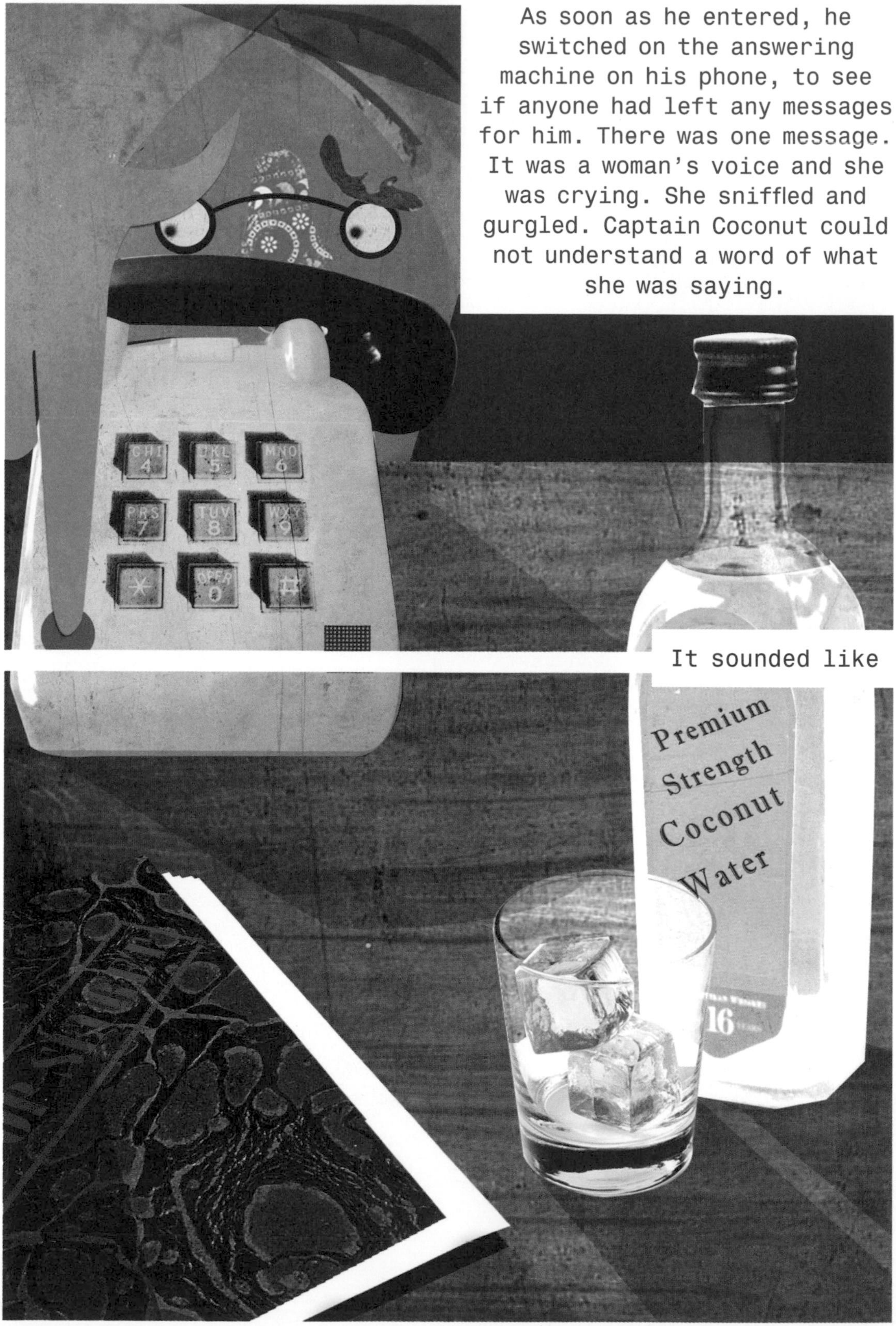
As soon as he entered, he switched on the answering machine on his phone, to see if anyone had left any messages for him. There was one message. It was a woman's voice and she was crying. She sniffled and gurgled. Captain Coconut could not understand a word of what she was saying.
It sounded like
Premium Strength Coconut Water
16

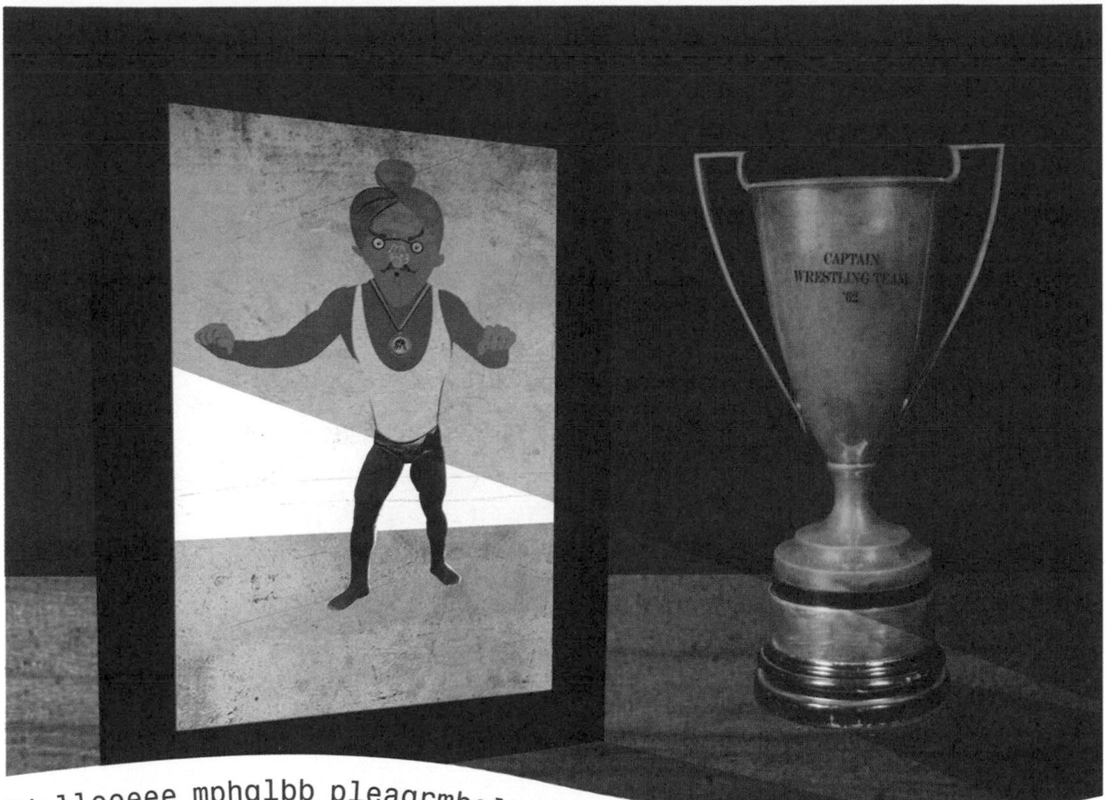
CAPTAIN
WRESTLING TEAM
'62

'Helleeeee mphglbb pleagrmbglbgls cooooohoohoo m...' and so on.

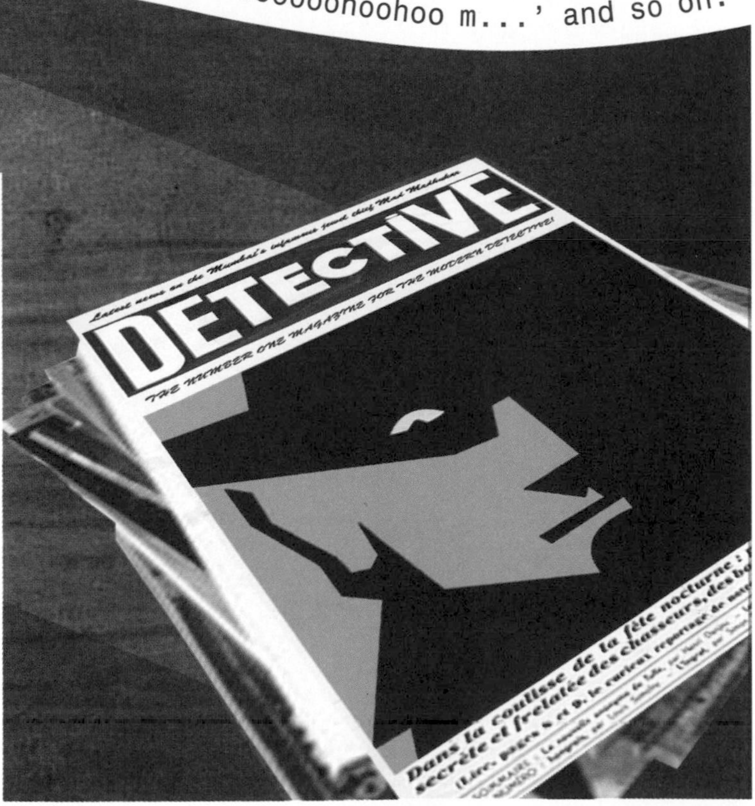
DETECTIVE
THE NUMBER ONE MAGAZINE FOR THE MODERN DETECTIVE!

Captain Coconut played the message again and again. After he had listened to it twenty-seven times, he finally managed to get the name and address of the woman.

He wasn't sure exactly what had happened, but he heard the word 'missing' and the word 'banana'.

'Hmm,' thought Captain Coconut. 'Missing. Banana. What could that mean?' He walked a few times around the room.

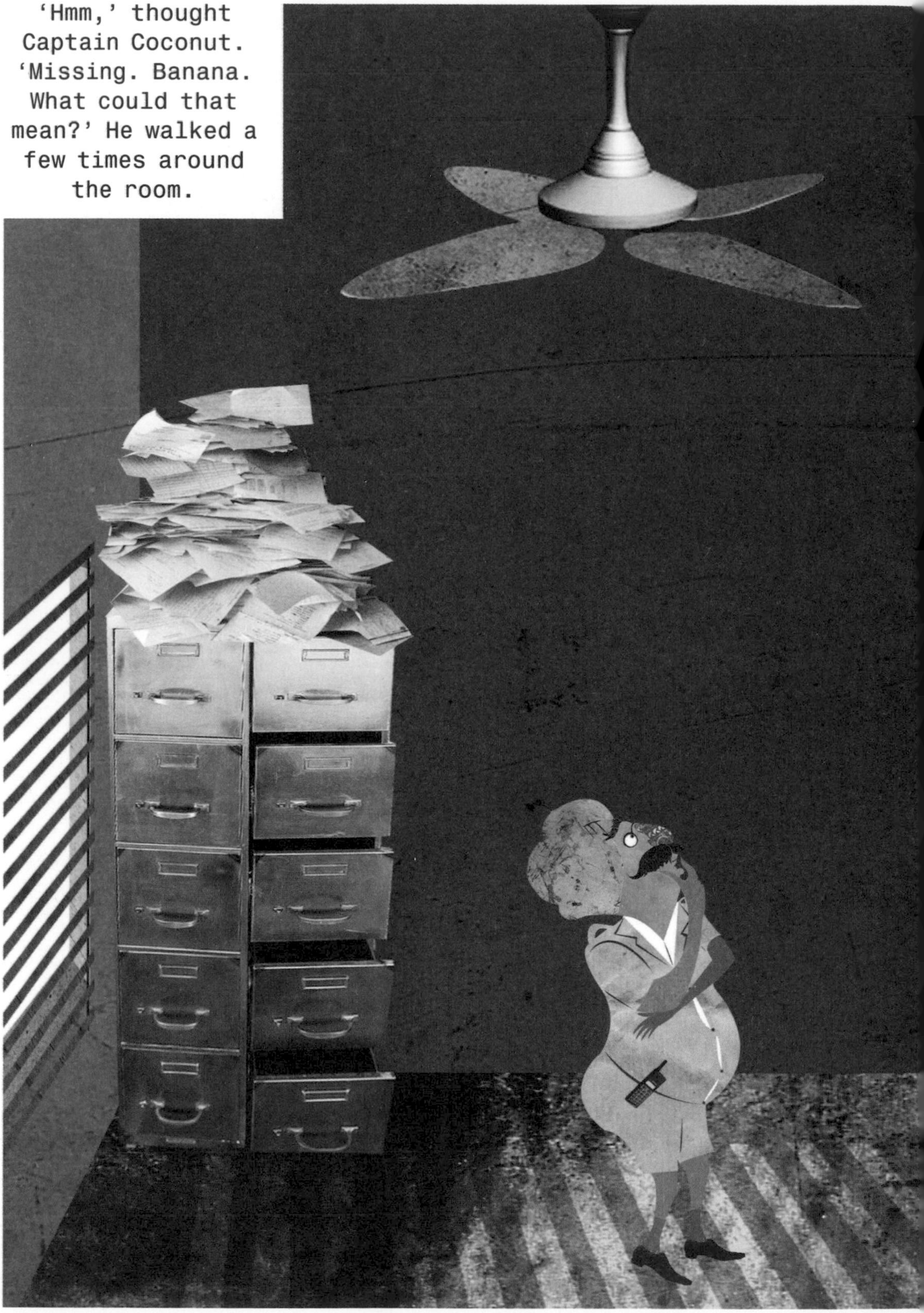

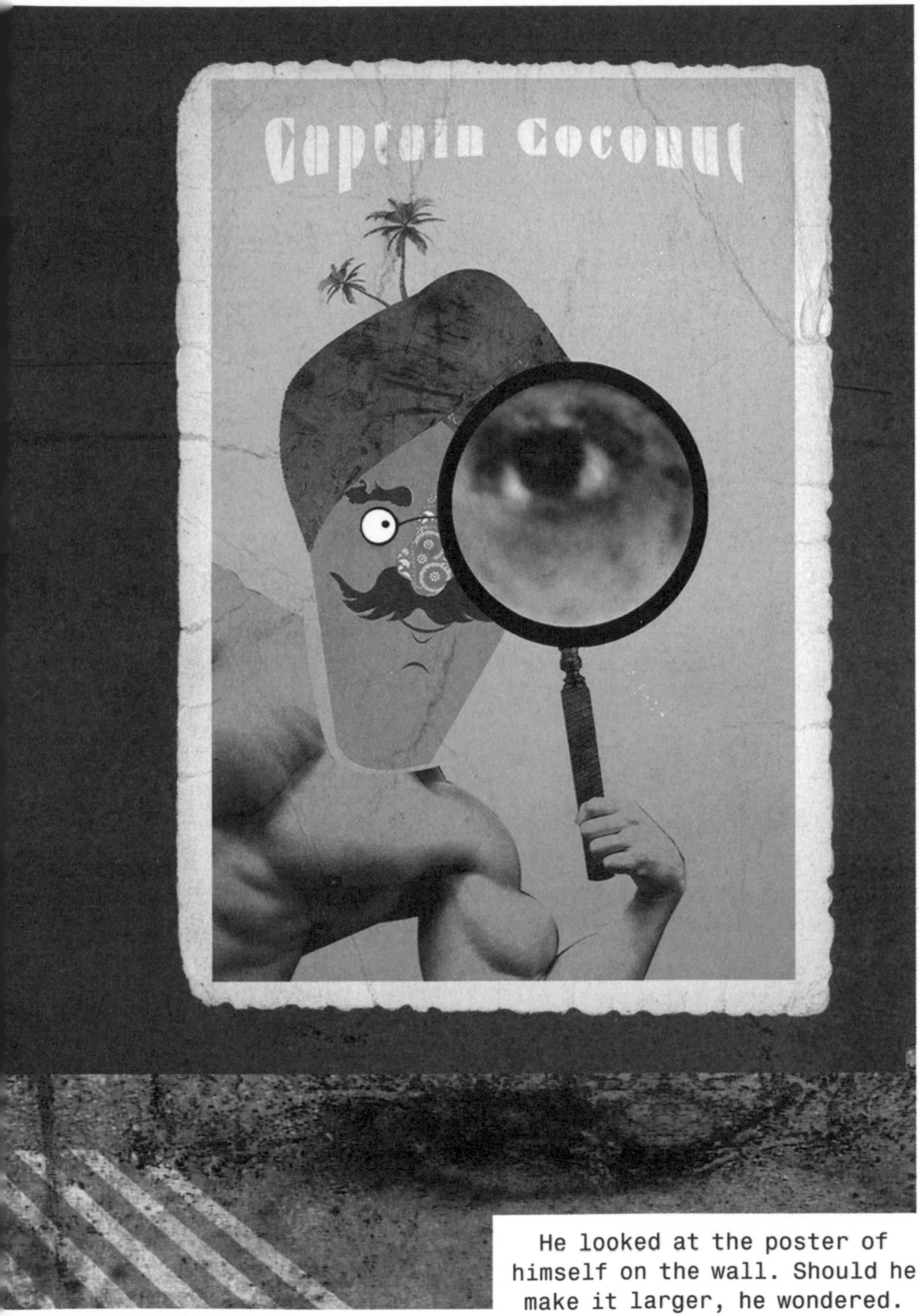
Captain Coconut

He looked at the poster of himself on the wall. Should he make it larger, he wondered.

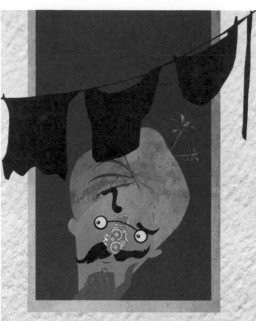

He looked out
thoughtfully
at the window
of the opposite
building.

He moved away quickly.

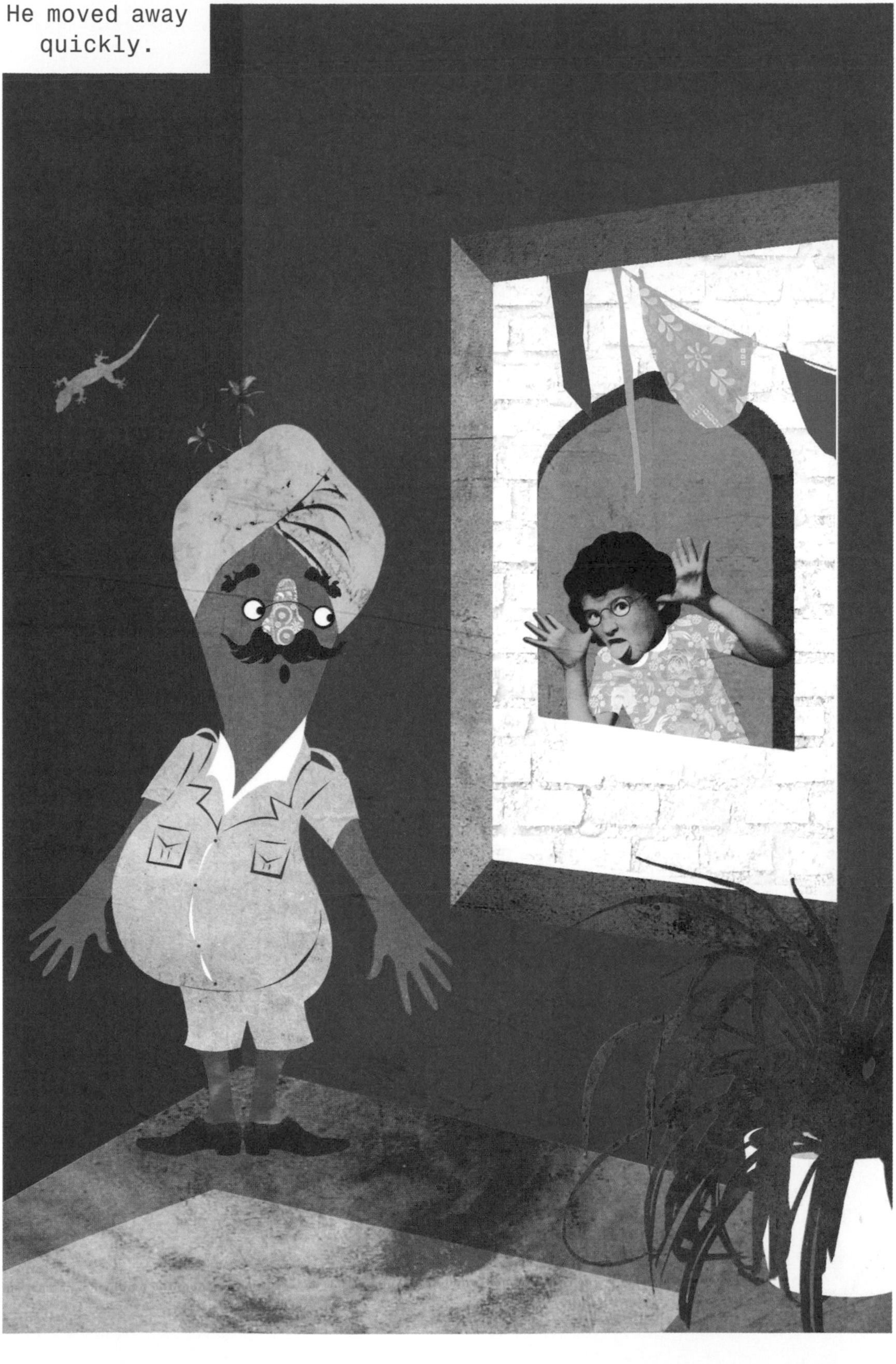

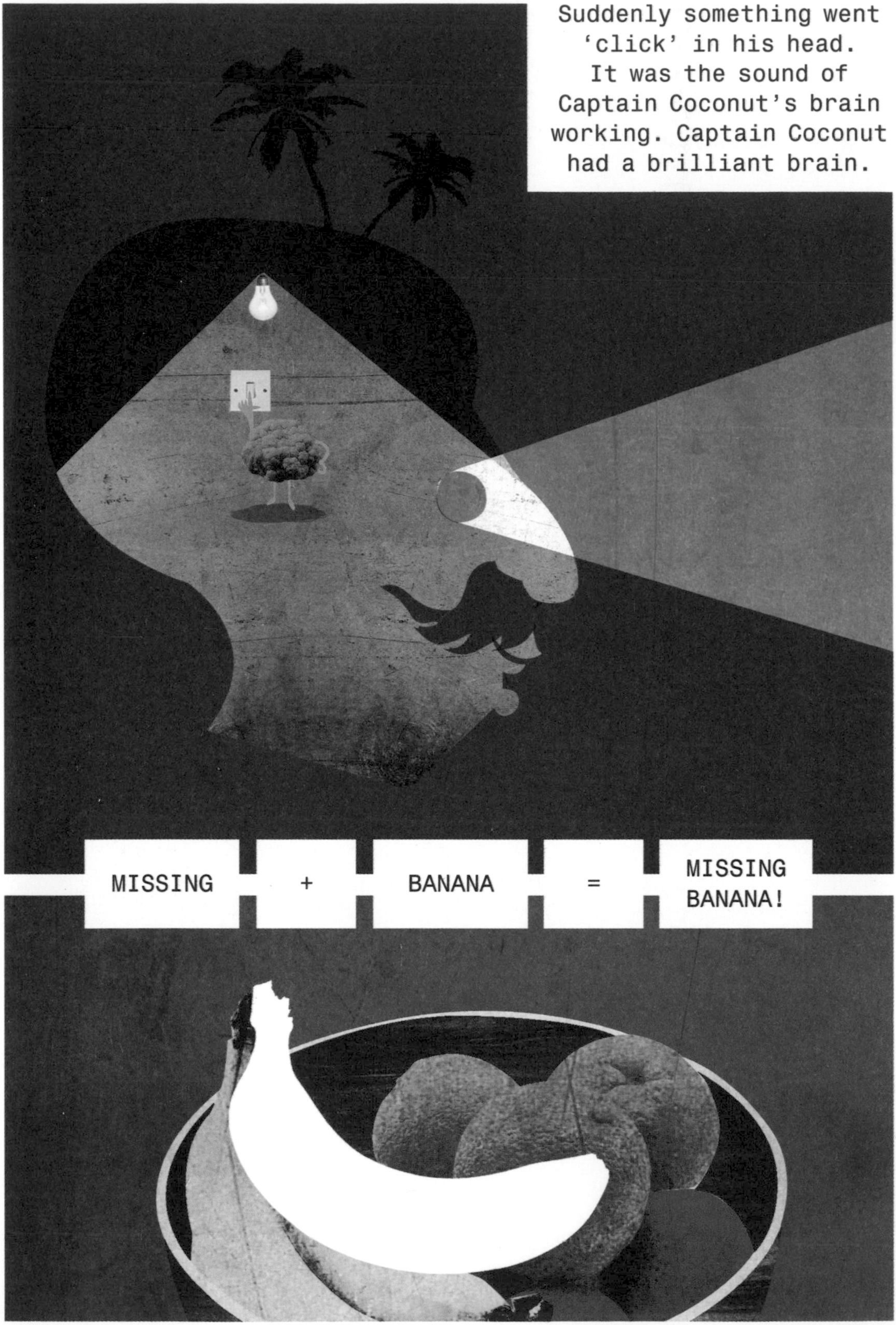
Suddenly something went 'click' in his head. It was the sound of Captain Coconut's brain working. Captain Coconut had a brilliant brain.
MISSING
+
BANANA
=
MISSING BANANA!

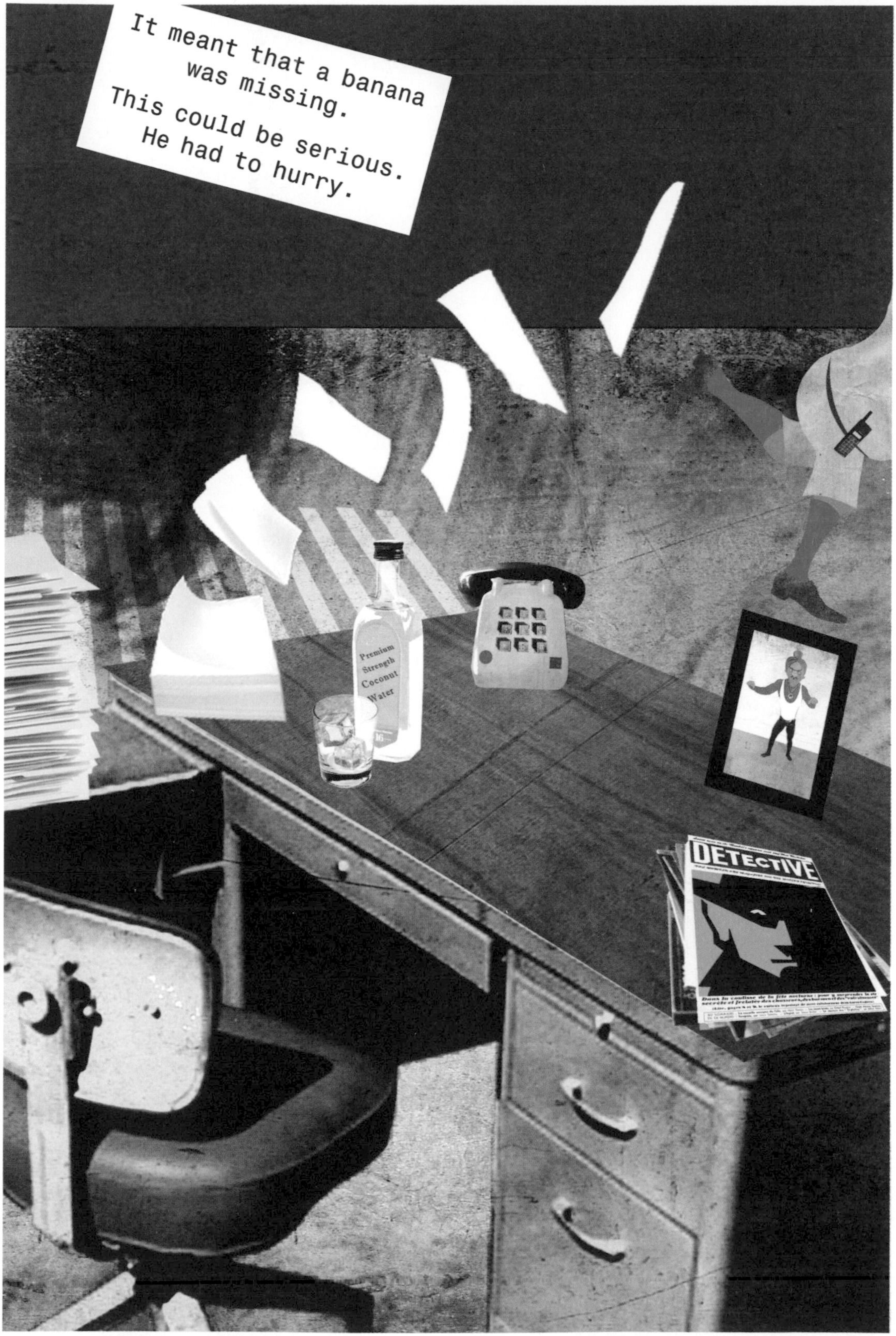
It meant that a banana was missing.
This could be serious.
He had to hurry.
Premium Strength Coconut Water
DETECTIVE

Captain Coconut leaped onto his scooter and turned up the accelerator. The scooter did not move. Captain Coconut wondered why, but only for a moment. Captain Coconut's brain worked like lightning. 'Aha!' he said, rubbing his hands together. 'I have found the answer!'

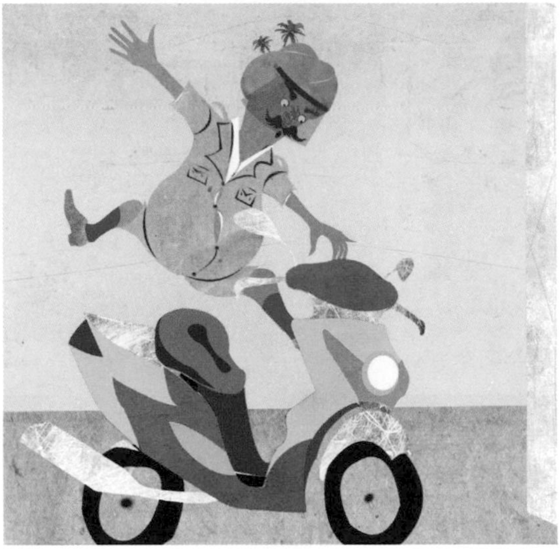

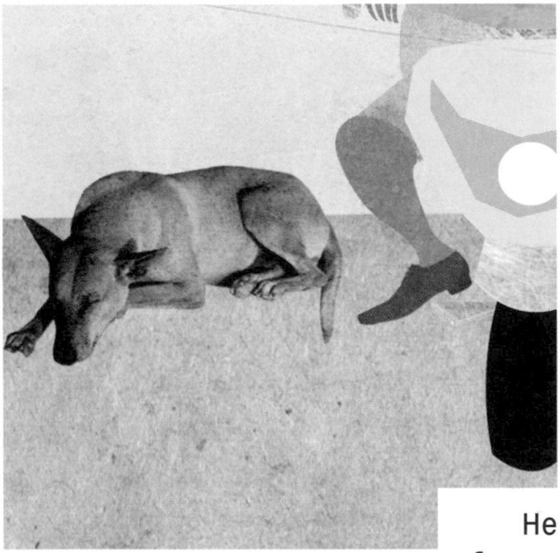

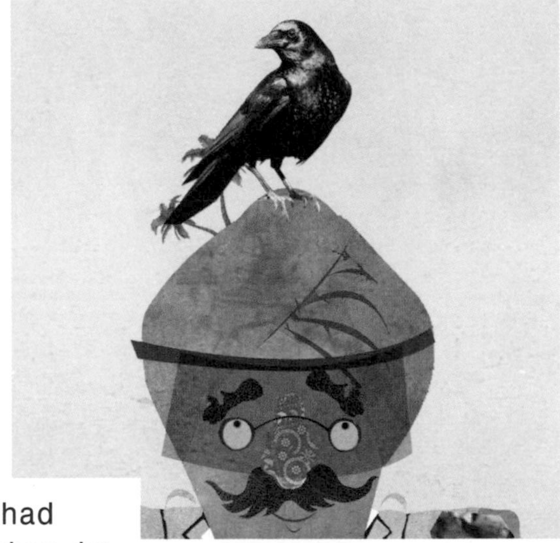

He had forgotten to start it.

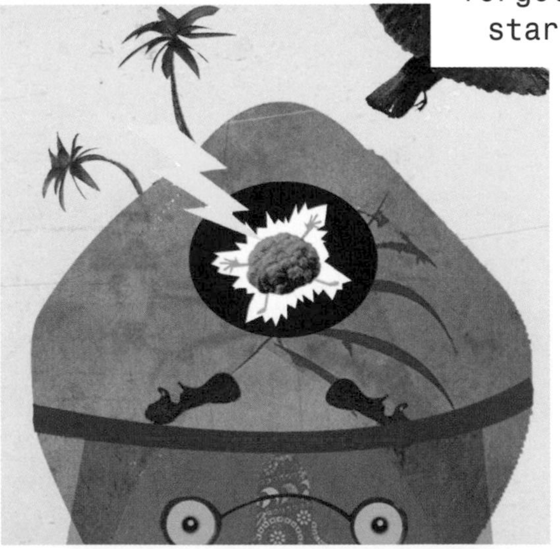

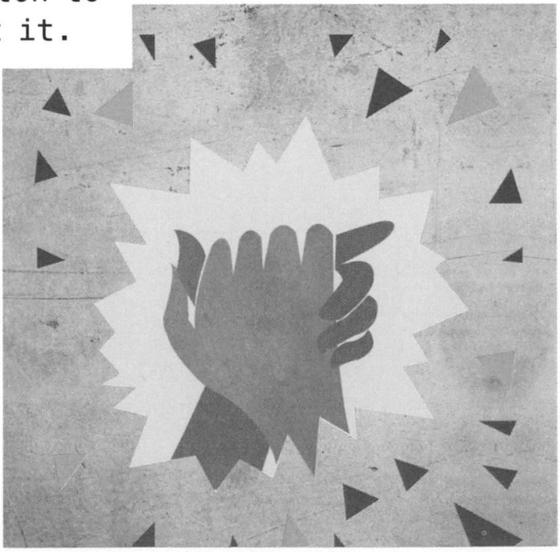

He started the scooter, and set off for the place where the bananas had gone missing.

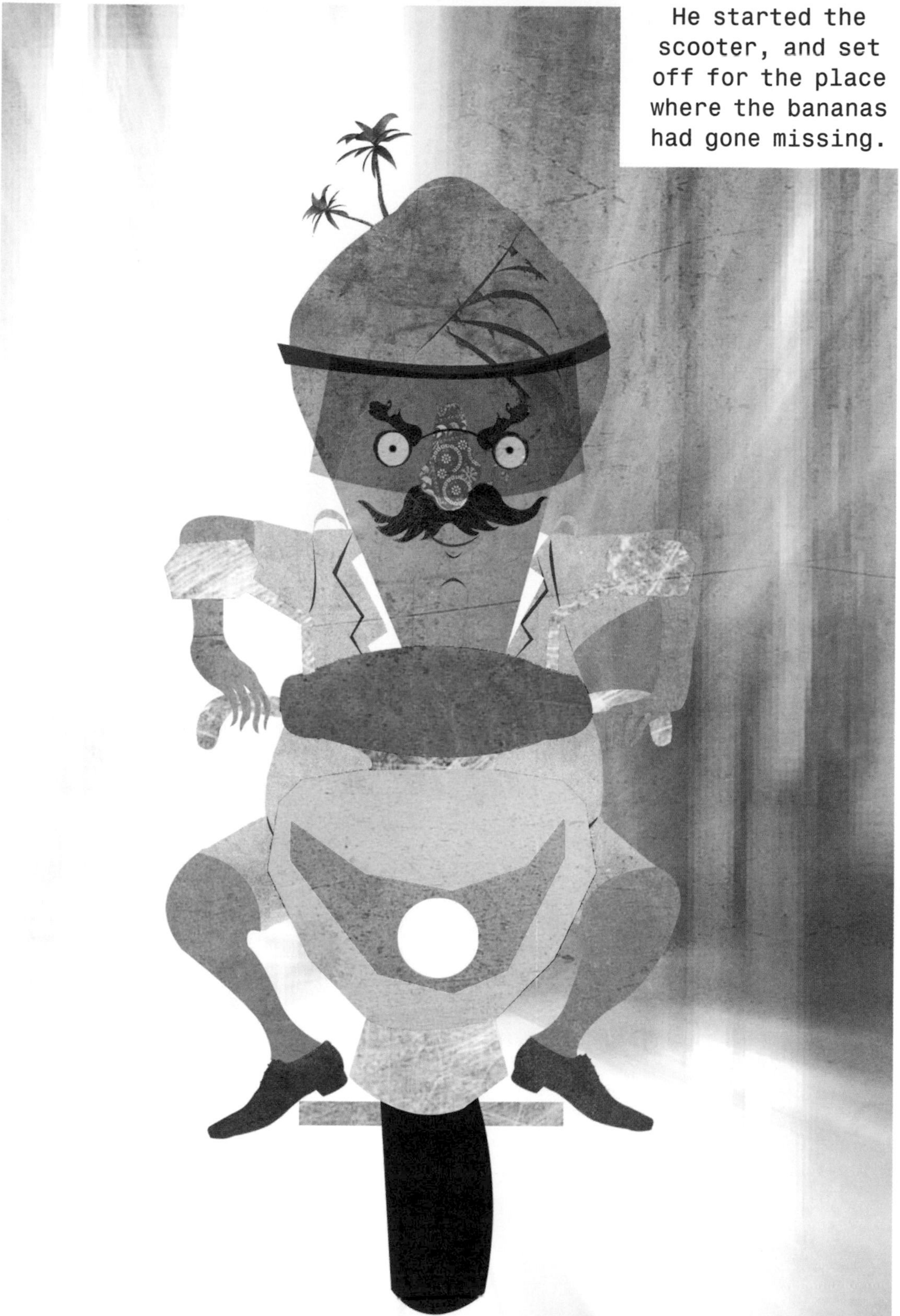

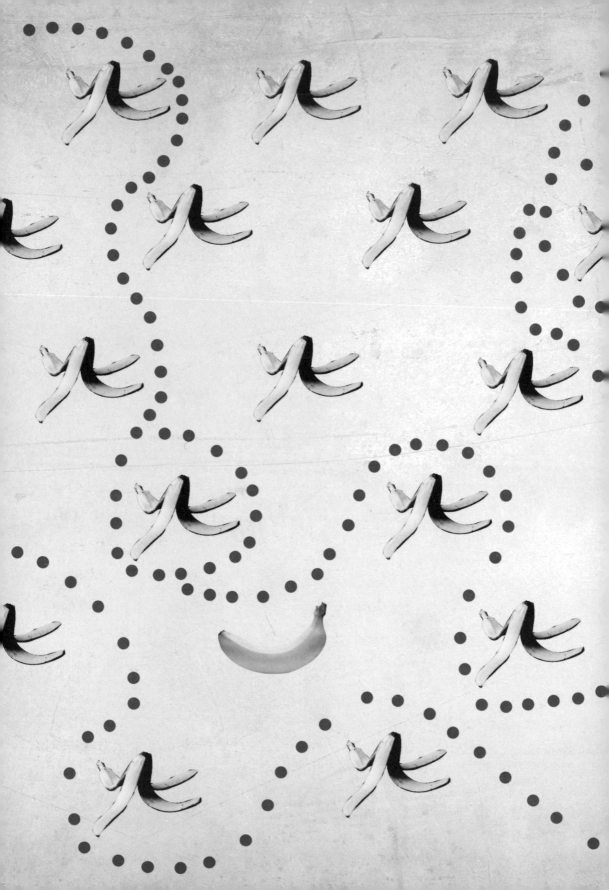

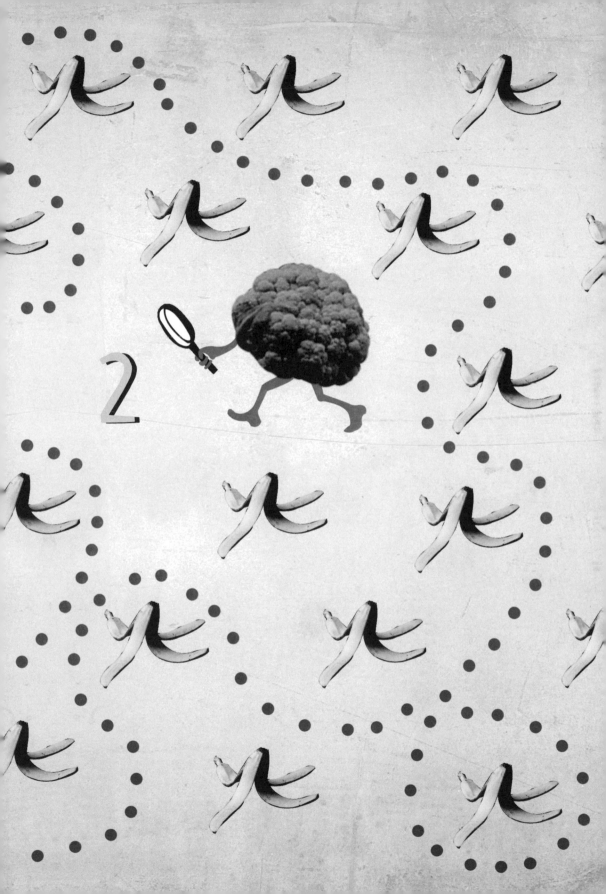

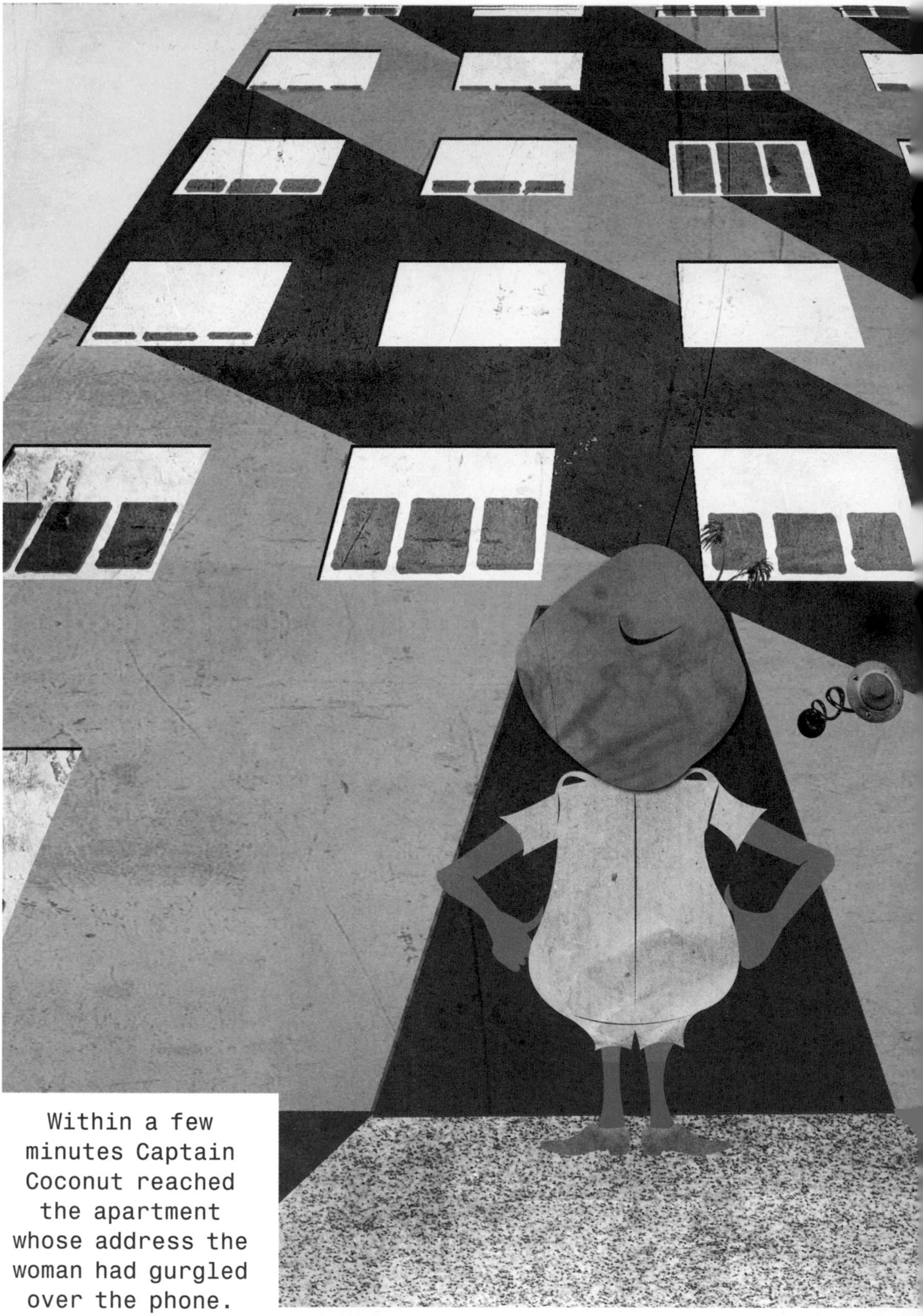

Within a few minutes Captain Coconut reached the apartment whose address the woman had gurgled over the phone.

He looked for the doorbell and found it was broken. But Captain Coconut was never at a loss.

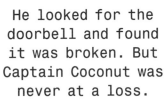

He knocked.

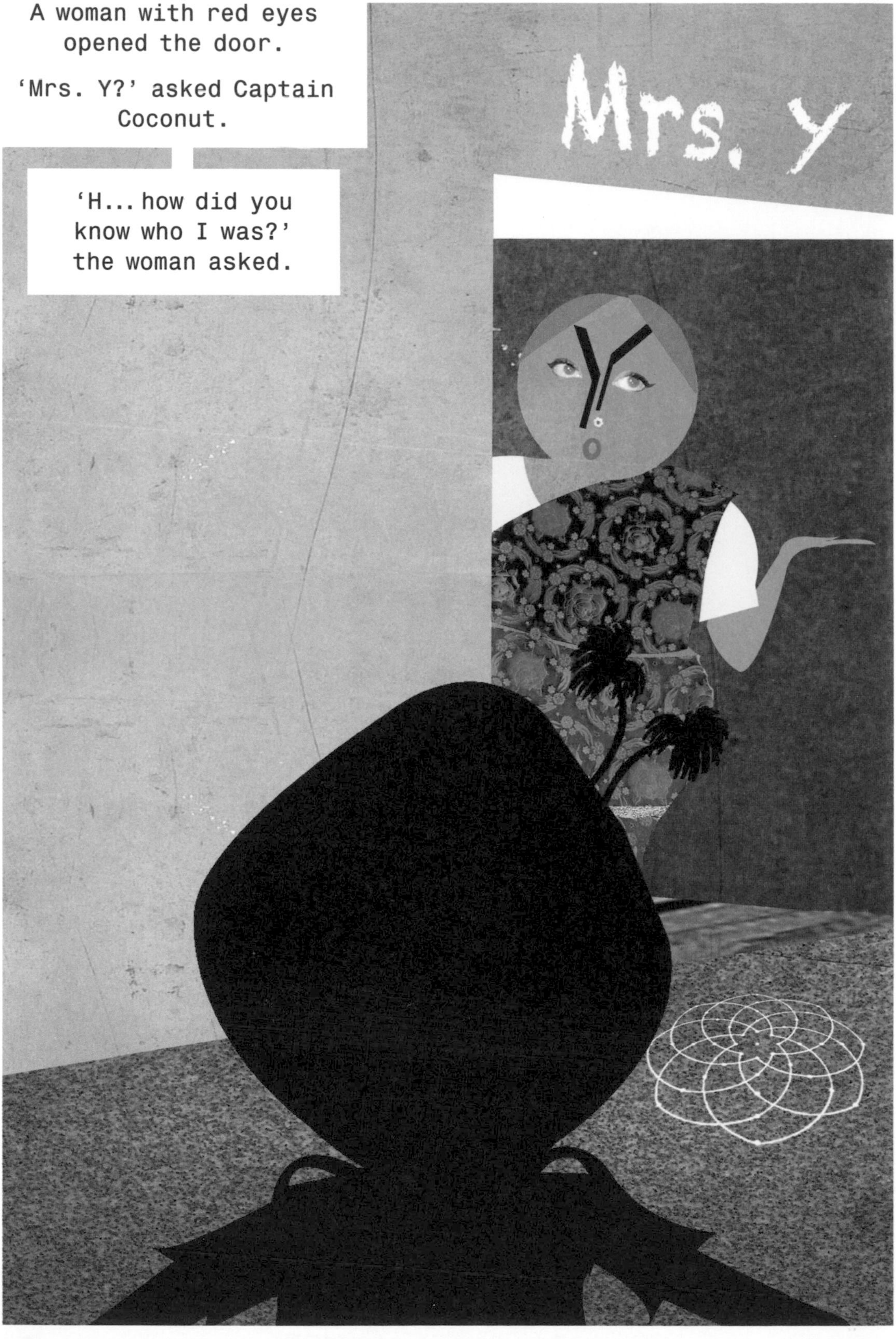
A woman with red eyes opened the door.
'Mrs. Y?' asked Captain Coconut.
'H... how did you know who I was?' the woman asked.
Mrs. Y

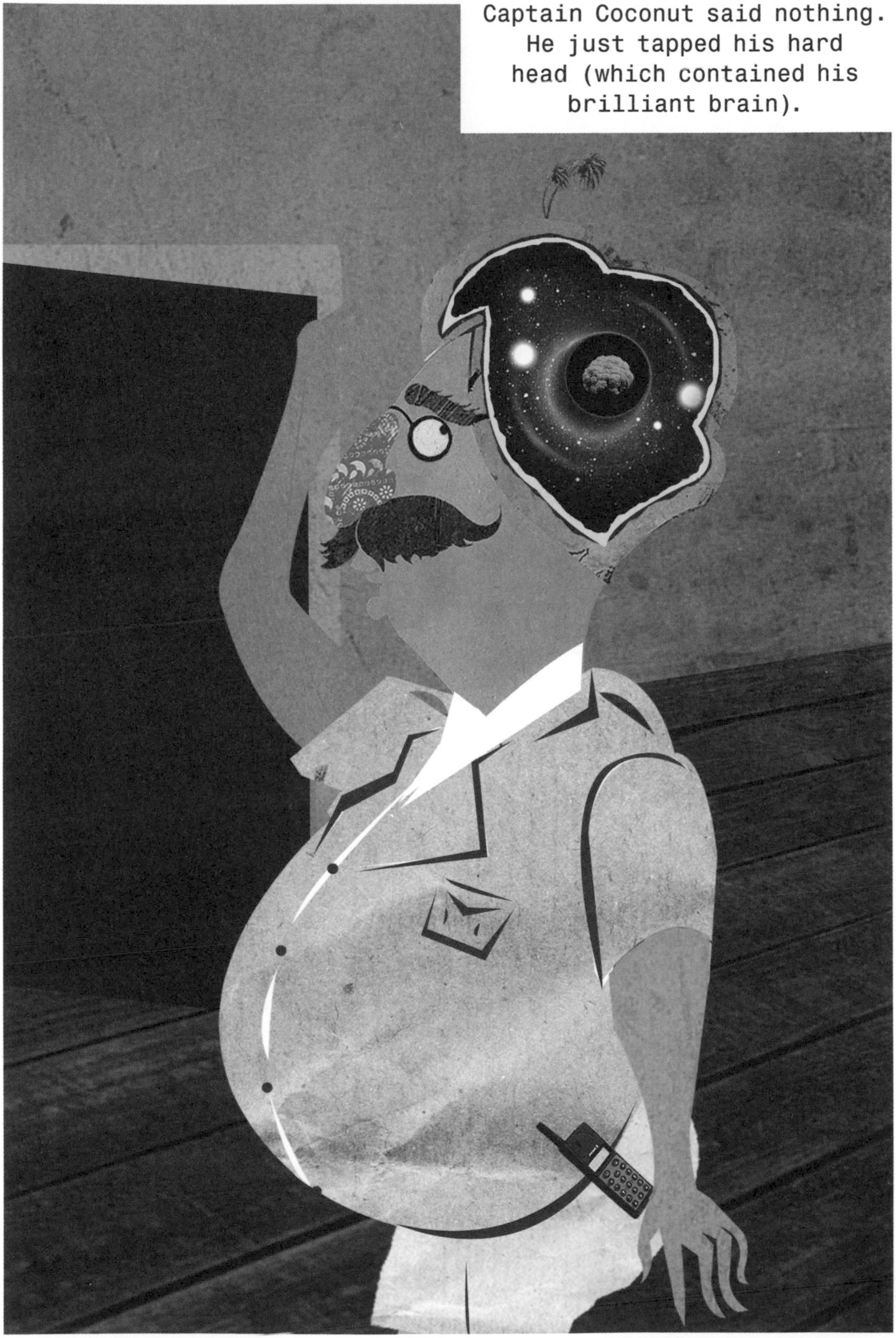
Captain Coconut said nothing. He just tapped his hard head (which contained his brilliant brain).

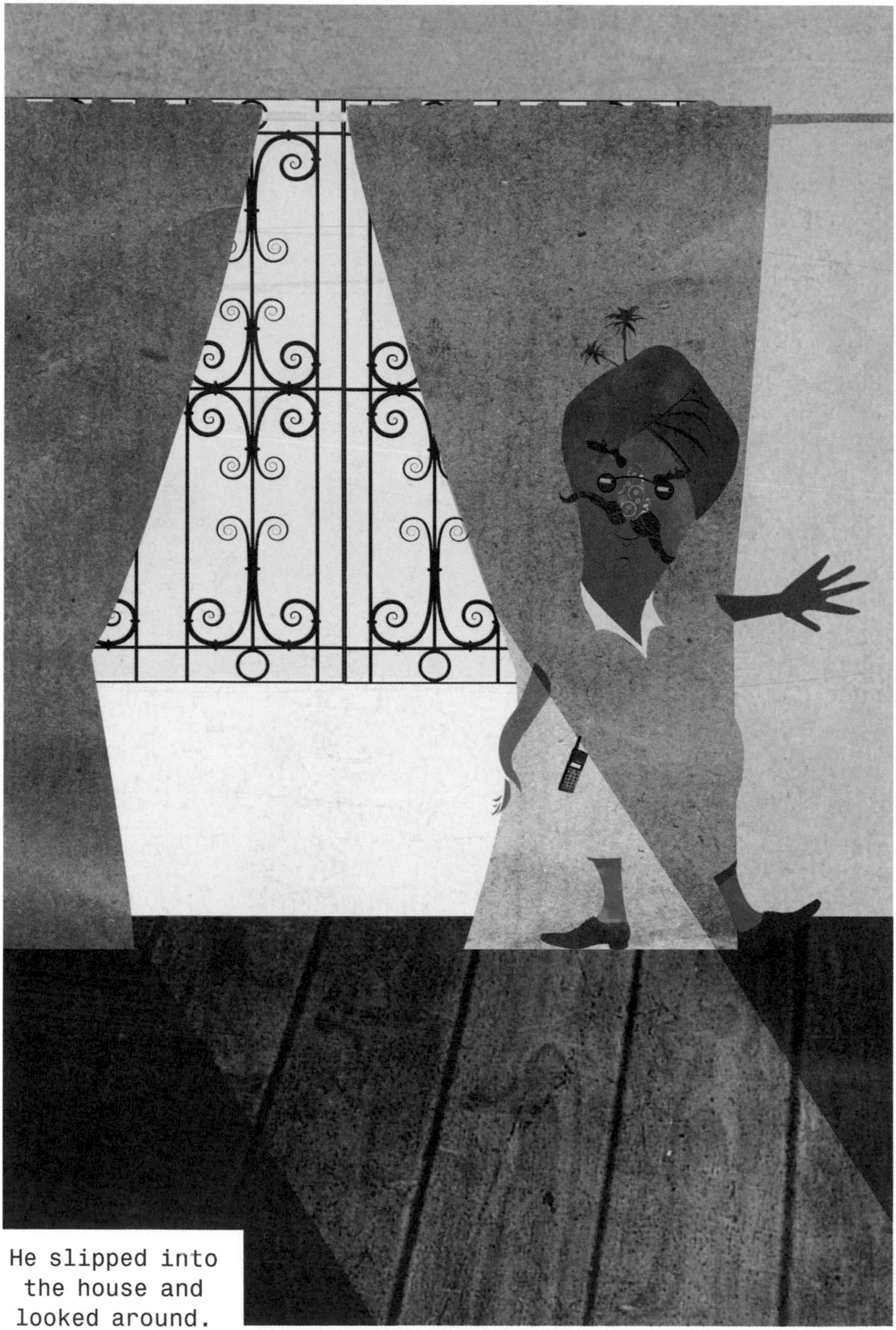

He slipped into the house and looked around.

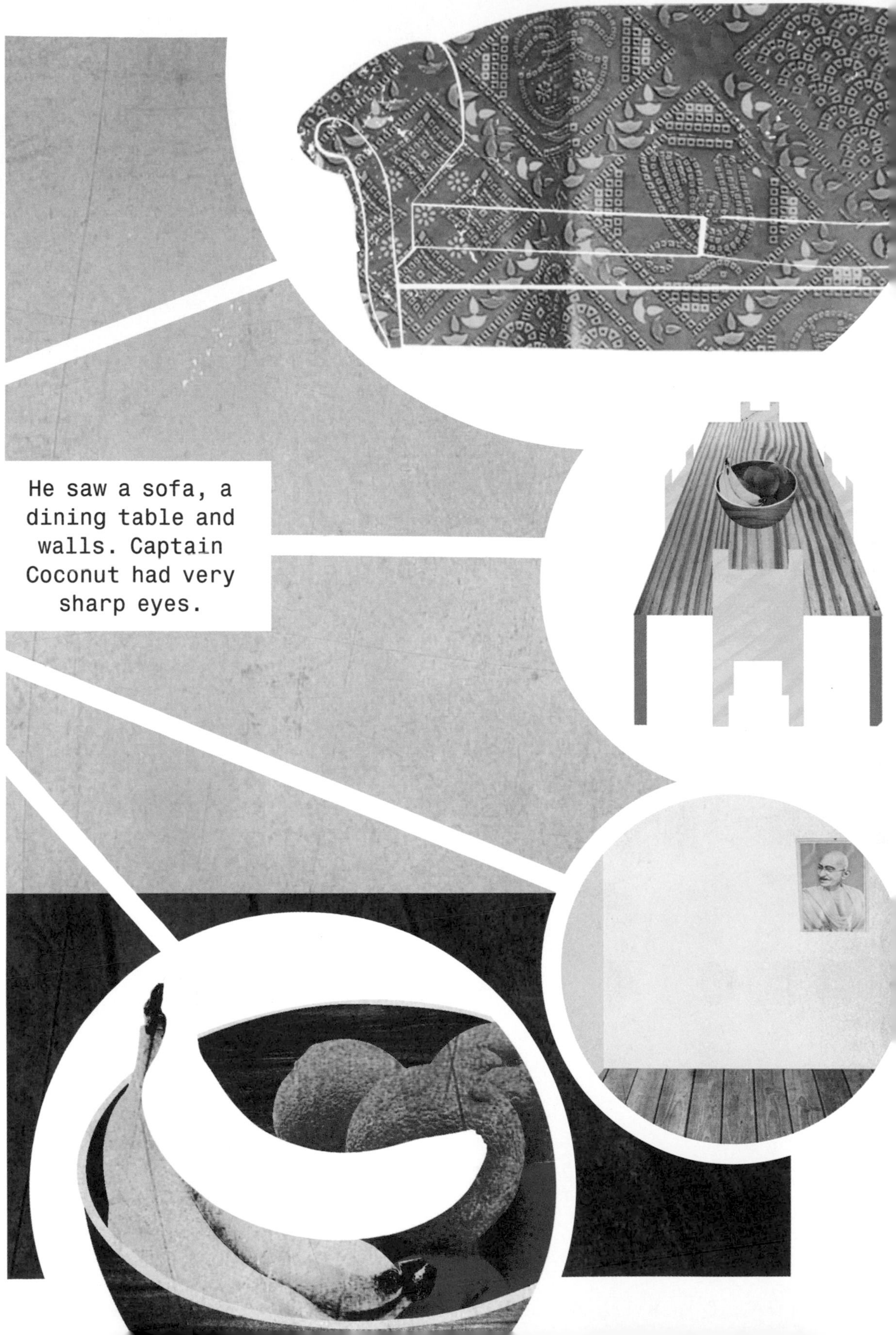
He saw a sofa, a dining table and walls. Captain Coconut had very sharp eyes.

On the table he
spotted a bunch
of bananas.
His nose twitched.

'Bananas?'
he asked Mrs. Y,
recognising the
fruit immediately.

Mrs. Y started
sobbing.

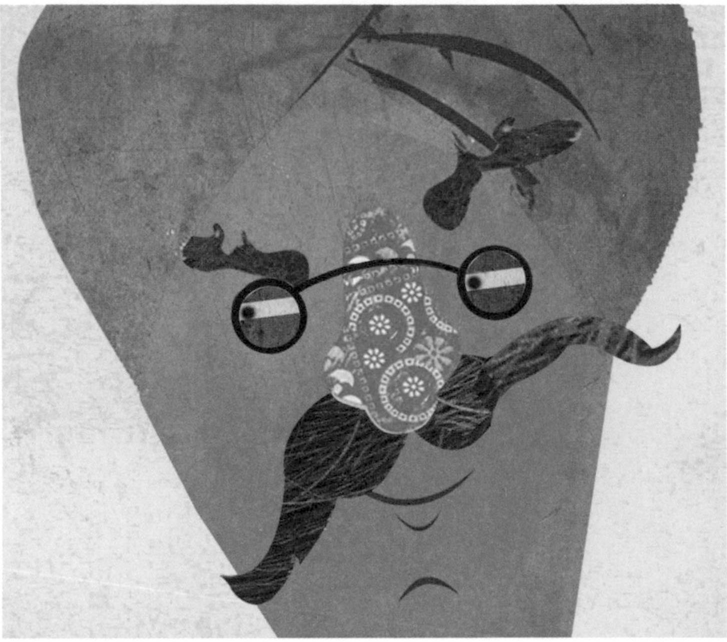

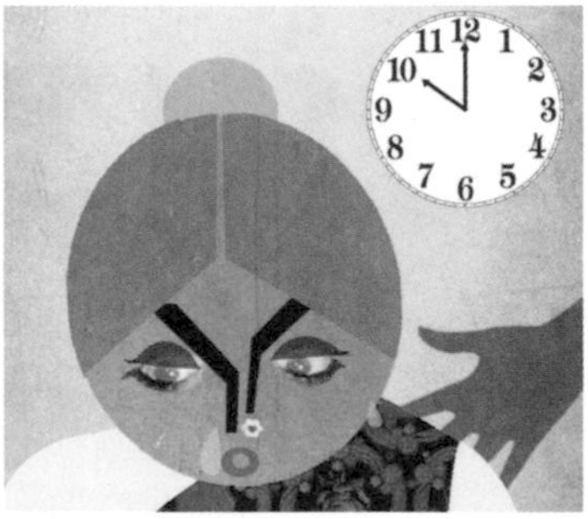

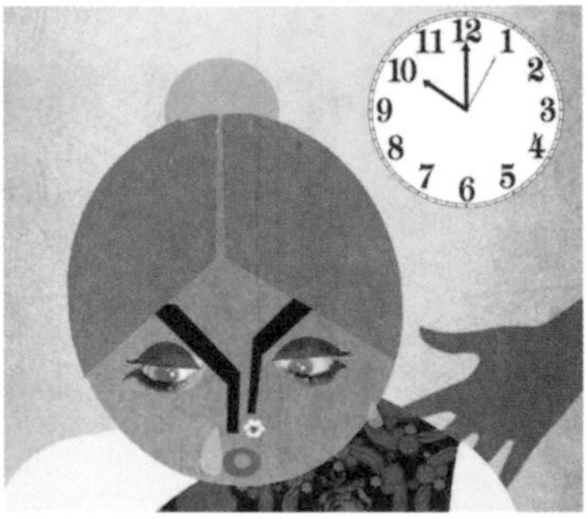

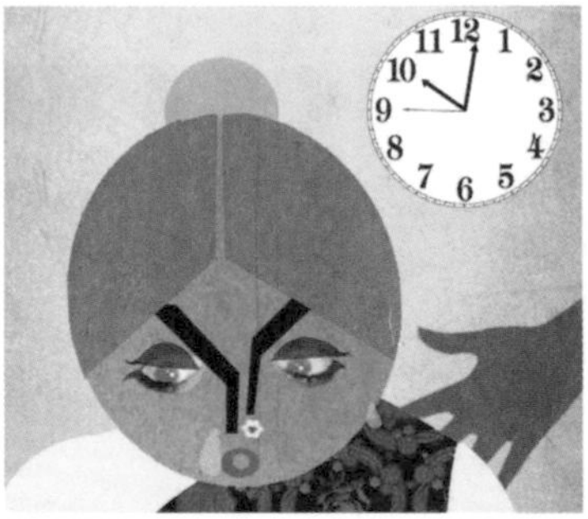

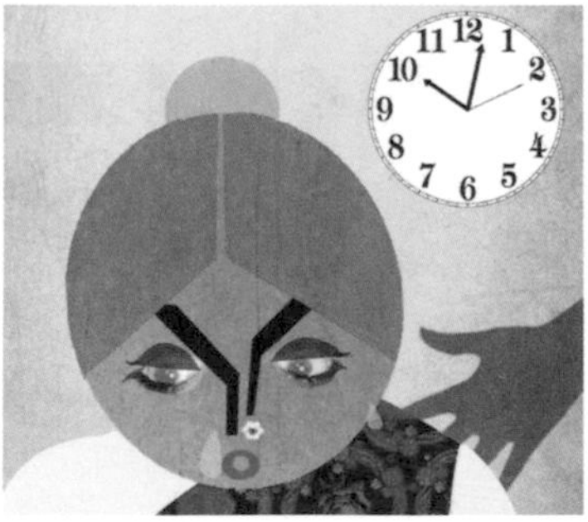

'There, there,
there, there,
there,'
the Captain said,
patting the woman
on the back.

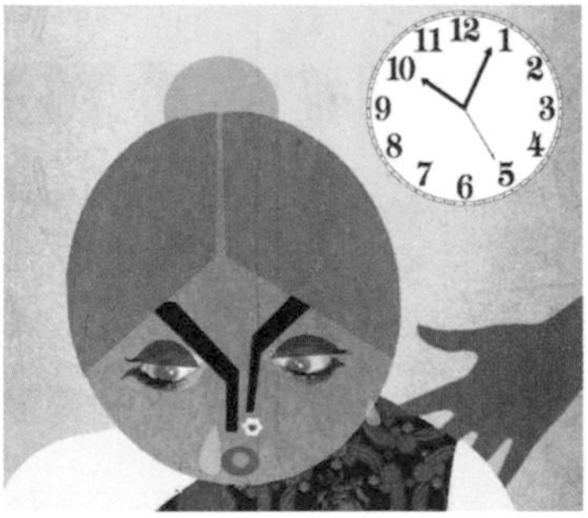

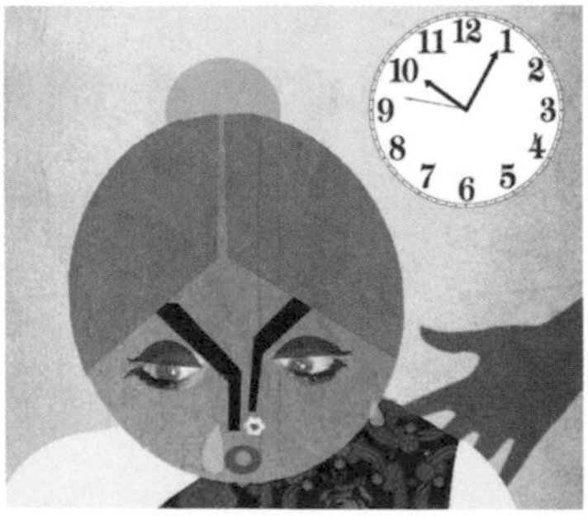

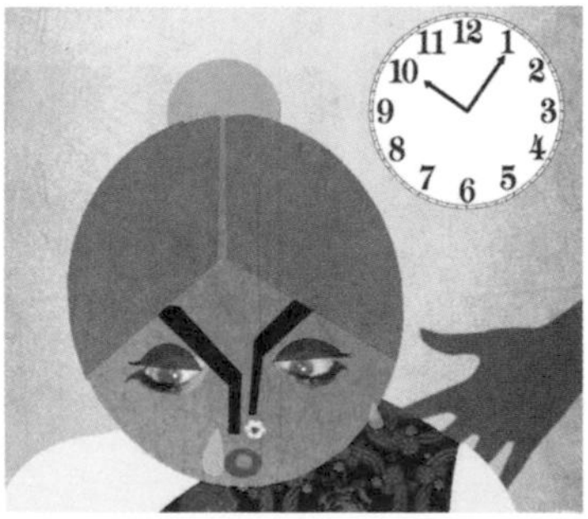

After a few minutes
she stopped crying
and began to tell
Captain Coconut
what had happened.

'Yesterday evening, on my way home from work, I bought a bunch of fourteen bananas.'

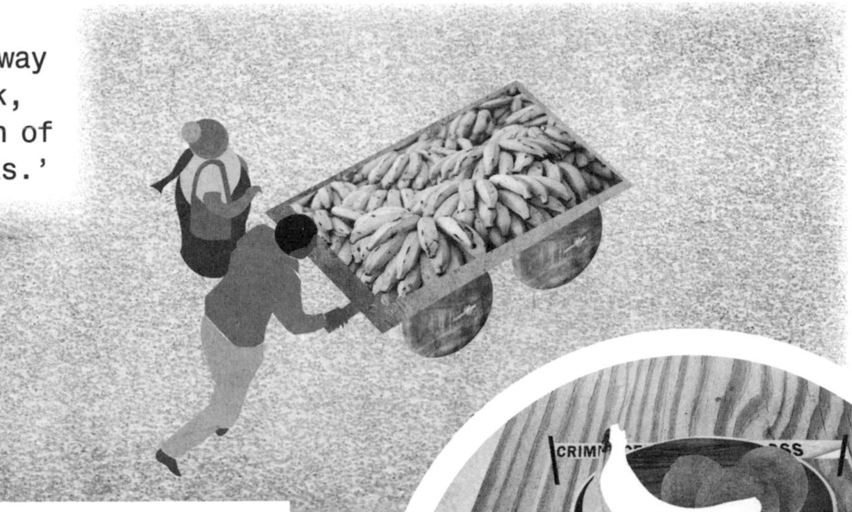

'That bunch?' asked Captain Coconut, nodding at the bunch he had seen earlier.

'Yes,' said Mrs. Y. 'How clever of you to guess!'

Captain Coconut smiled.

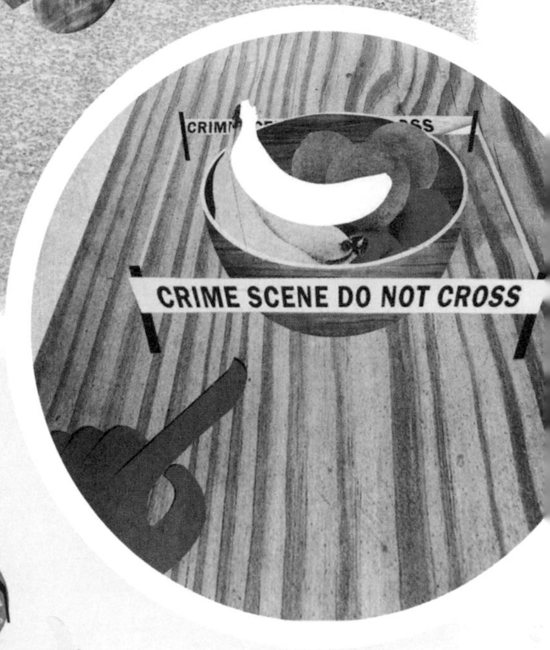
CRIME SCENE DO NOT CROSS

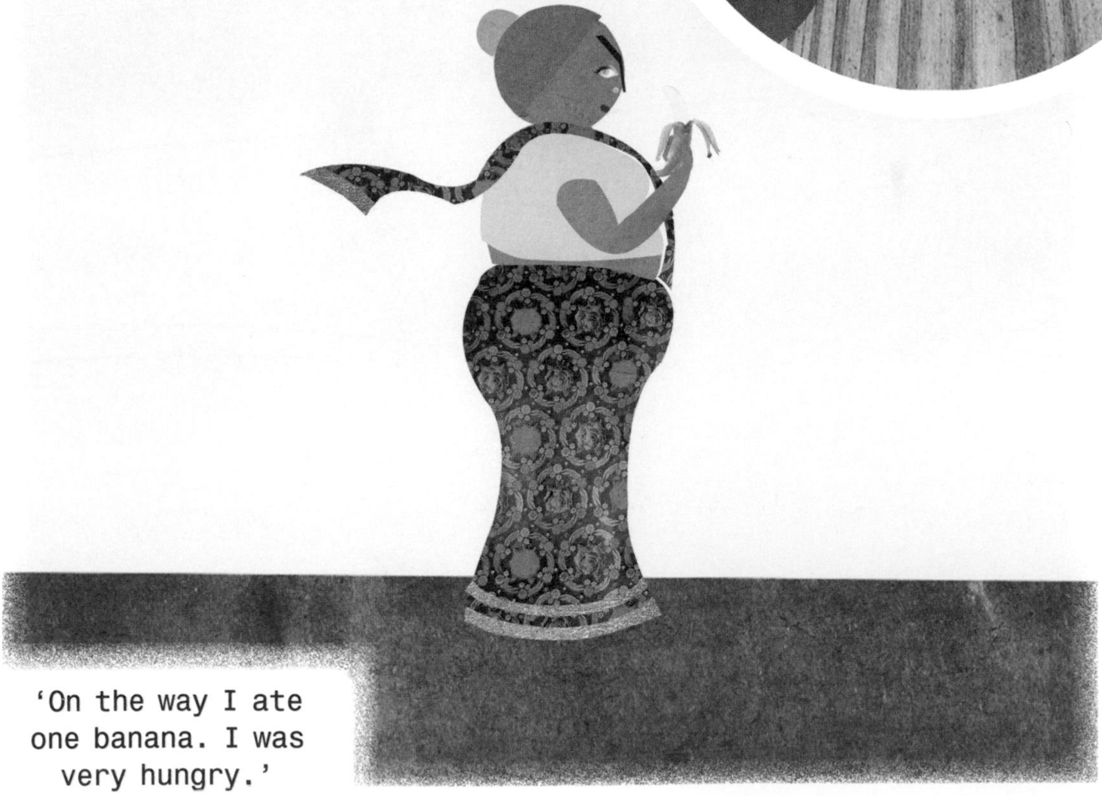

'On the way I ate one banana. I was very hungry.'

'I hope you threw the peel into a dustbin?' asked Captain Coconut.

'Oh yes! It was one of those green cans. I remember, because it matched my bag. Then I came home, and kept the bananas on the table.'

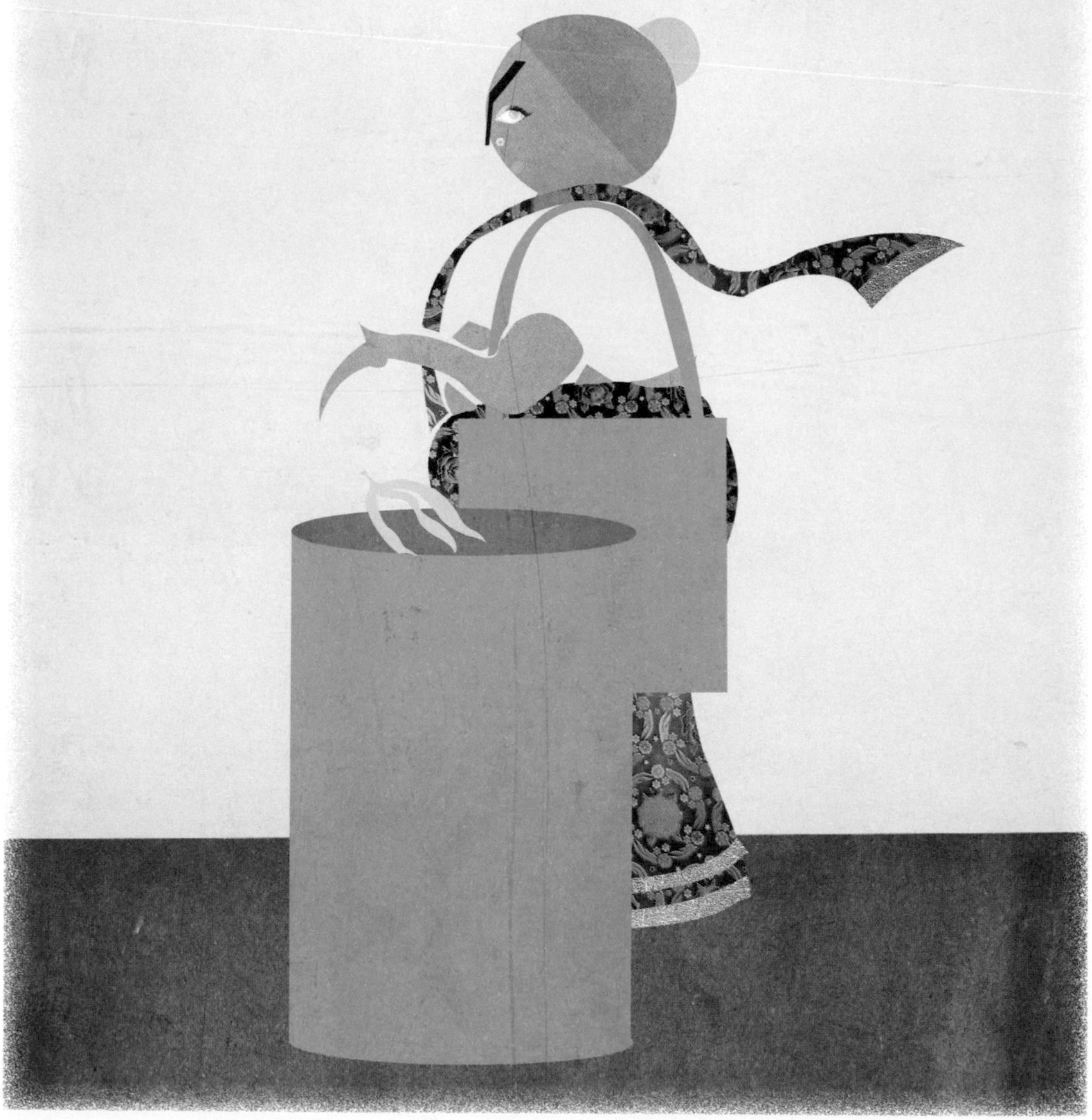

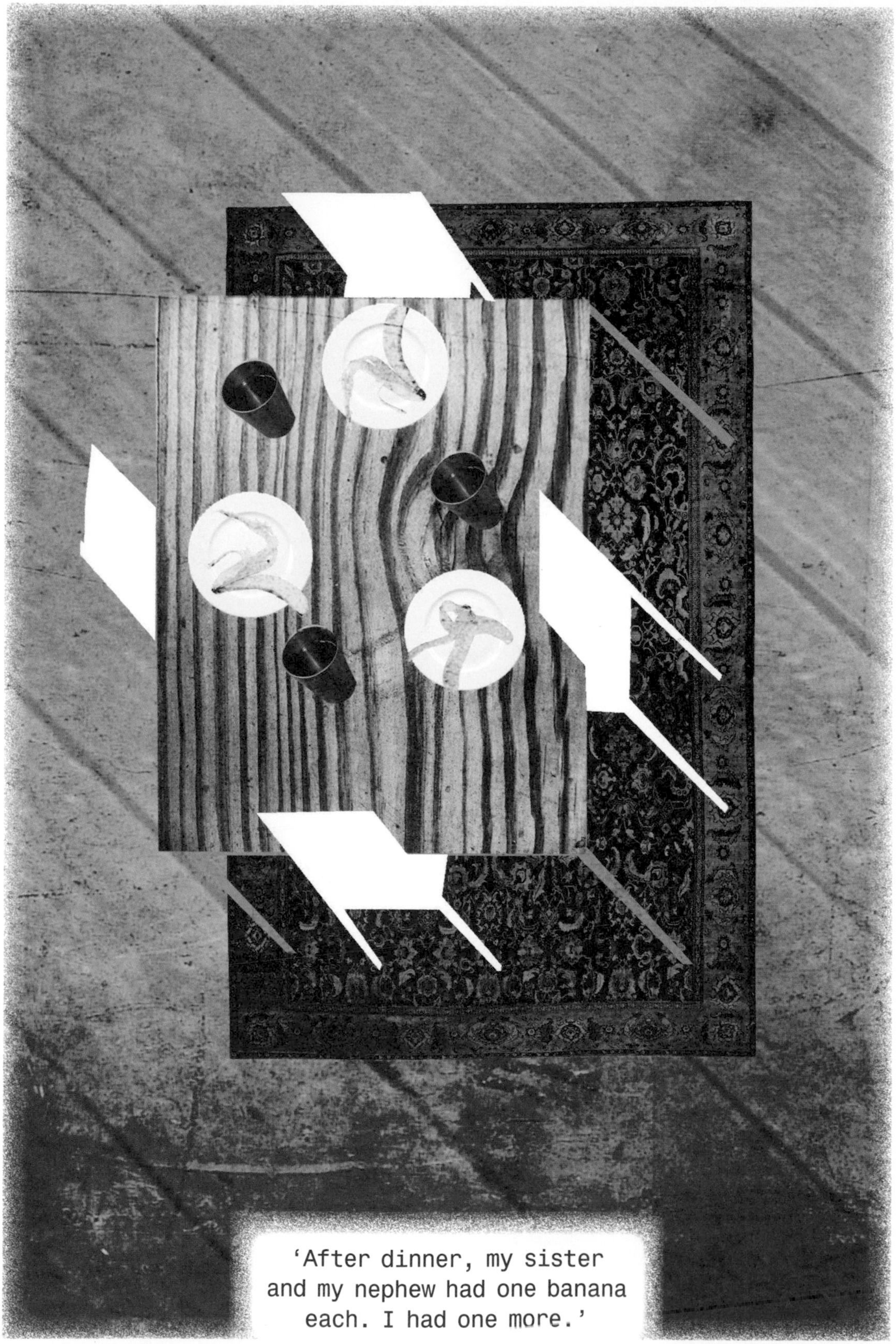
'After dinner, my sister
and my nephew had one banana
each. I had one more.'

Captain Coconut whipped out a calculator and did a quick calculation.

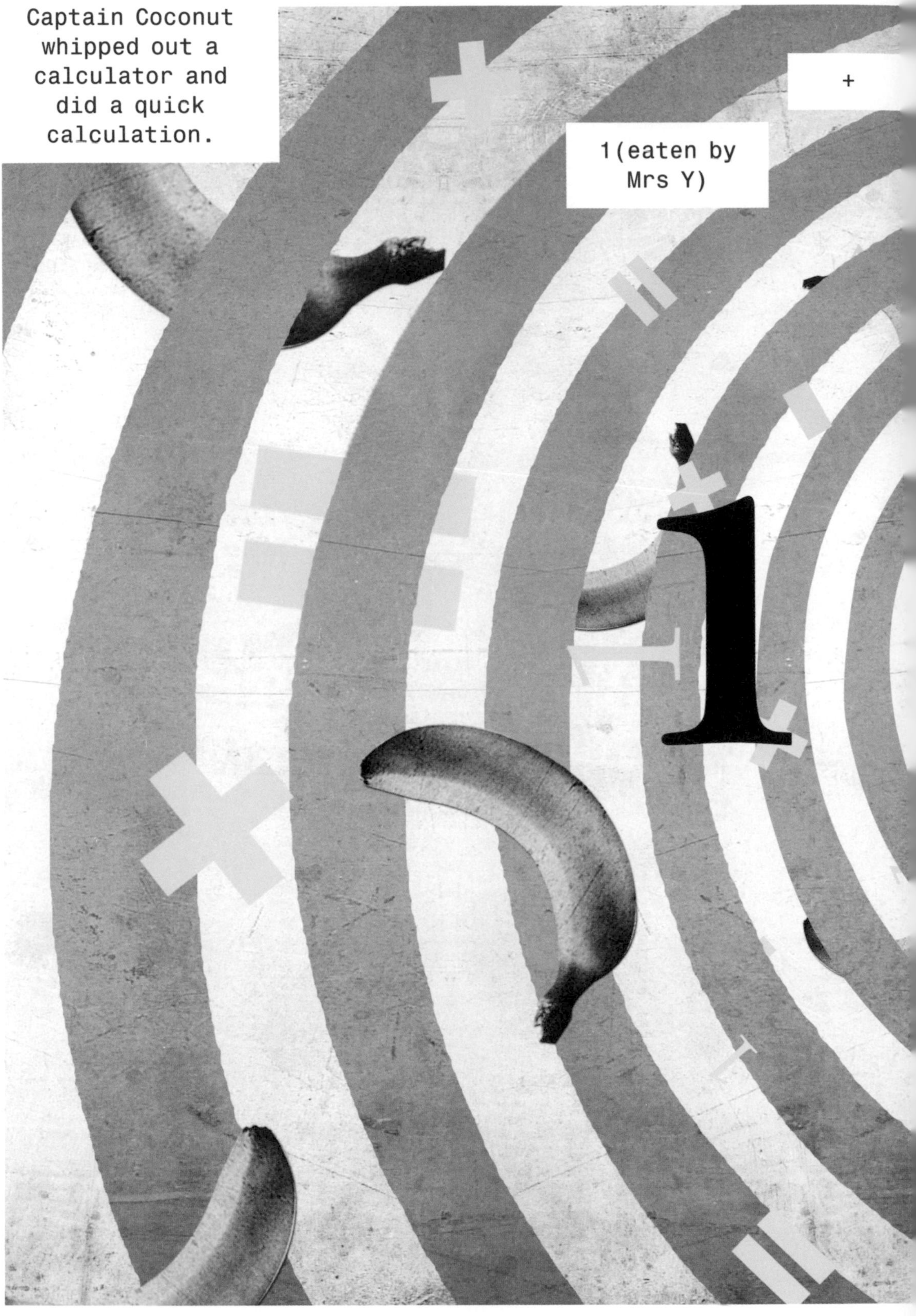
+
1(eaten by Mrs Y)
1

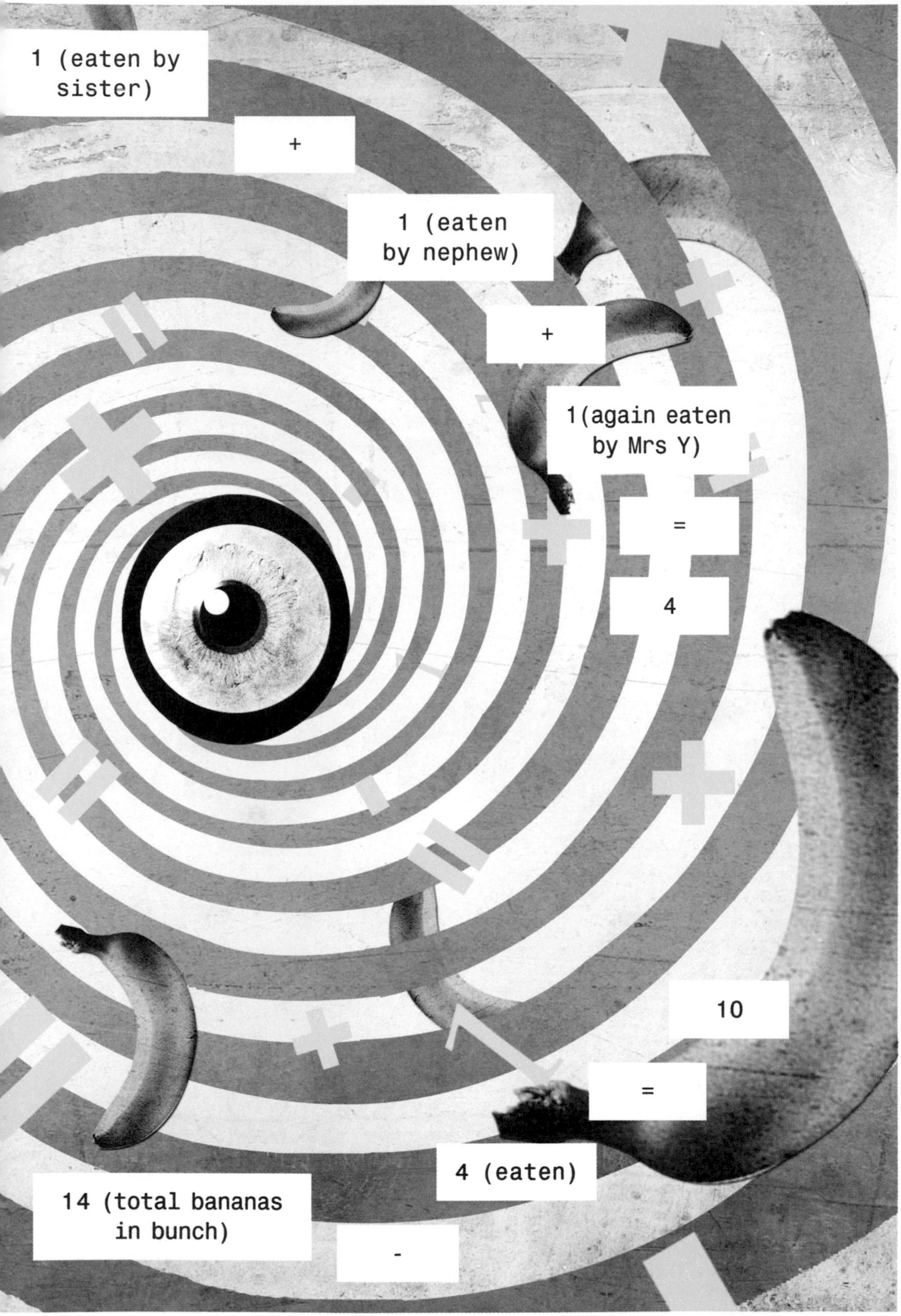

1 (eaten by sister)
+
1 (eaten by nephew)
+
1(again eaten by Mrs Y)
=
4
14 (total bananas in bunch)
-
4 (eaten)
=
10

'So there should be ten bananas left,' he said cleverly.

Mrs. Y gasped in admiration.

'You're a genius! I'm so glad I called you. I can see you're a man with a hard head.'

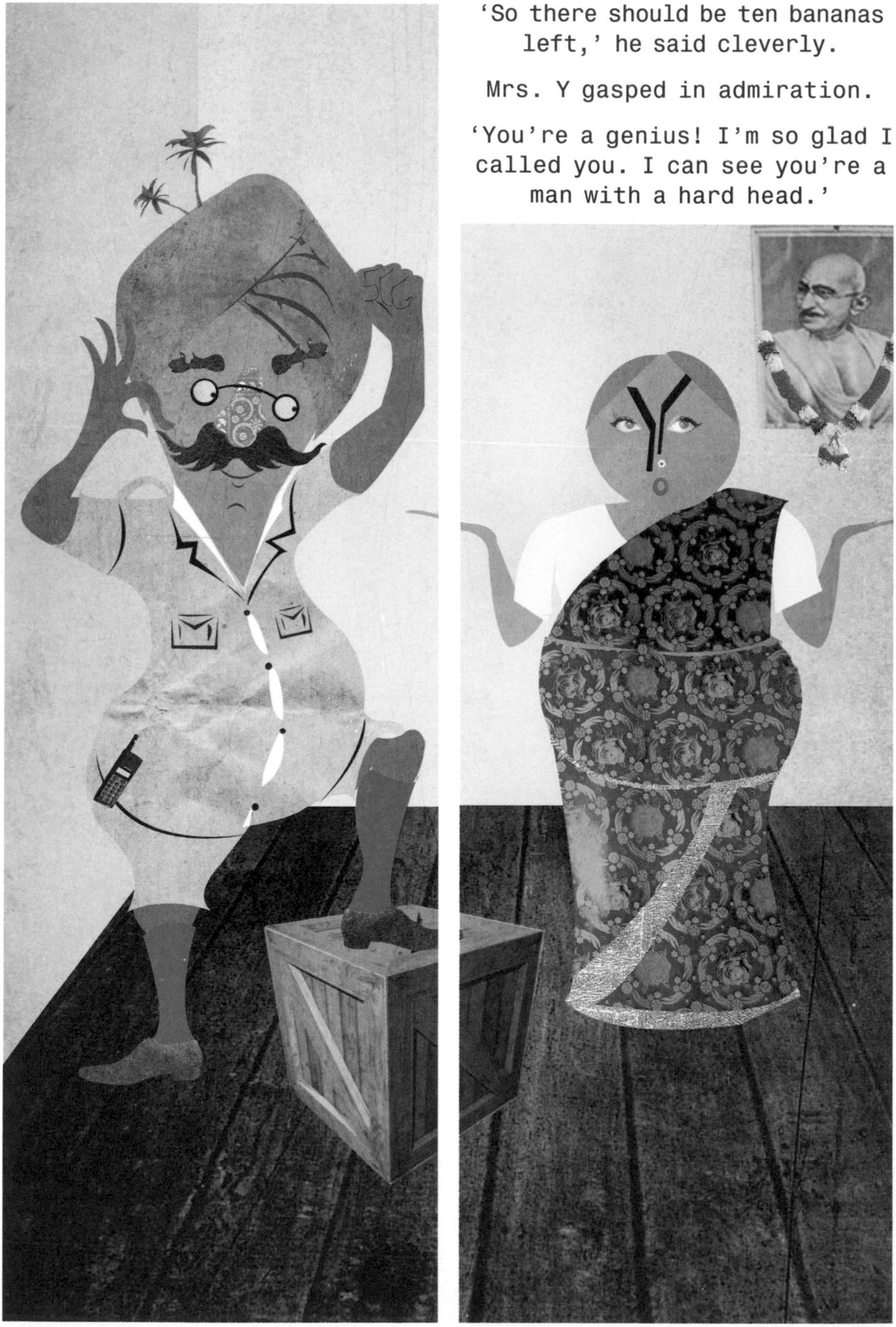

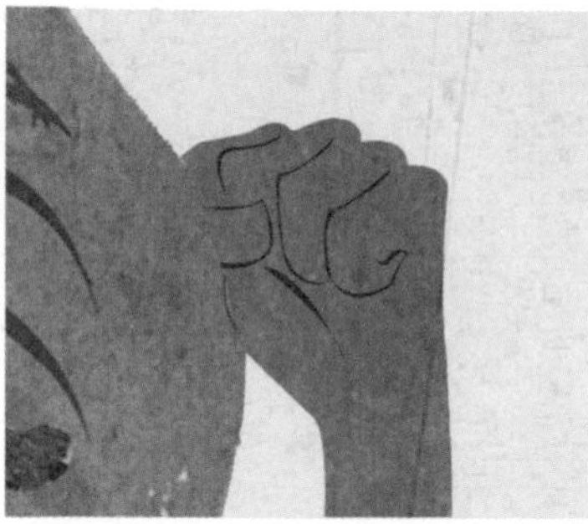

'Yes, I'm a tough nut to crack,' said Captain Coconut, twirling his moustache with one hand, tapping his forehead with the other and beaming at the woman, all at the same time. 'Tough nut, Coconut, get it?' he asked.

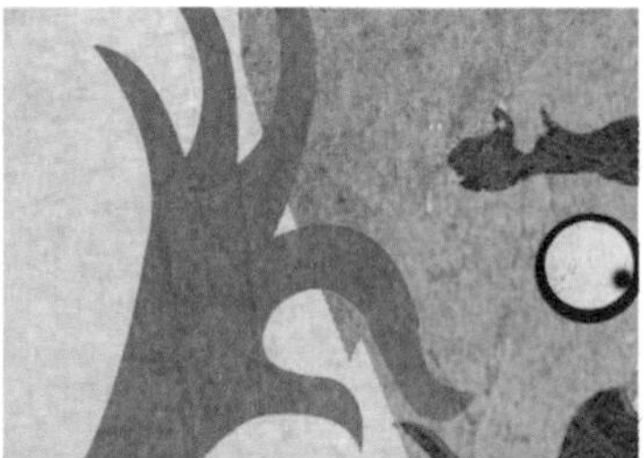

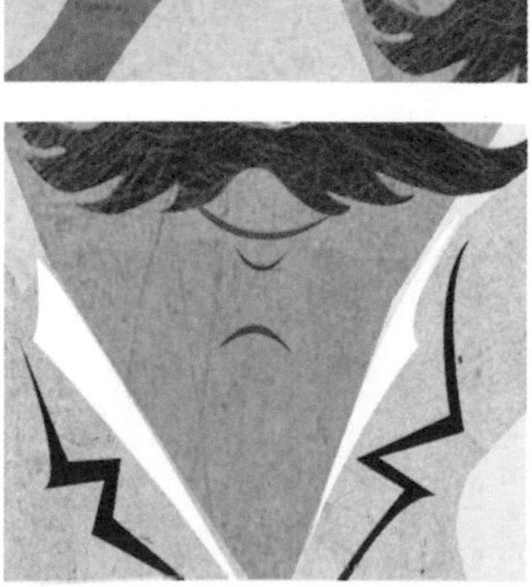

'Eh?' asked Mrs Y. 'Anyway, as you say, there should have been ten bananas. But I woke up in the morning and there were only...' Mrs. Y choked. Her eyes began to fill up with tears.

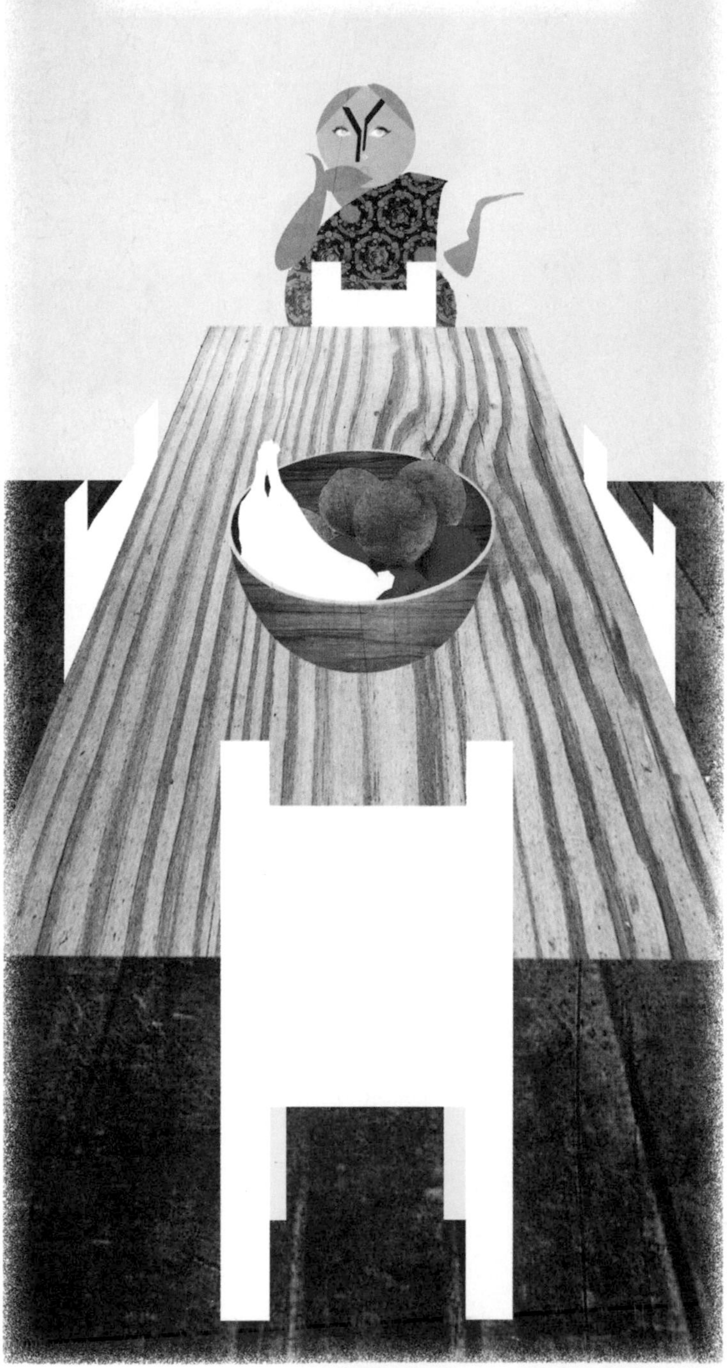

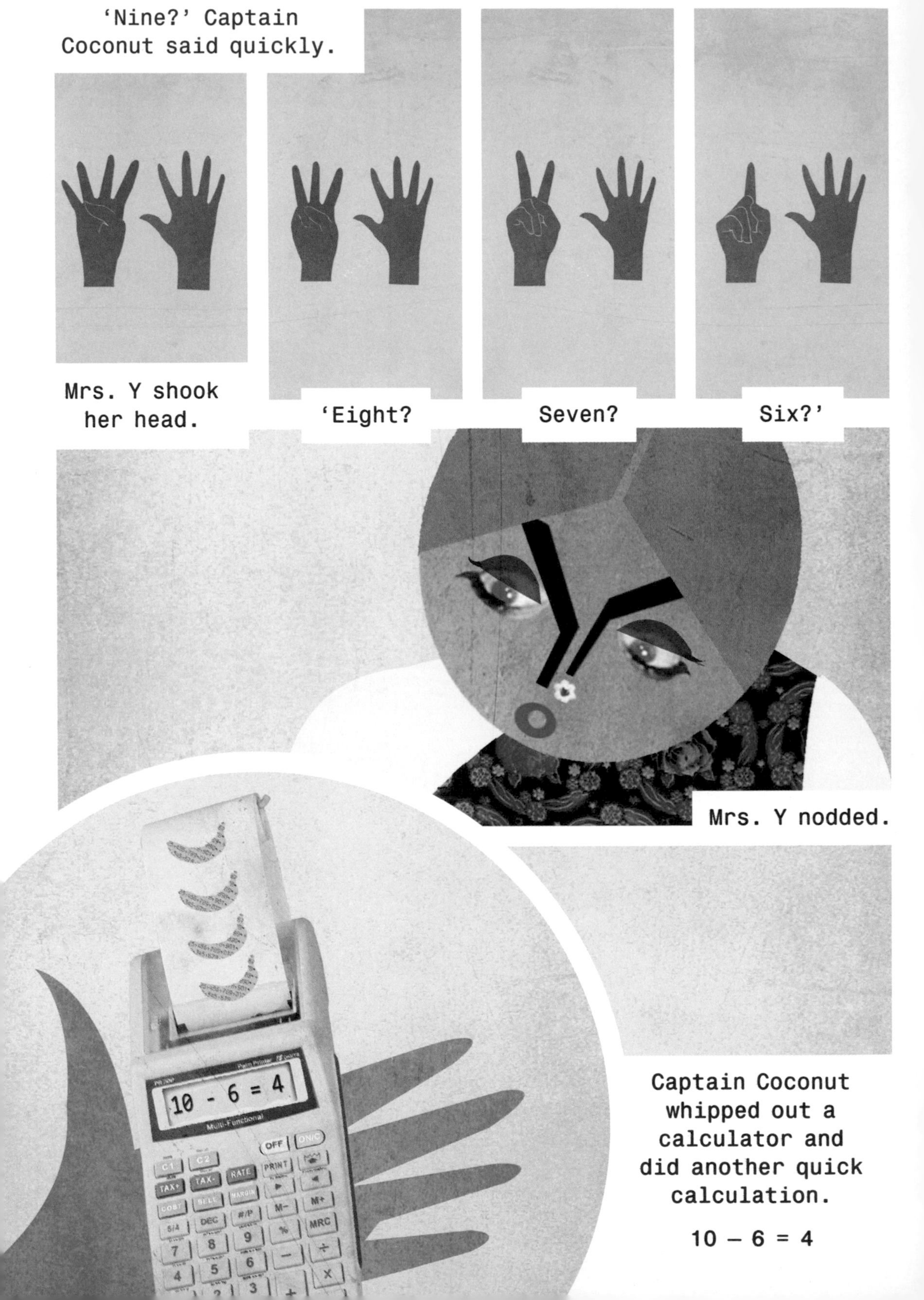
'Nine?' Captain Coconut said quickly.
Mrs. Y shook her head.
'Eight?
Seven?
Six?'
Mrs. Y nodded.
10 - 6 = 4
Captain Coconut whipped out a calculator and did another quick calculation.
10 – 6 = 4

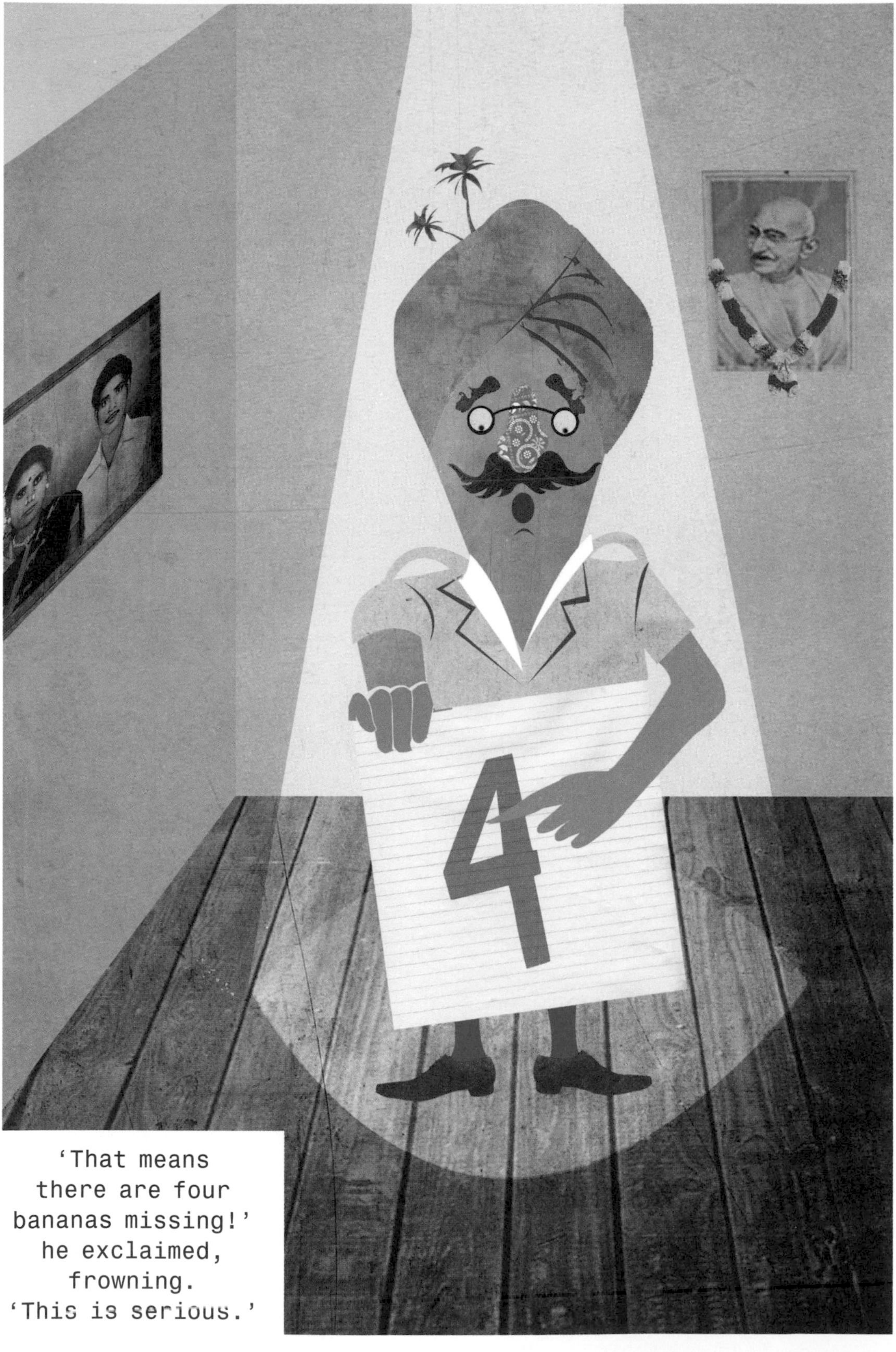
4

'That means there are four bananas missing!' he exclaimed, frowning. 'This is serious.'

Then he had a brainwave. Captain Coconut was known far and wide for his brainwaves. His brainwaves were so famous that whenever a detective got a sudden idea, it was called 'doing a Coconut'.

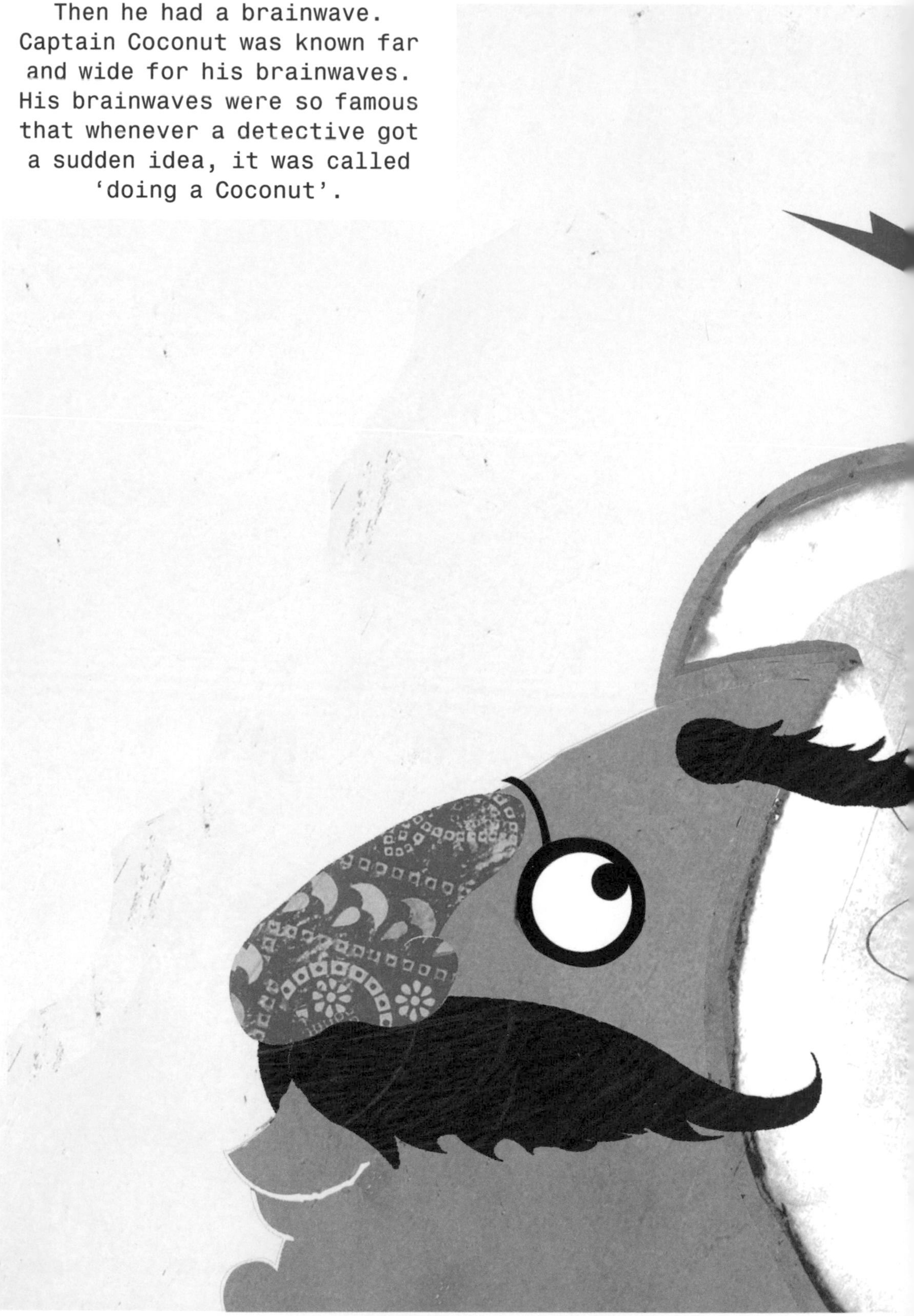

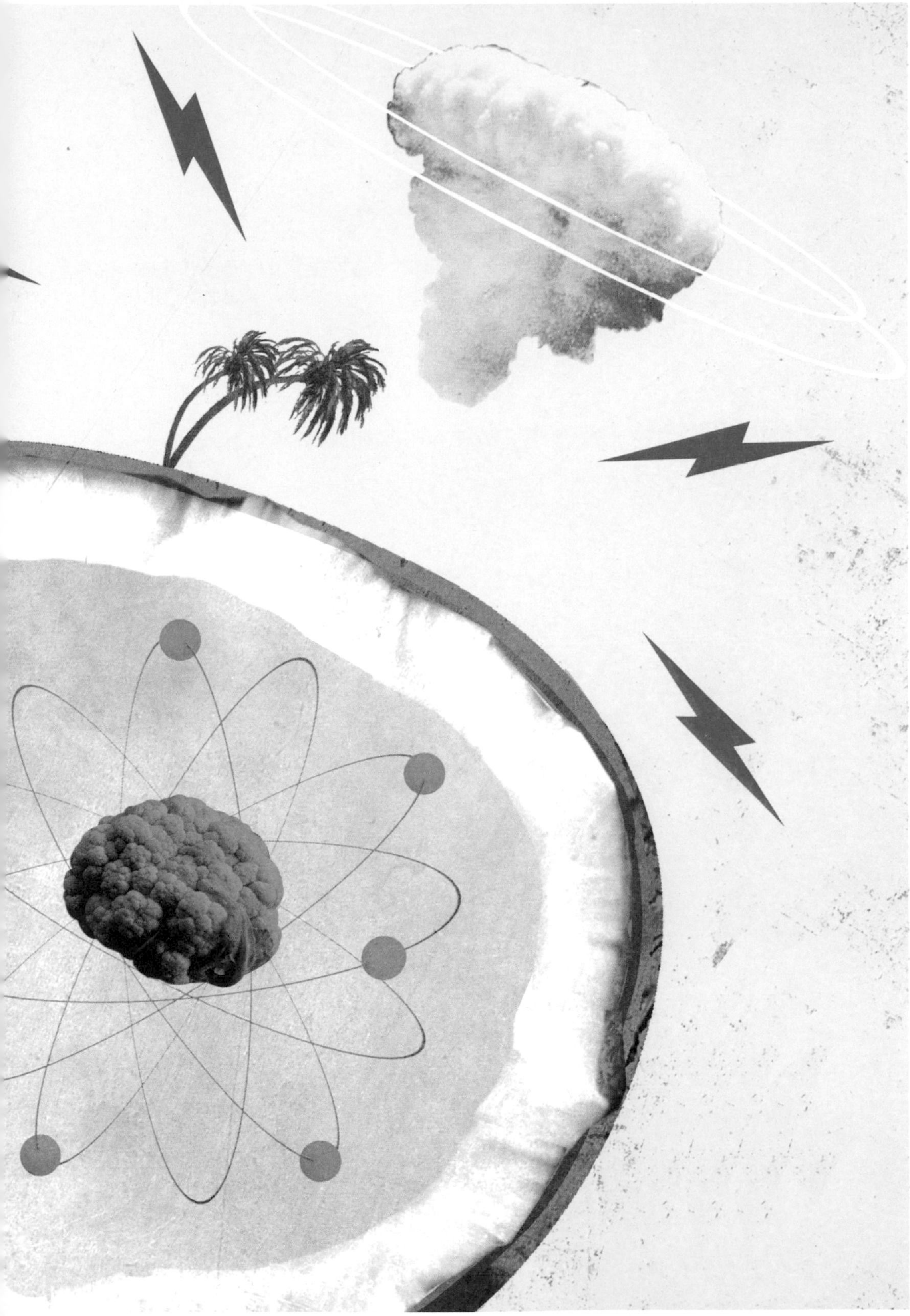

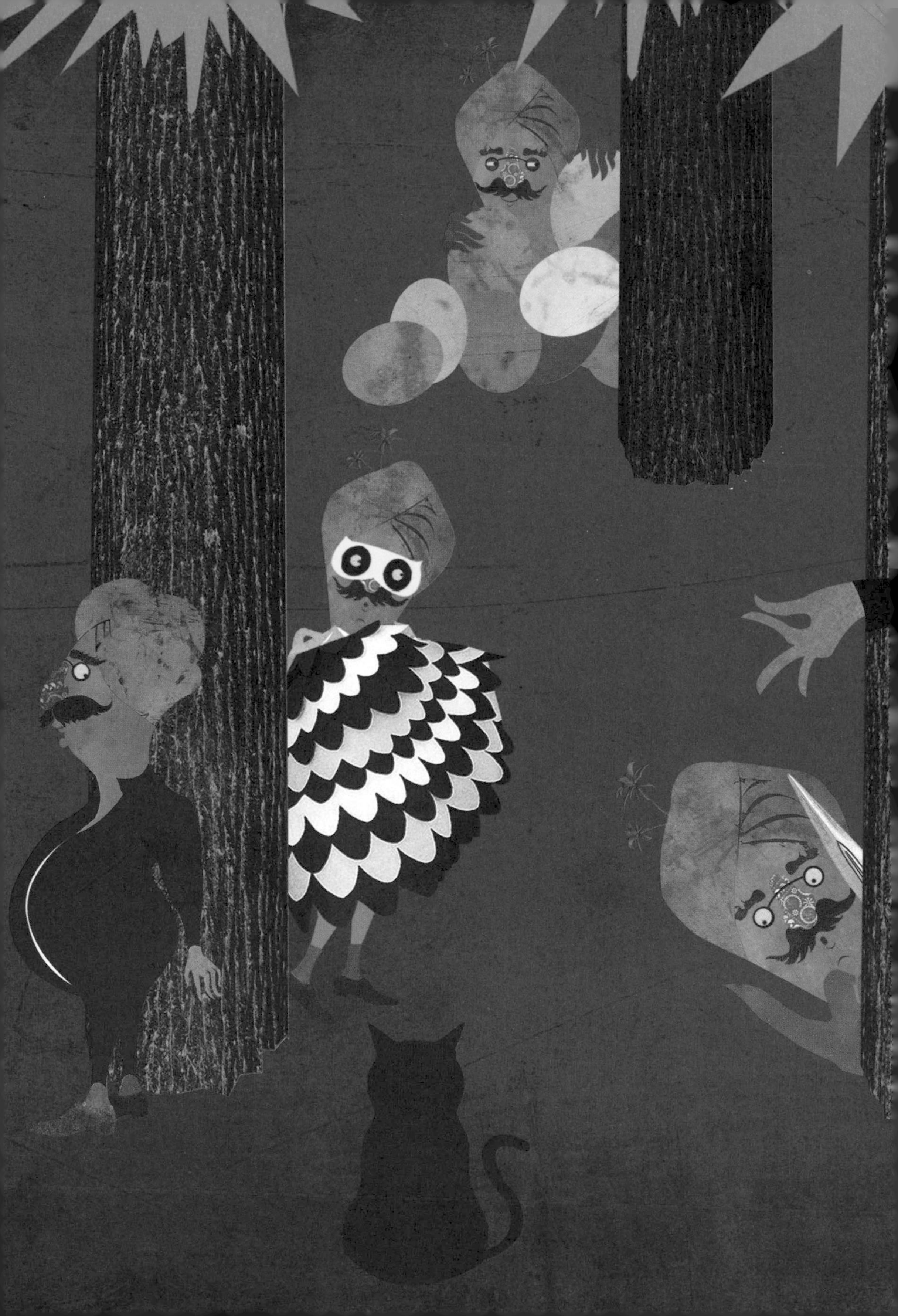

SONG:
DO A COCONUT

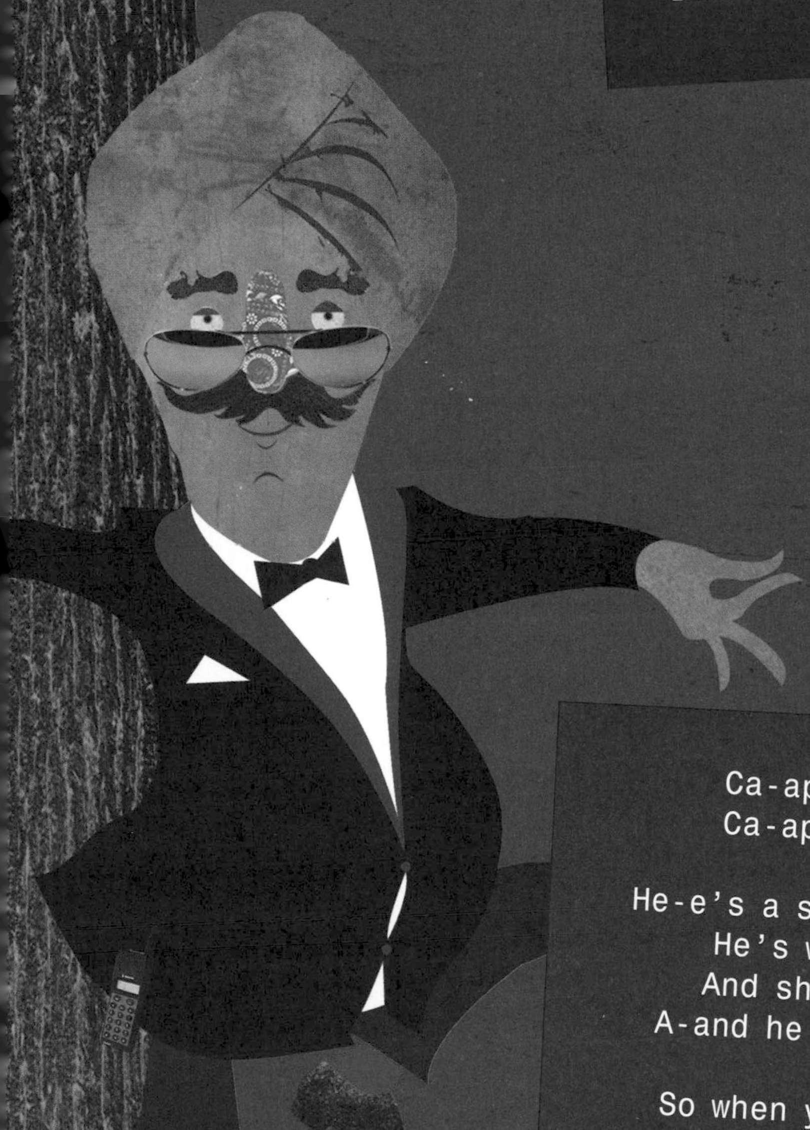

Ca-aptain Coconut!
Ca-aptain Coconut!

He-e's a special kind of guy
He's wise as an owl
And sharp as a sword
A-and he has an eagle eye

So when you're stuck and
the spot is tight
When you can't see any
glimmer of light

Do-o a Coconut
Do-o a Coconut

And everything will be alright!

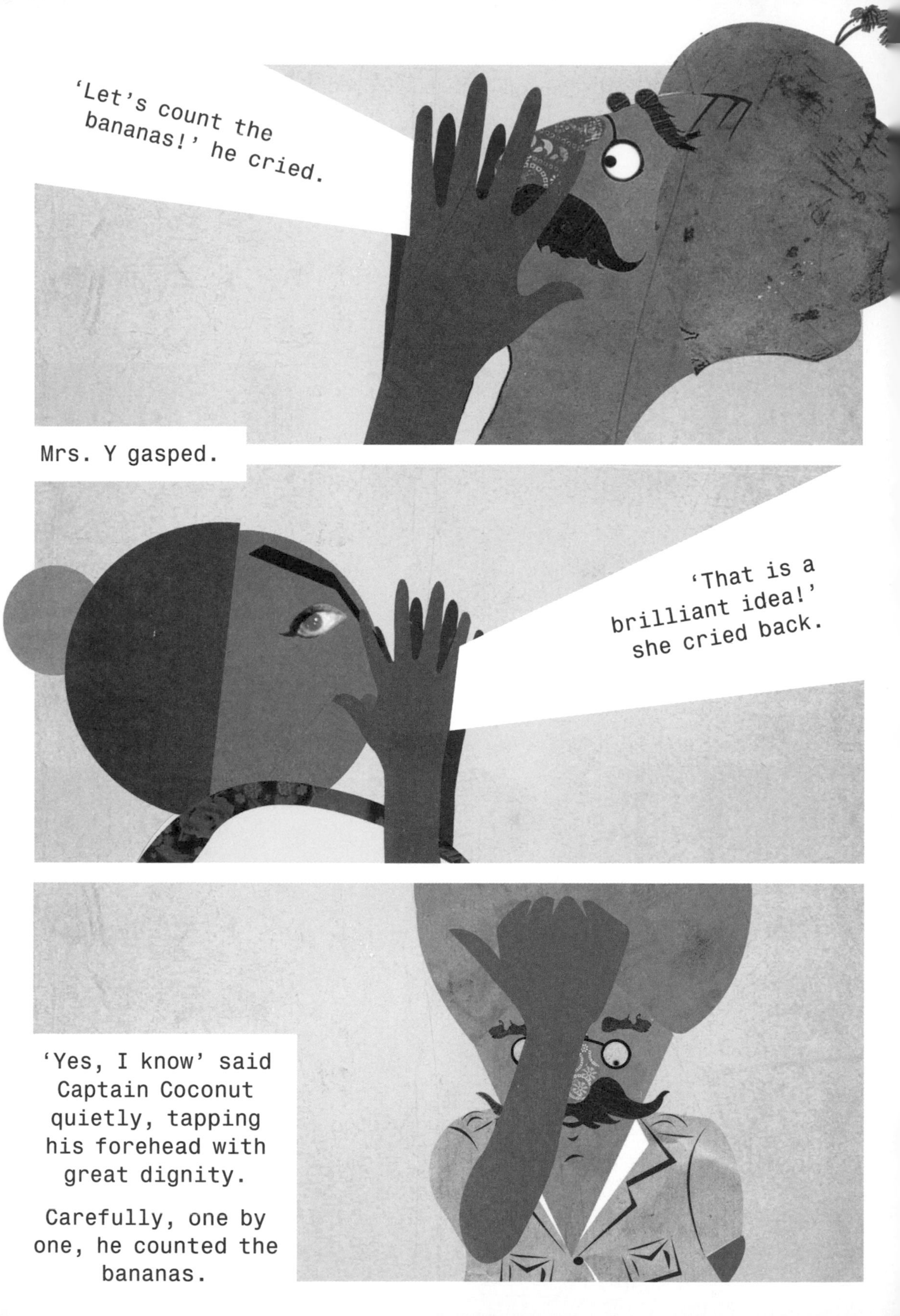
'Let's count the bananas!,' he cried.
Mrs. Y gasped.
'That is a brilliant idea!' she cried back.
'Yes, I know' said Captain Coconut quietly, tapping his forehead with great dignity.
Carefully, one by one, he counted the bananas.

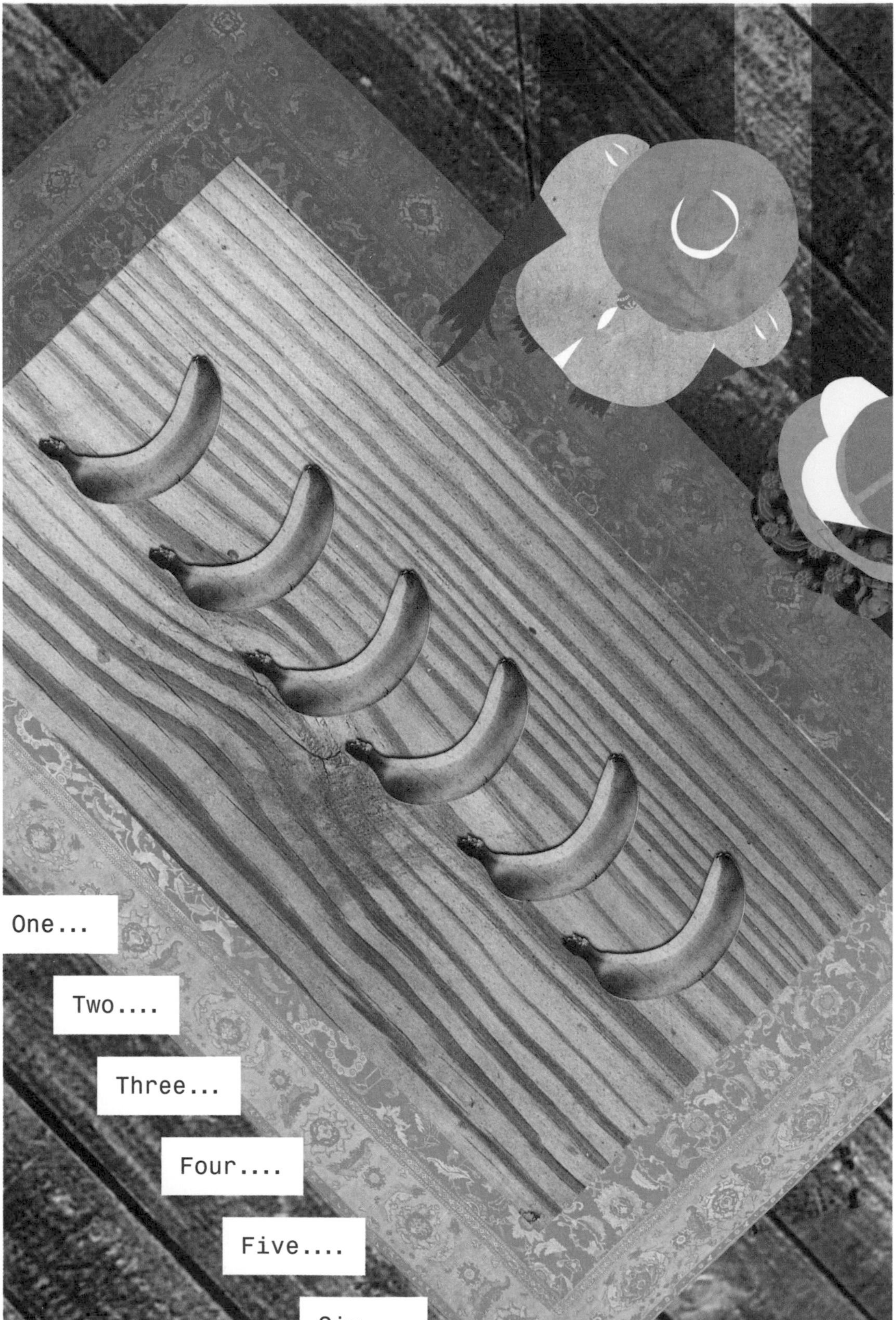
One...
Two....
Three...
Four....
Five....
Six....

He whipped out his
notebook and noted:

'Six bananas on the table.
Counted and checked.'

Captain Coconut felt that he had made good progress. He noted it all down:

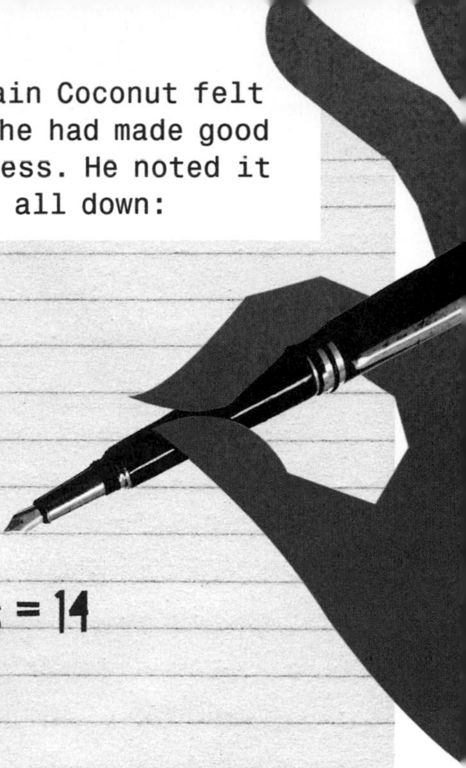

Total number of bananas = 14

Total number eaten = 4

Should remain = 14 – 4 = 10

Actually remaining = 6

Number missing = 10 – 6 = 4

'Hmm,' said Captain Coconut. There was nothing else to say.

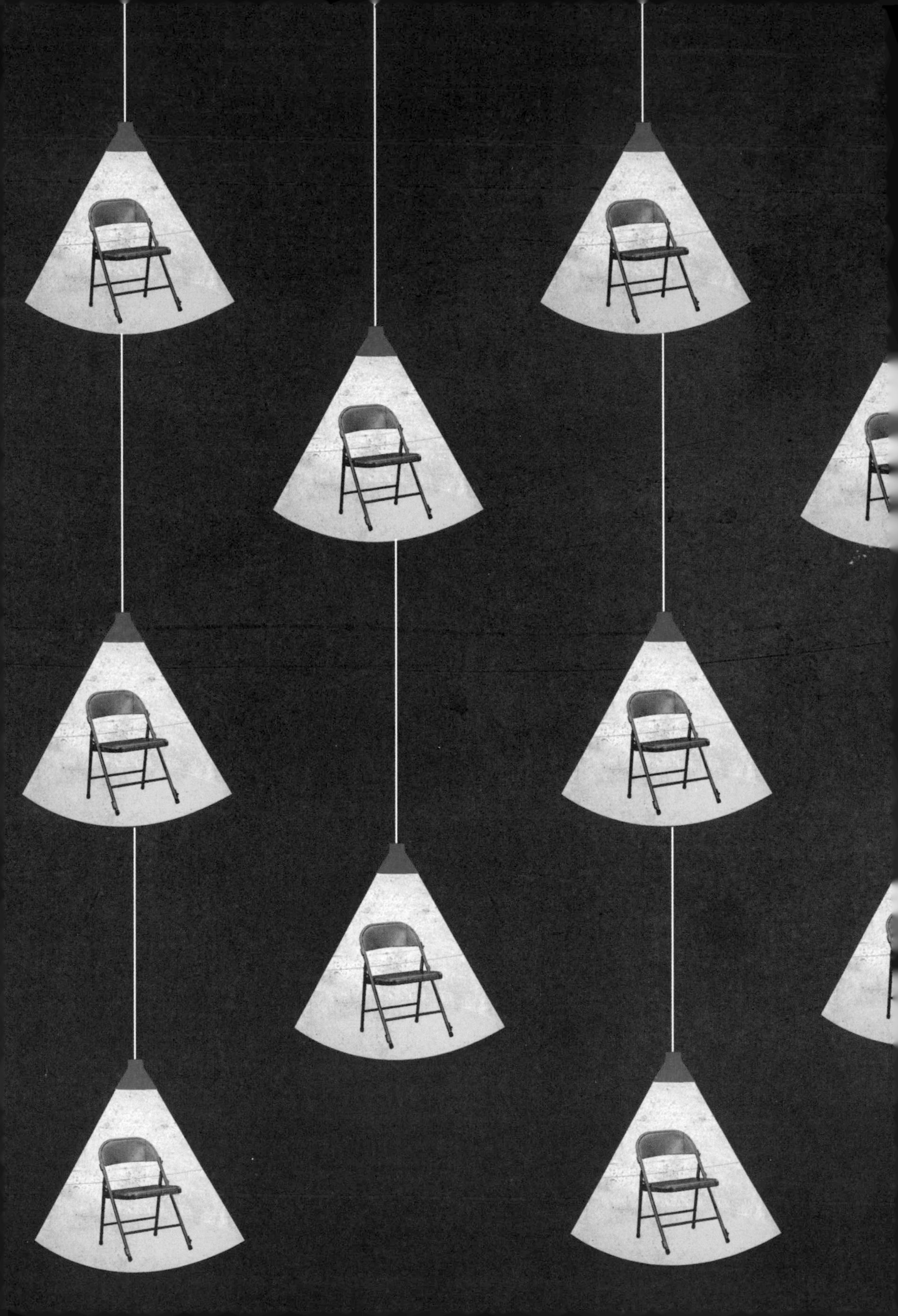

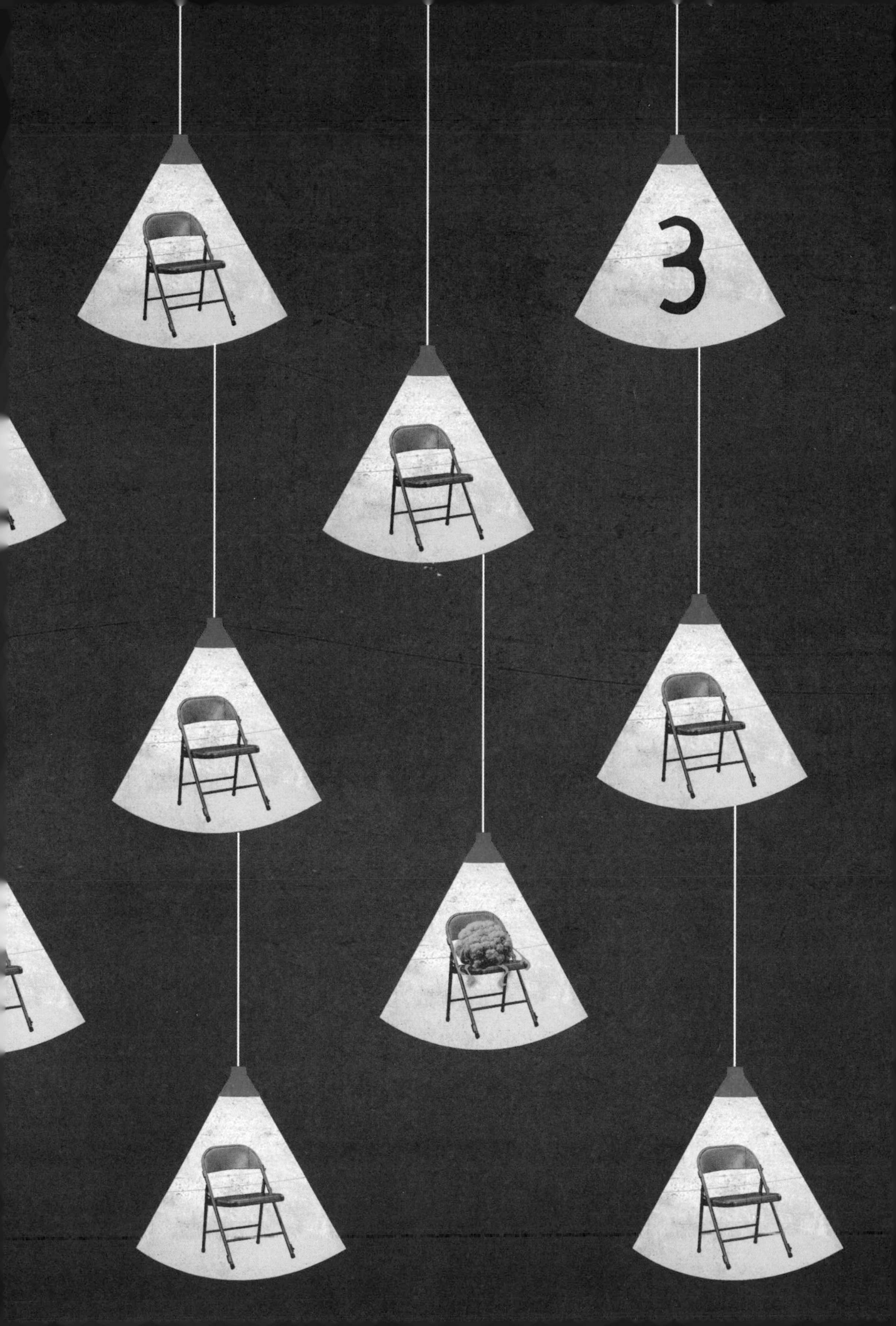
3

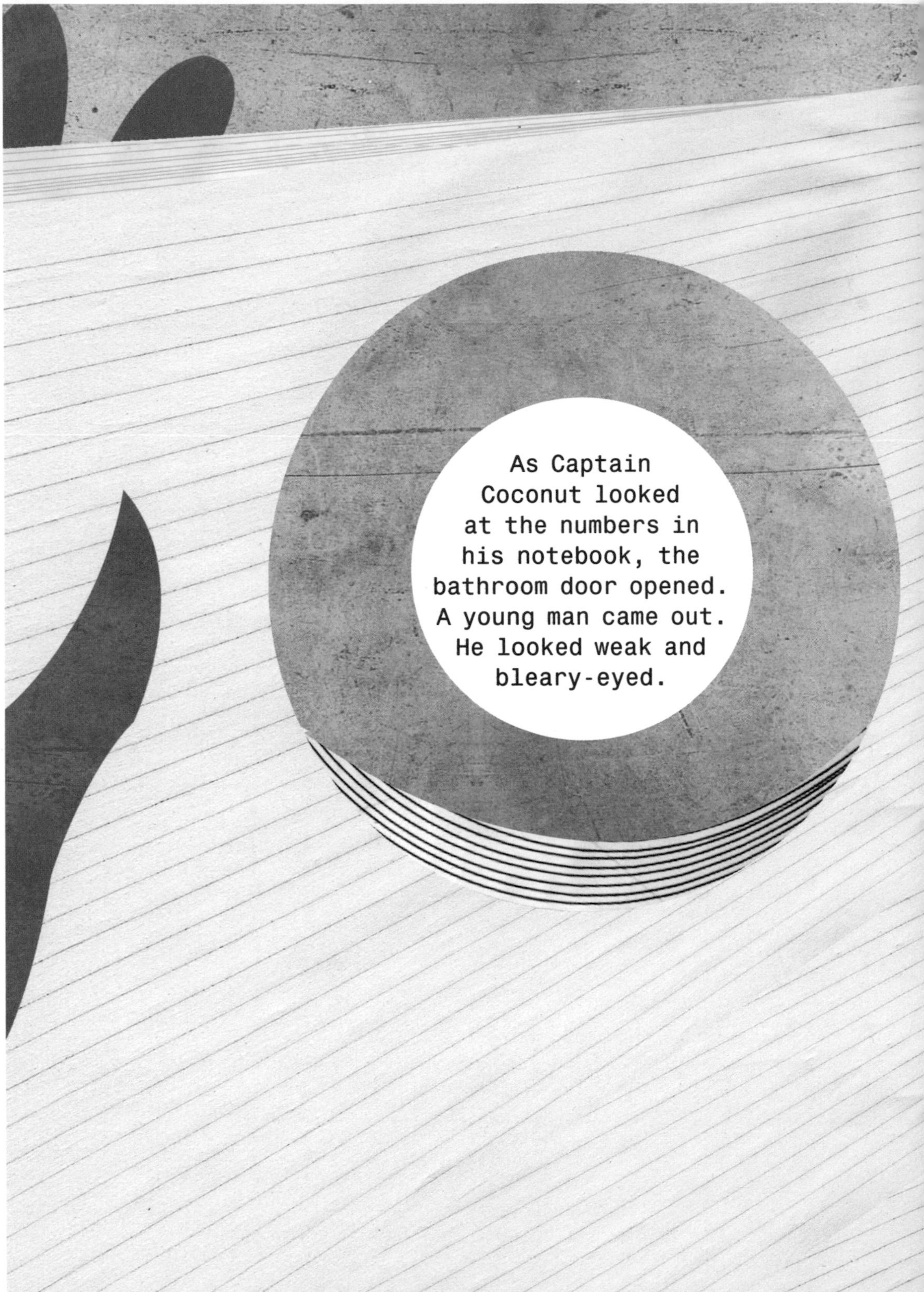
As Captain Coconut looked at the numbers in his notebook, the bathroom door opened. A young man came out. He looked weak and bleary-eyed.

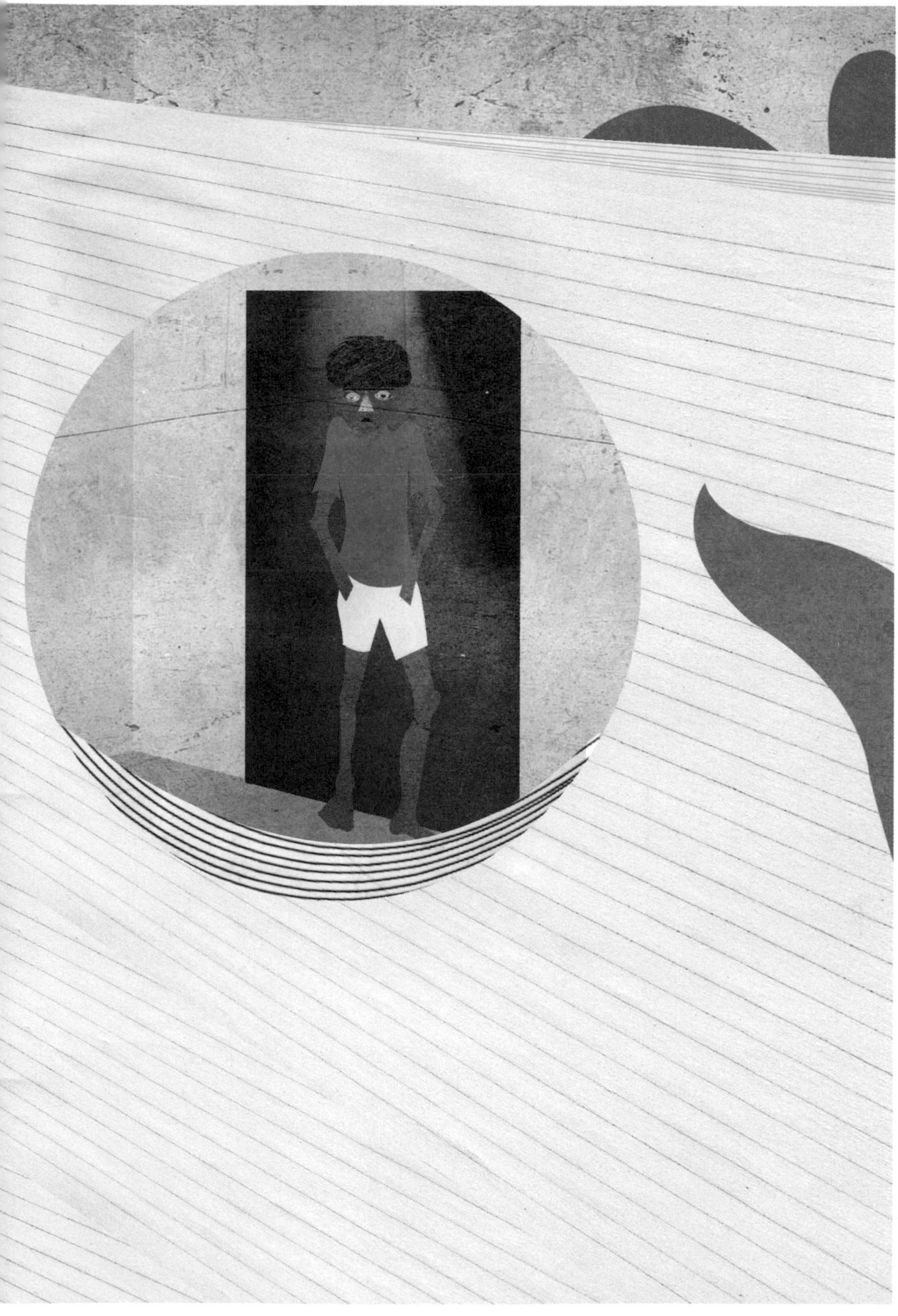

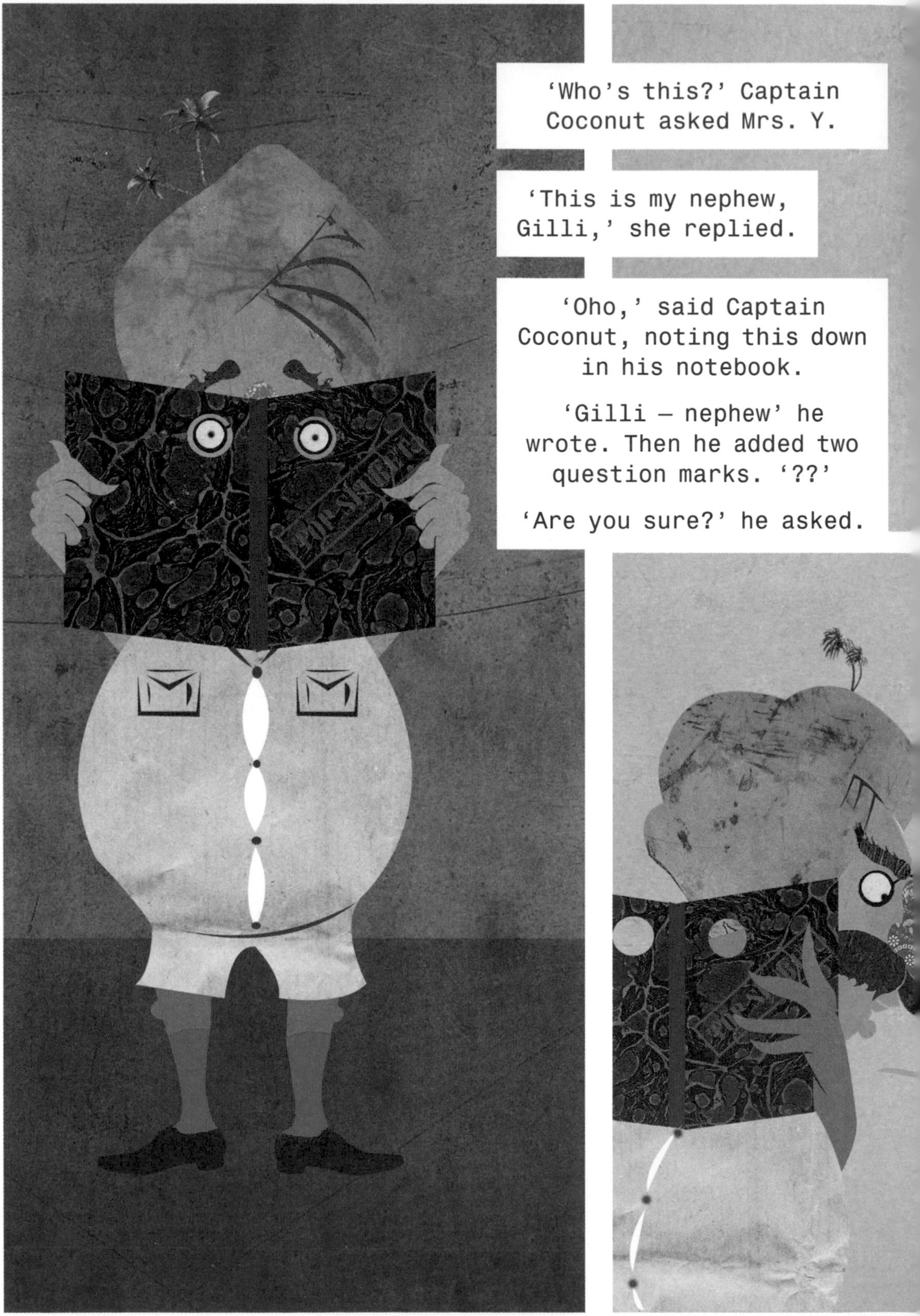
'Who's this?' Captain Coconut asked Mrs. Y.
'This is my nephew, Gilli,' she replied.
'Oho,' said Captain Coconut, noting this down in his notebook.
'Gilli – nephew' he wrote. Then he added two question marks. '??'
'Are you sure?' he asked.

It was
the first rule
that they taught in
detective school.
Always confirm your
facts.

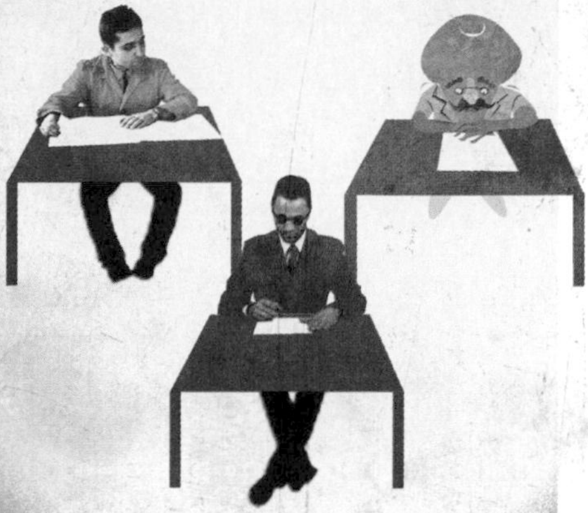

'Yes' said Mrs.Y

'Confirmed,' Captain Coconut wrote in his notebook.

'Where were you last night?' he asked Gilli, who had collapsed on the sofa and was groaning softly.

'Eh?' asked Gilli.

'He's not very bright,' Mrs. Y said.

'Are you sure?' asked Captain Coconut.

'Yes,' said Mrs. Y.

'Not very bright, checked and confirmed,' Captain Coconut wrote in his book.

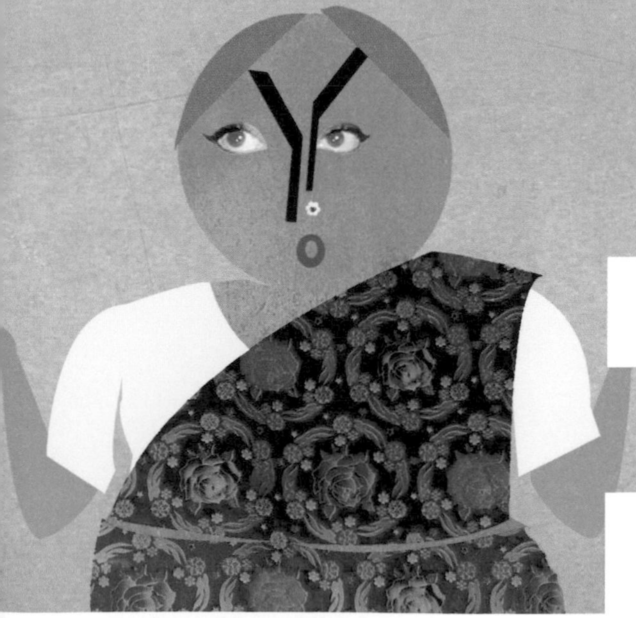

'Where were you last night?' he asked Gilli again. This time he accompanied his words with actions.

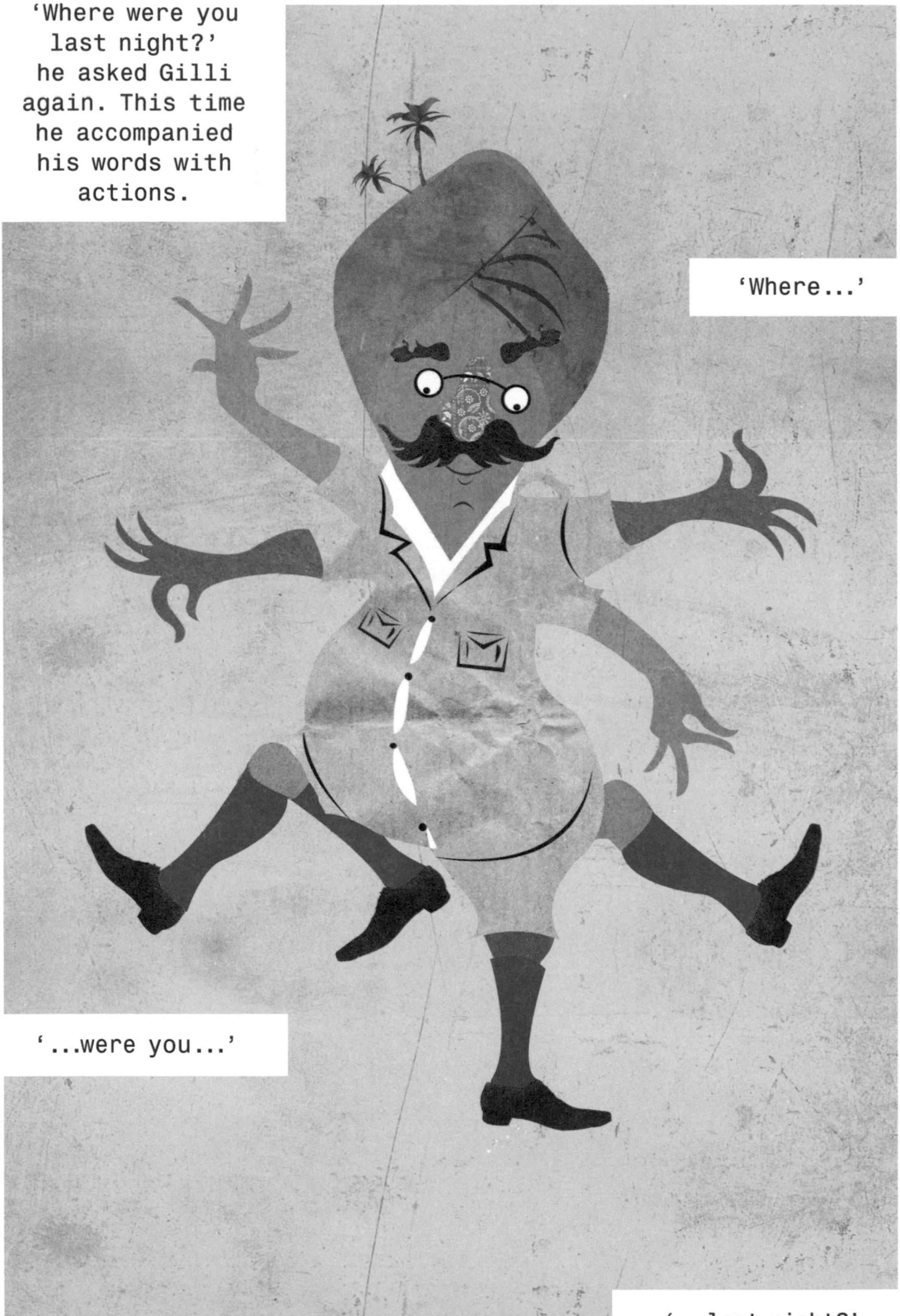

'Eh?' said Gilli again. He wondered why the man with the moustache was doing a strange dance in his house, and wished he would go away. 'I wish you would go away,' he said.

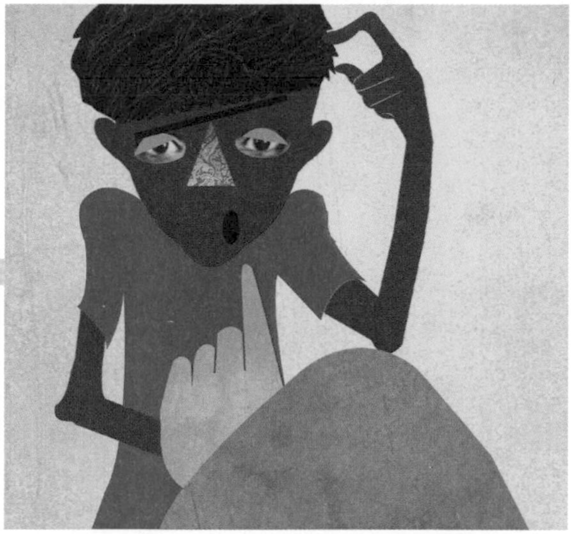

'Aha!' said the Captain. 'You do, do you? That is very interesting. Tell me, he said,' patting Gilli on the head, like a fond uncle 'Do you like bananas?'

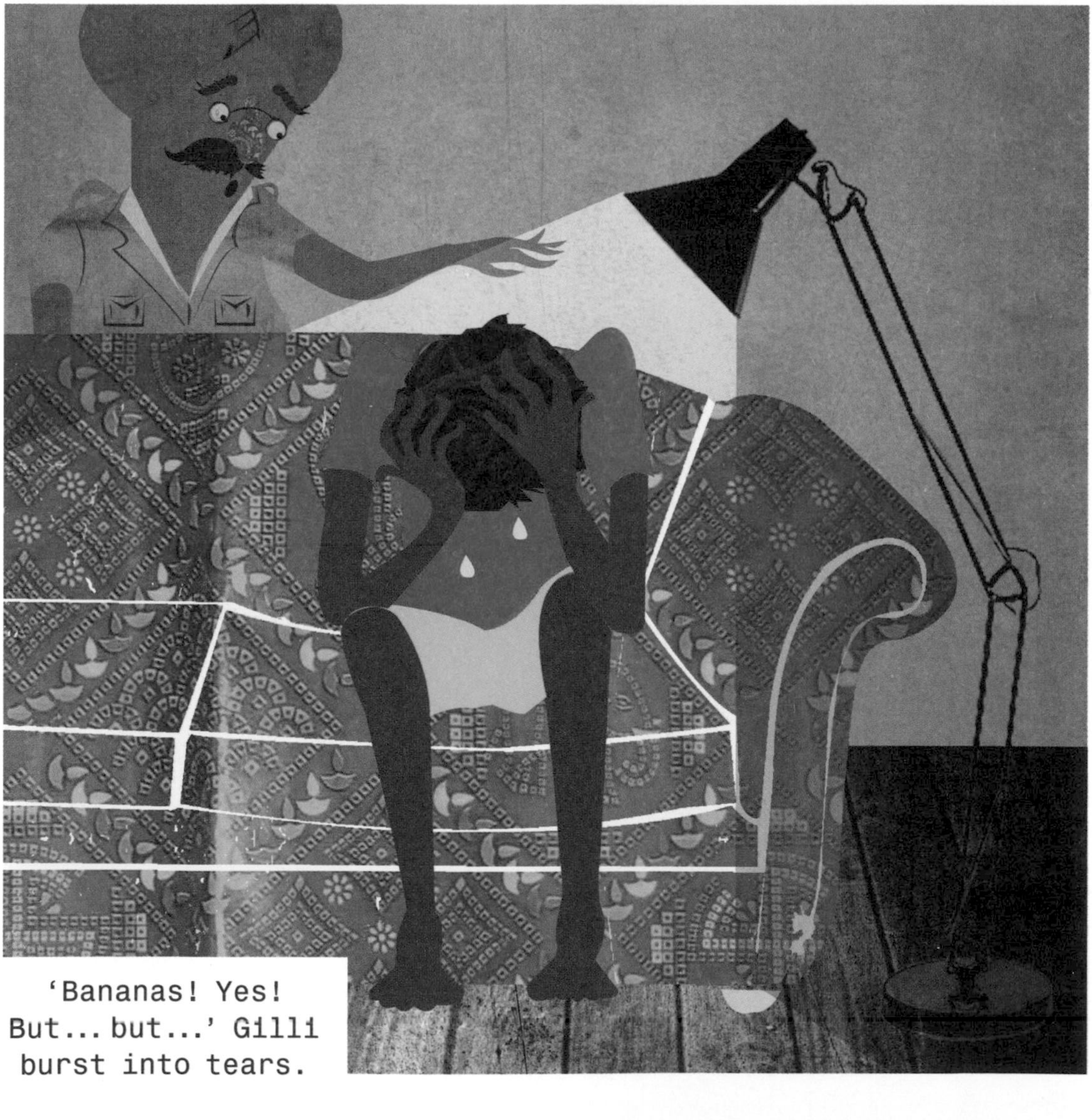

'Bananas! Yes! But... but...' Gilli burst into tears.

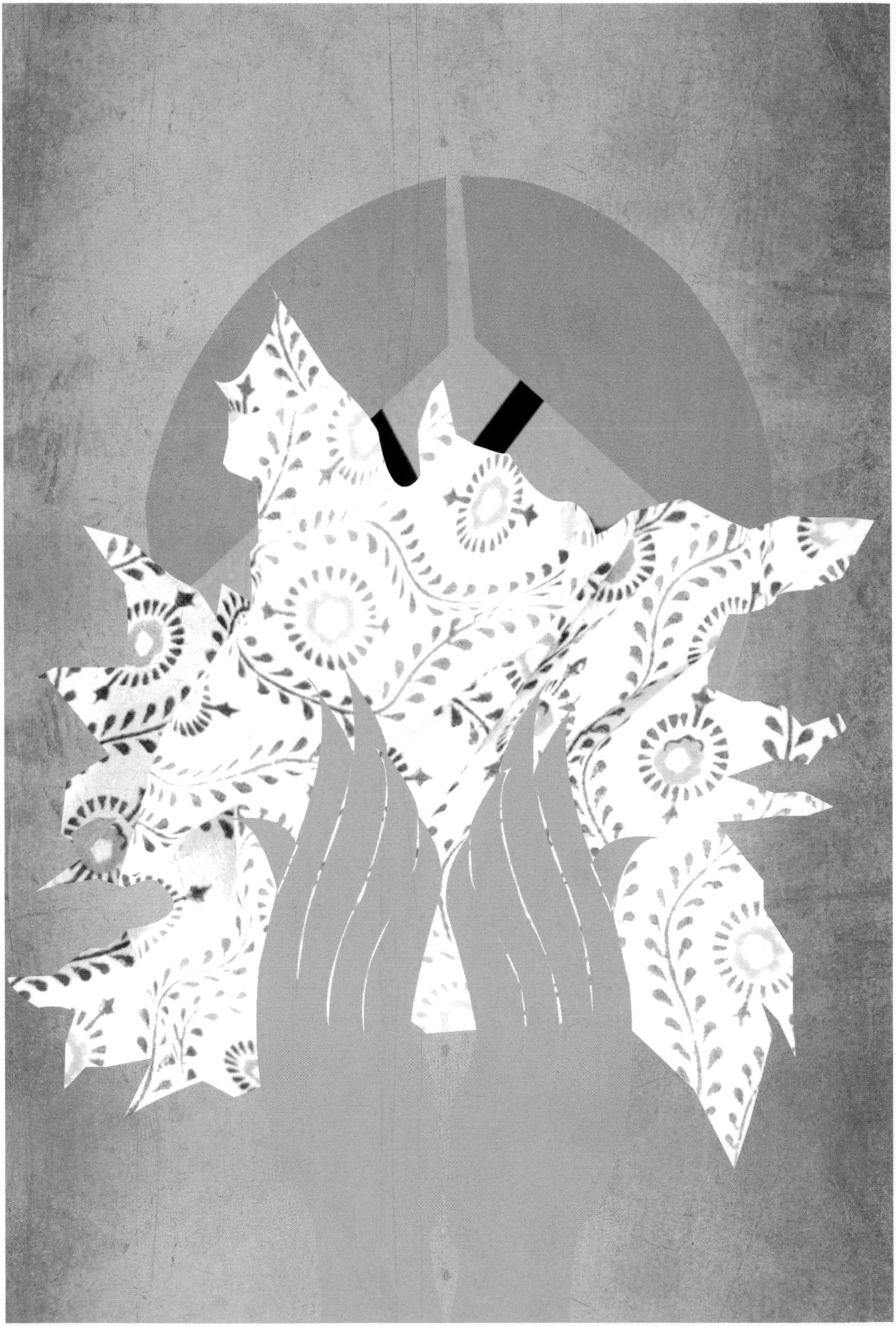

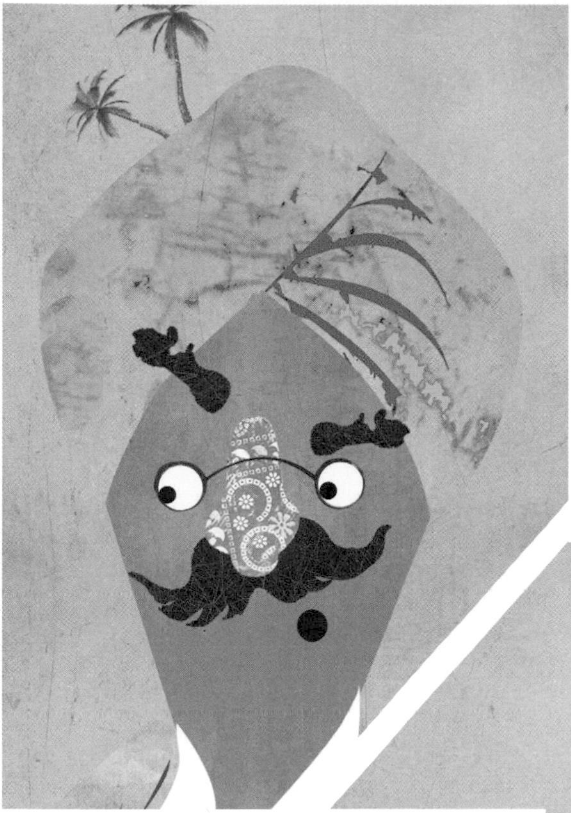

'Does everyone in this family cry a lot?' Captain Coconut asked Mrs. Y, whose eyes were filling up at the sight of her crying nephew.

Mrs. Y did not answer, because she was busy blowing her nose.

Captain Coconut frowned. 'Refuses to answer question about family,' he wrote in his notebook. Then he remembered that Gilli had not finished his sentence.

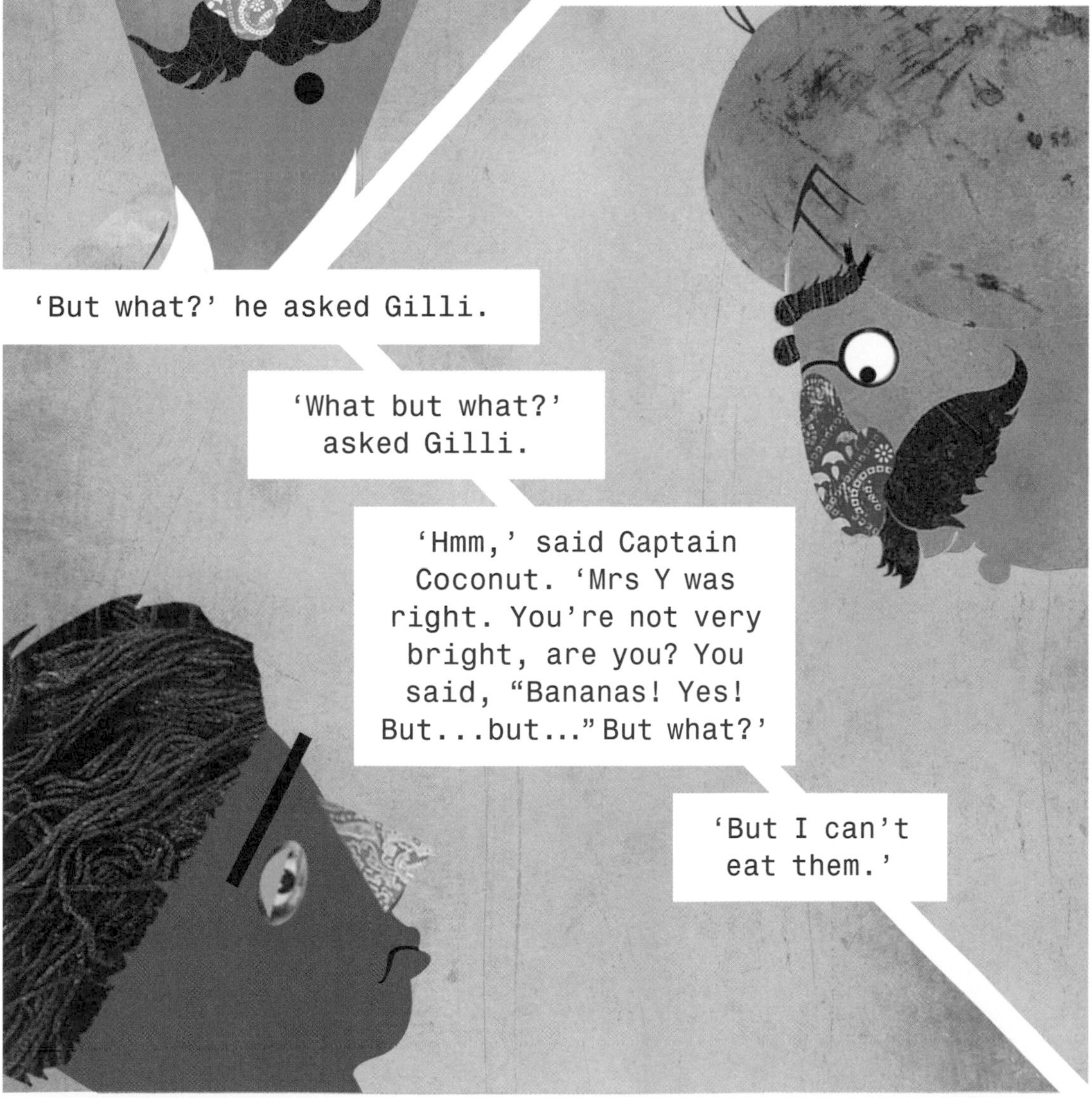

'But what?' he asked Gilli.

'What but what?' asked Gilli.

'Hmm,' said Captain Coconut. 'Mrs Y was right. You're not very bright, are you? You said, "Bananas! Yes! But...but..." But what?'

'But I can't eat them.'

Nouvelle Guinée
Nouvelle Zelande
de Capricorne
Cercle du Pôle Antarctique
Terre Australe et
Magel'an
Isles Açores
France
Mer de Nort
Archipelague de Sainct Lazare

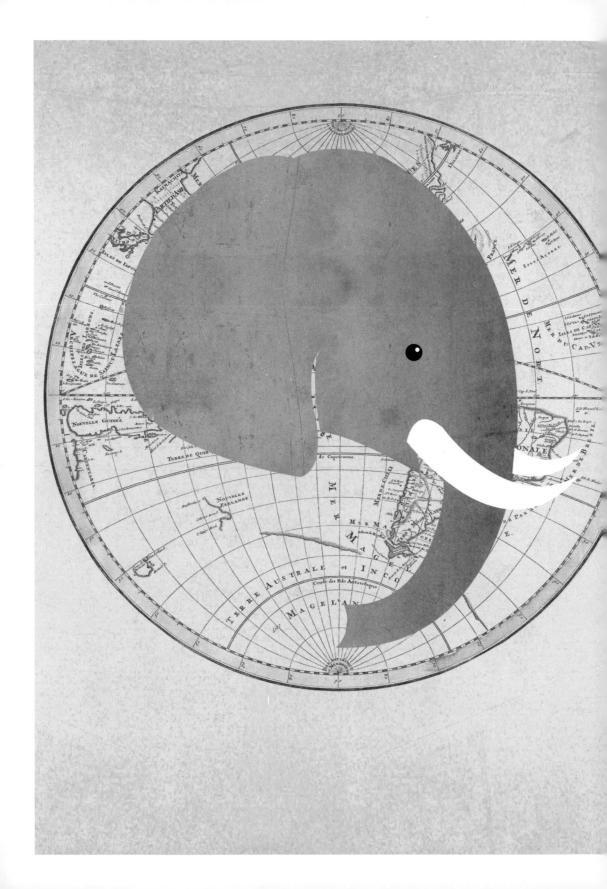

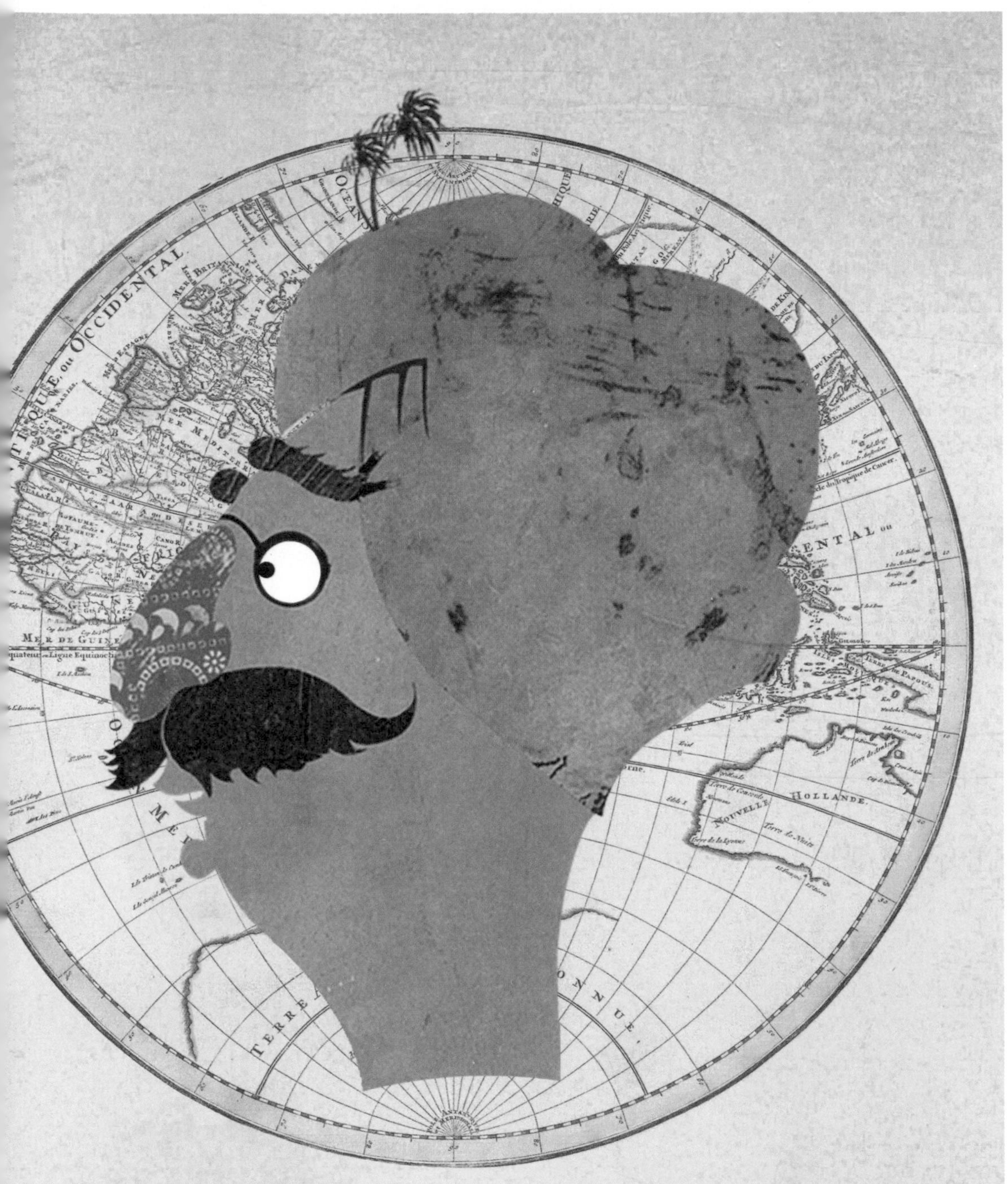
OCCIDENTAL
MER DE GUINEE
HOLLANDE.
TERRE

Captain Coconut was known far and wide as the man with the memory of an elephant. Whenever someone remembered a small fact, it was called 'doing a Coconut'.

SONG: MEMORY OF AN ELEPHANT

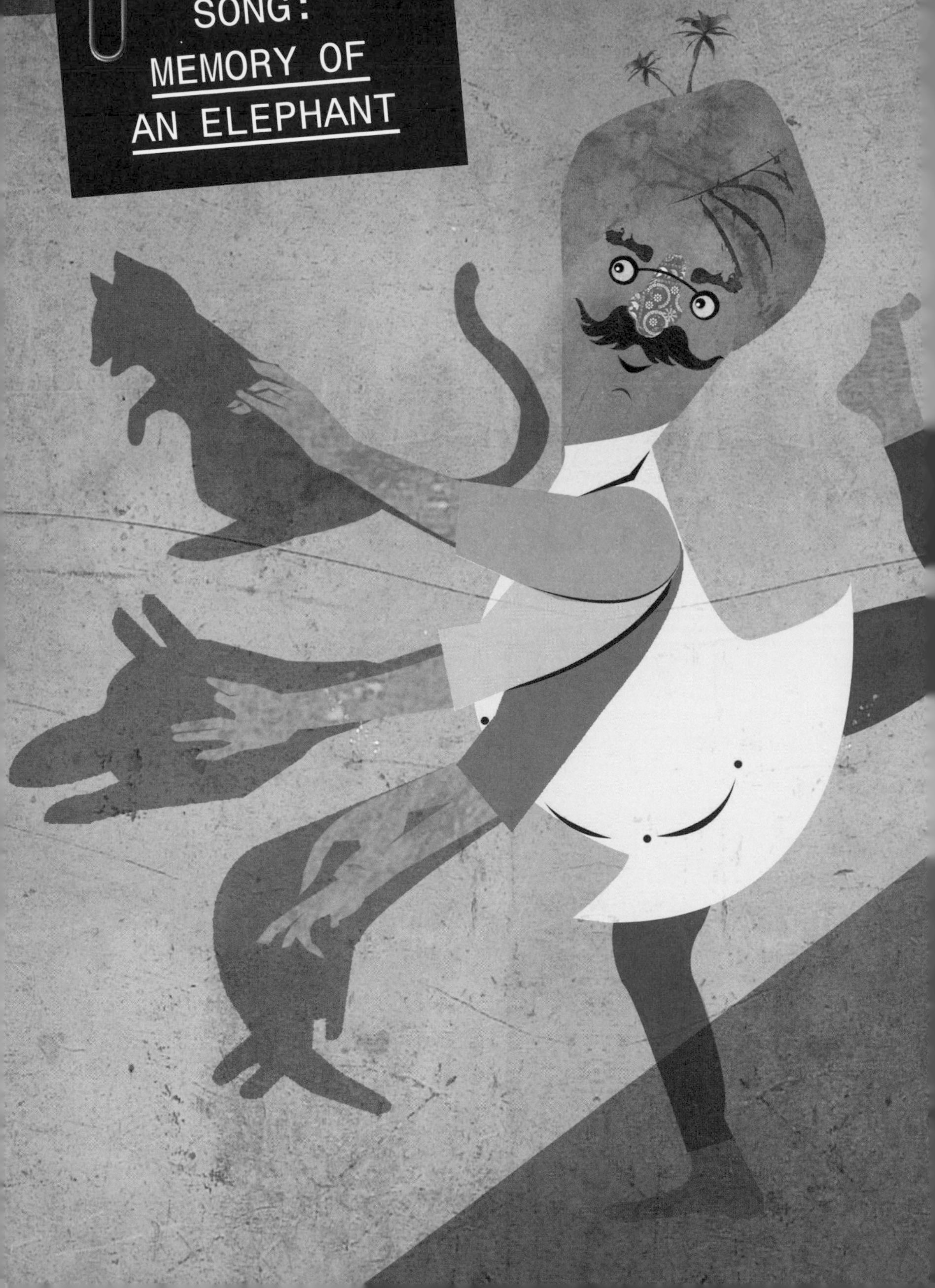

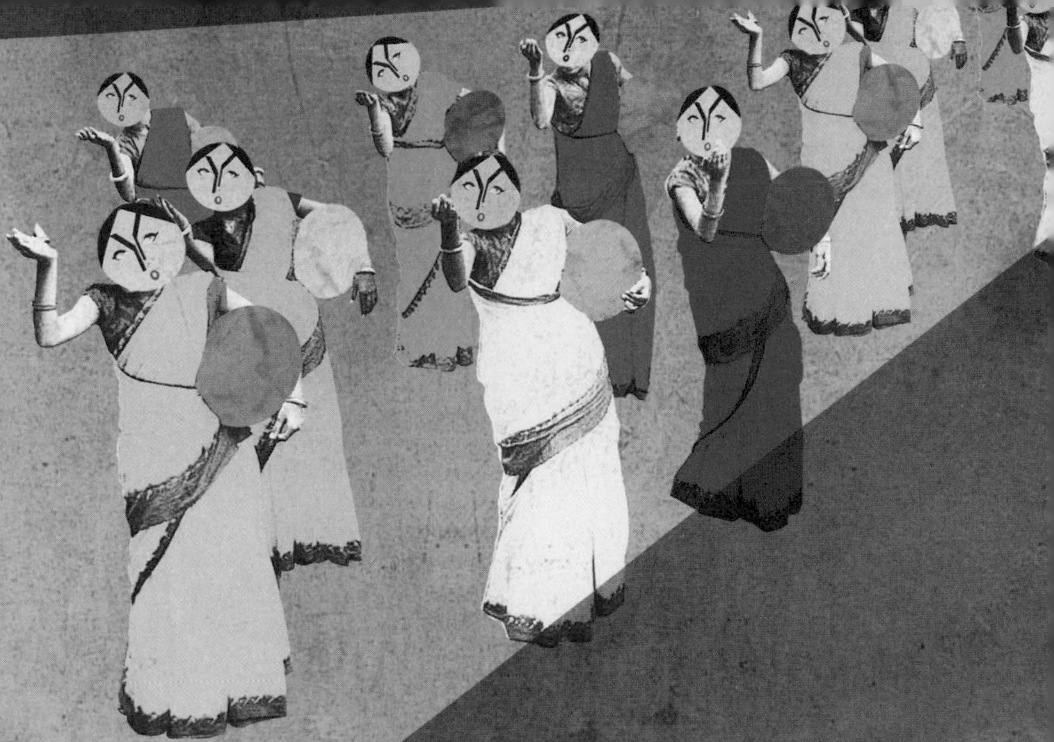

Ca-aptain Coconut!
Ca-aptain Coconut!

He-e's a special kind of gent
He's curious as a cat
And sharp-nosed as a dog
With the mem-ory of an elephant

So when the case is big and the
facts are small
When your mind is dim and you
can't recall

Do-o a Coconut
Do-o a Coconut

And you will remember it all!

'But I remember quite clearly a small fact that your aunt mentioned to me. She said you ate a banana last night!'
'Did I?' Gilli asked his aunt. Mrs. Y nodded. Captain Coconut took this to mean 'yes'.
'That might explain my diarrhoea,' Gilli groaned.
Captain Coconut did a bit of thinking in his notebook.

'Bananas – ate – diarrhoea. Ergo,' He considered the word 'ergo' for a few minutes. He wasn't sure he knew what it meant. So he cancelled it and wrote 'Therefore, bananas – diarrhoea.'

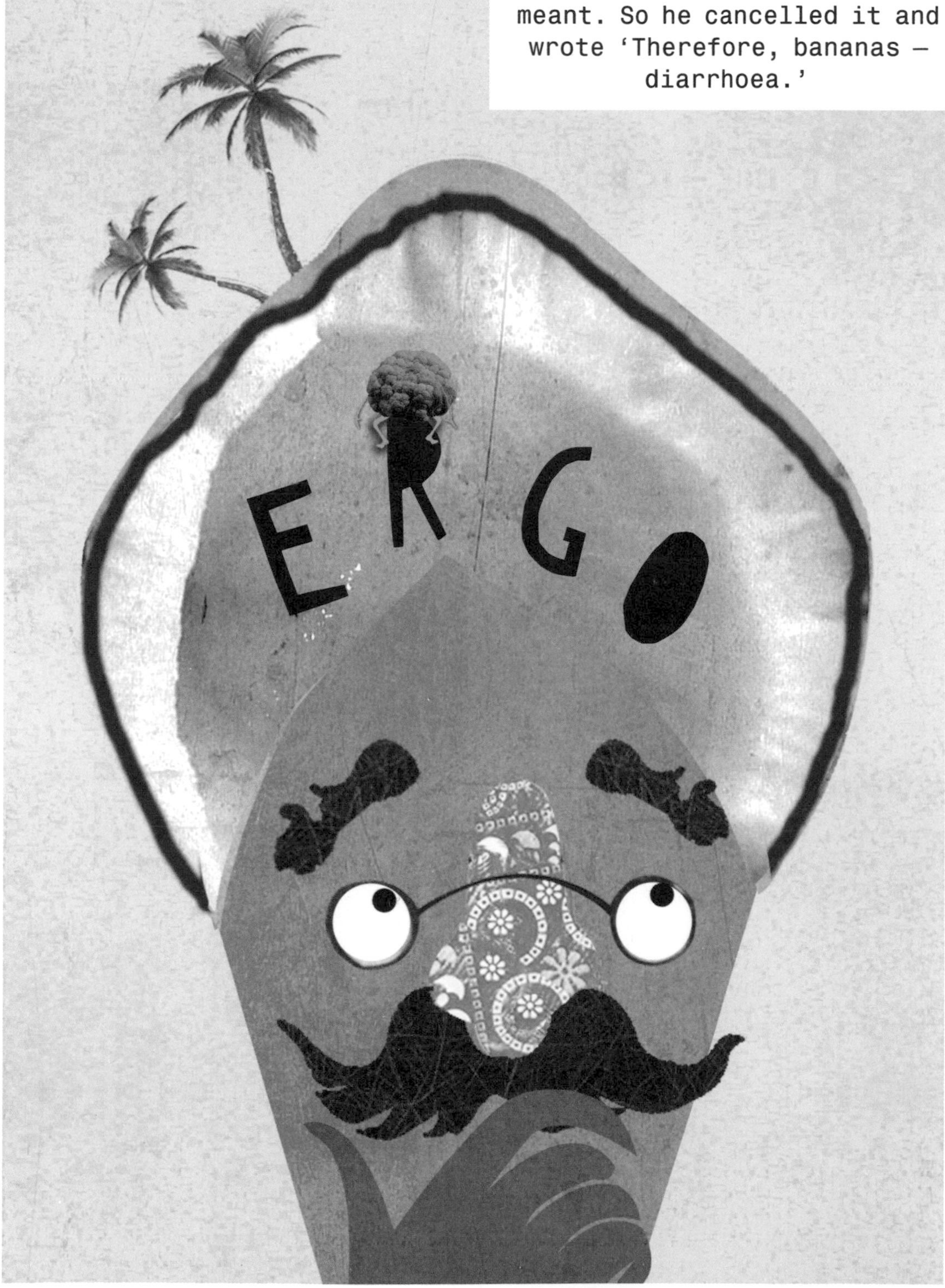
ERGO

'Aha!' he cried, understanding immediately. 'Bananas give you diarrhoea, do they?'

'Usually I just feel a bit queasy in my stomach. But once, I ate five bananas and got severe diarrhoea. I ate only one yesterday!'

'Are you sure?' asked Captain Coconut, with narrowed eyes.

'Yes,' said Mrs. Y. 'I gave it to him myself.'

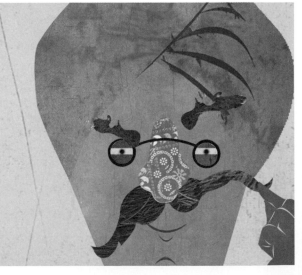

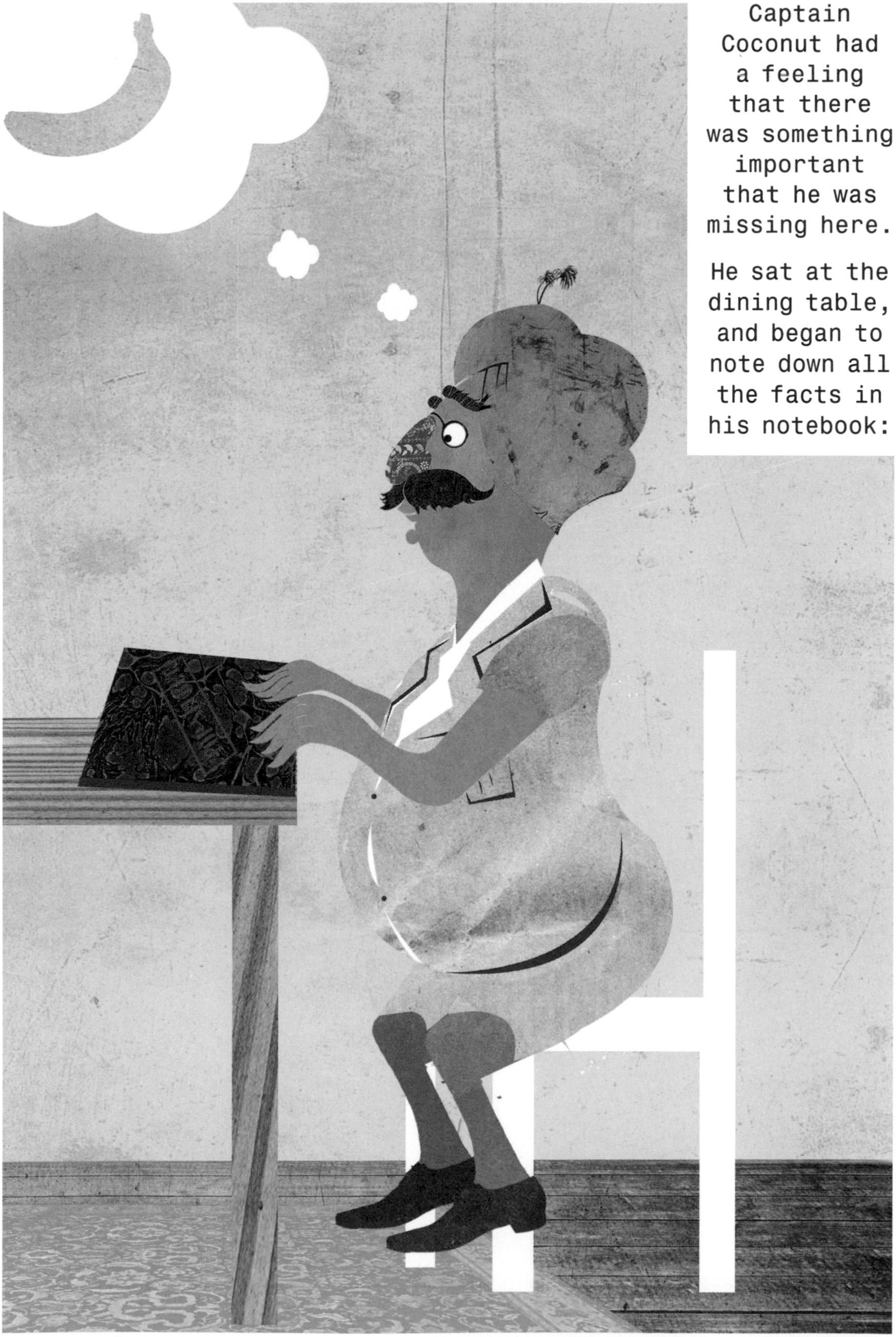

Captain Coconut had a feeling that there was something important that he was missing here.

He sat at the dining table, and began to note down all the facts in his notebook:

No. of bananas bought = 14

No. of bananas eaten by Mrs. Y
on the way = 1

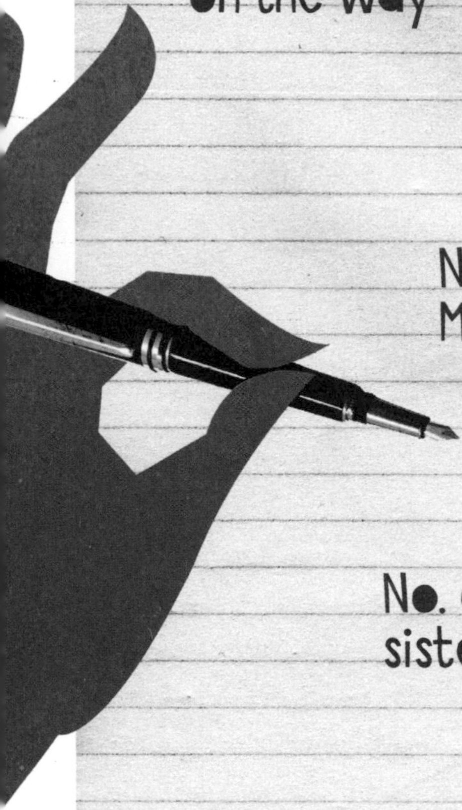

No. of bananas eaten by
Mrs. Y at night = 1

No. of bananas eaten by Mrs. Y's
sister at night = 1

No. of bananas eaten by Gilli at night = 1

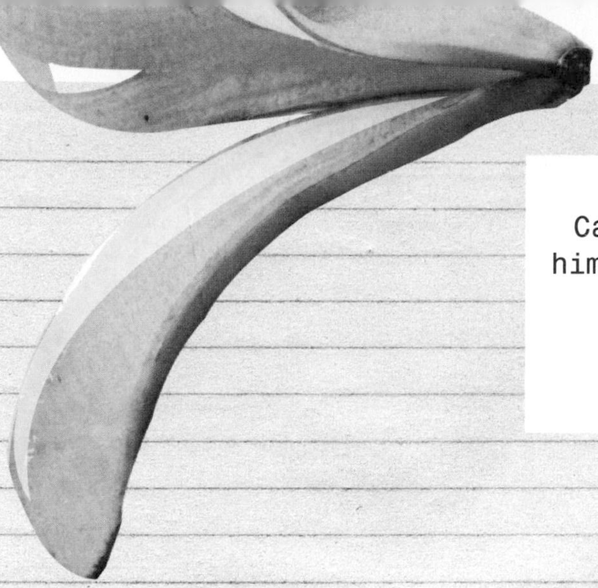

'All this is clear,' Captain Coconut muttered to himself, as he absent-mindedly ate a banana.

He then noted down some more facts:

No. of bananas that cause Gilli to get diarrhoea = 5

No. of bananas eaten by Gilli = 1

No. of bananas more that Gilli should have eaten to get diarrhoea = 4

No. of bananas missing = 4

Four, and four.
This had to mean something.

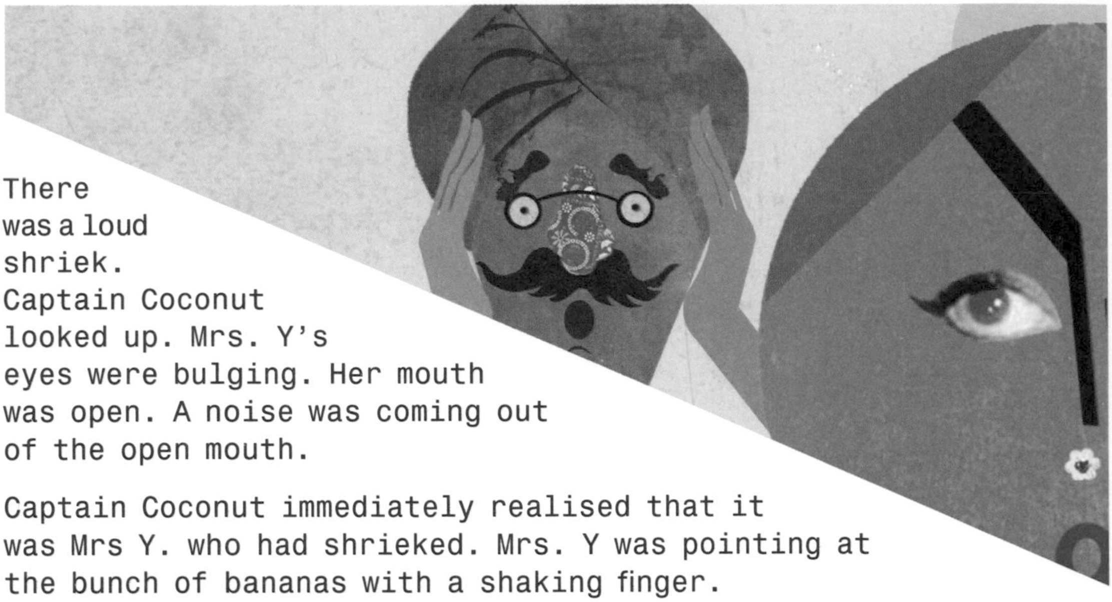
There was a loud shriek. Captain Coconut looked up. Mrs. Y's eyes were bulging. Her mouth was open. A noise was coming out of the open mouth.
Captain Coconut immediately realised that it was Mrs Y. who had shrieked. Mrs. Y was pointing at the bunch of bananas with a shaking finger.

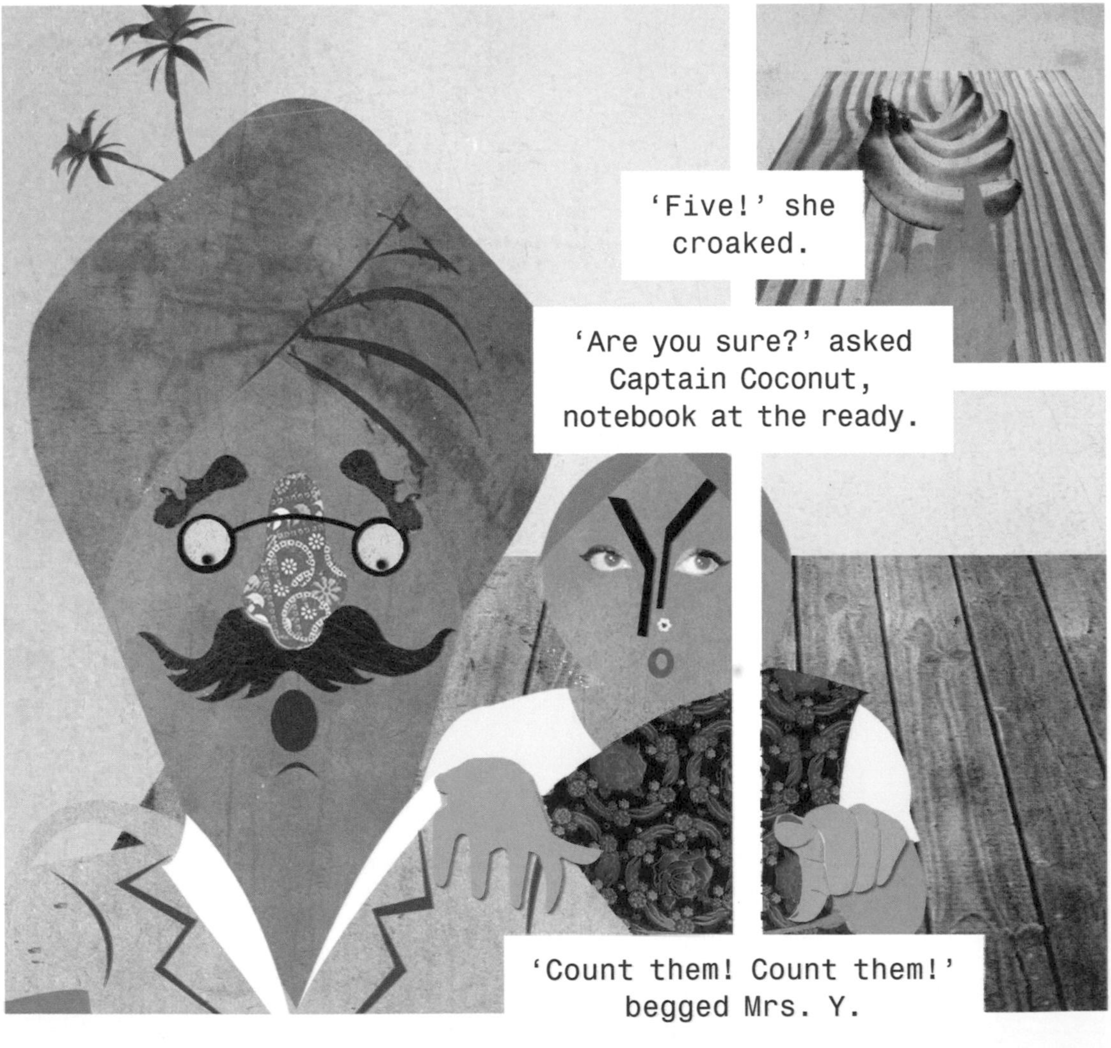
'Five!' she croaked.
'Are you sure?' asked Captain Coconut, notebook at the ready.
'Count them! Count them!' begged Mrs. Y.

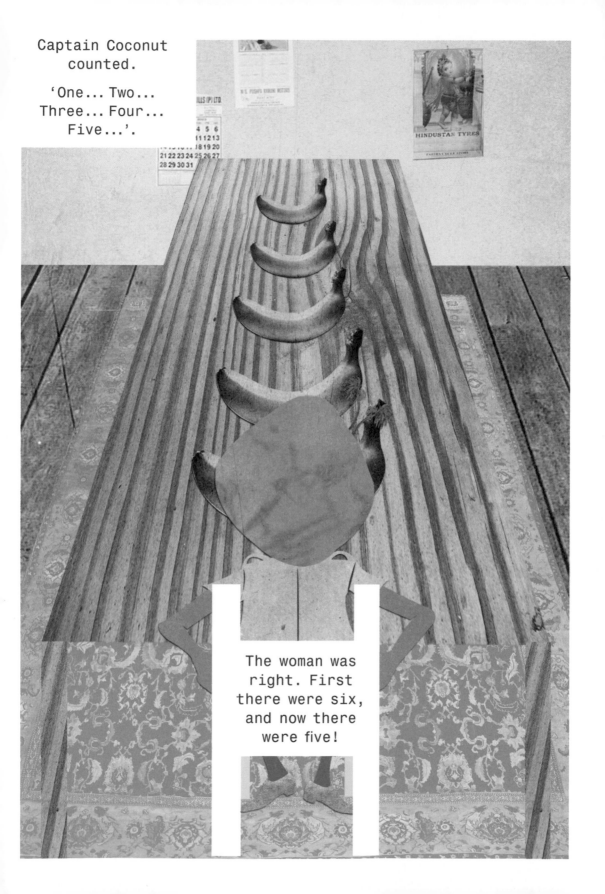

Captain Coconut counted.

'One... Two... Three... Four... Five...'.

The woman was right. First there were six, and now there were five!

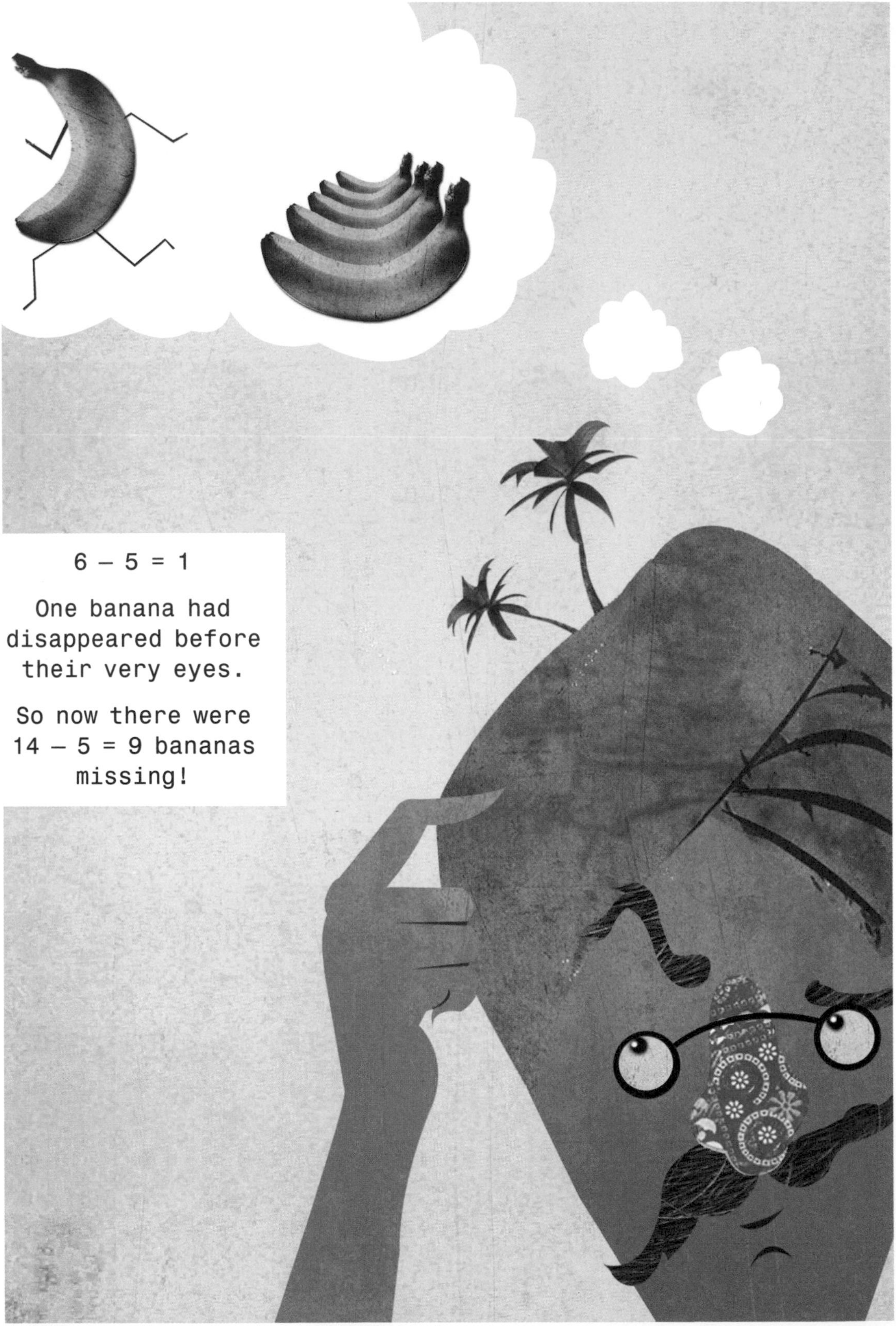

$6 - 5 = 1$

One banana had disappeared before their very eyes.

So now there were $14 - 5 = 9$ bananas missing!

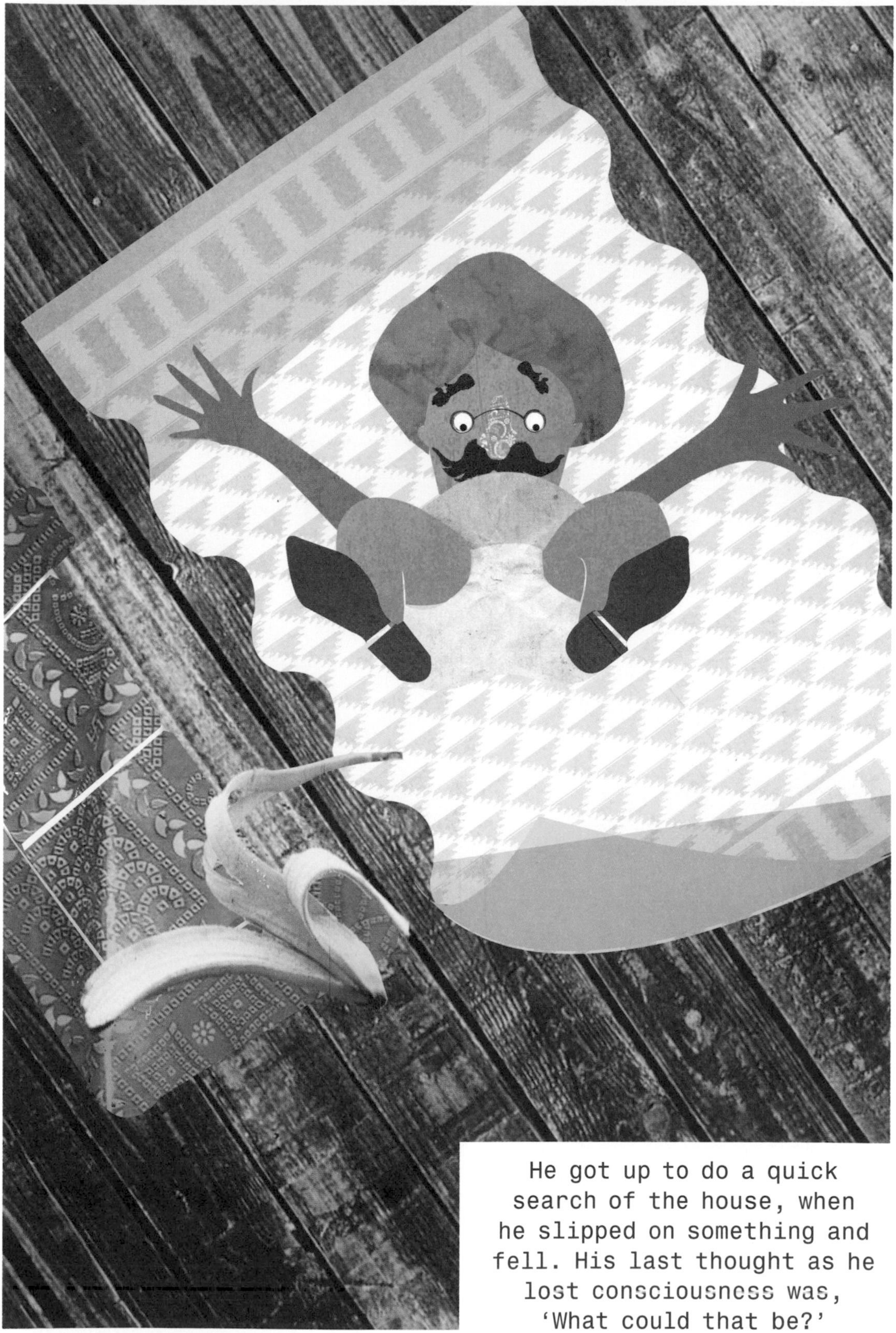

He got up to do a quick search of the house, when he slipped on something and fell. His last thought as he lost consciousness was, 'What could that be?'

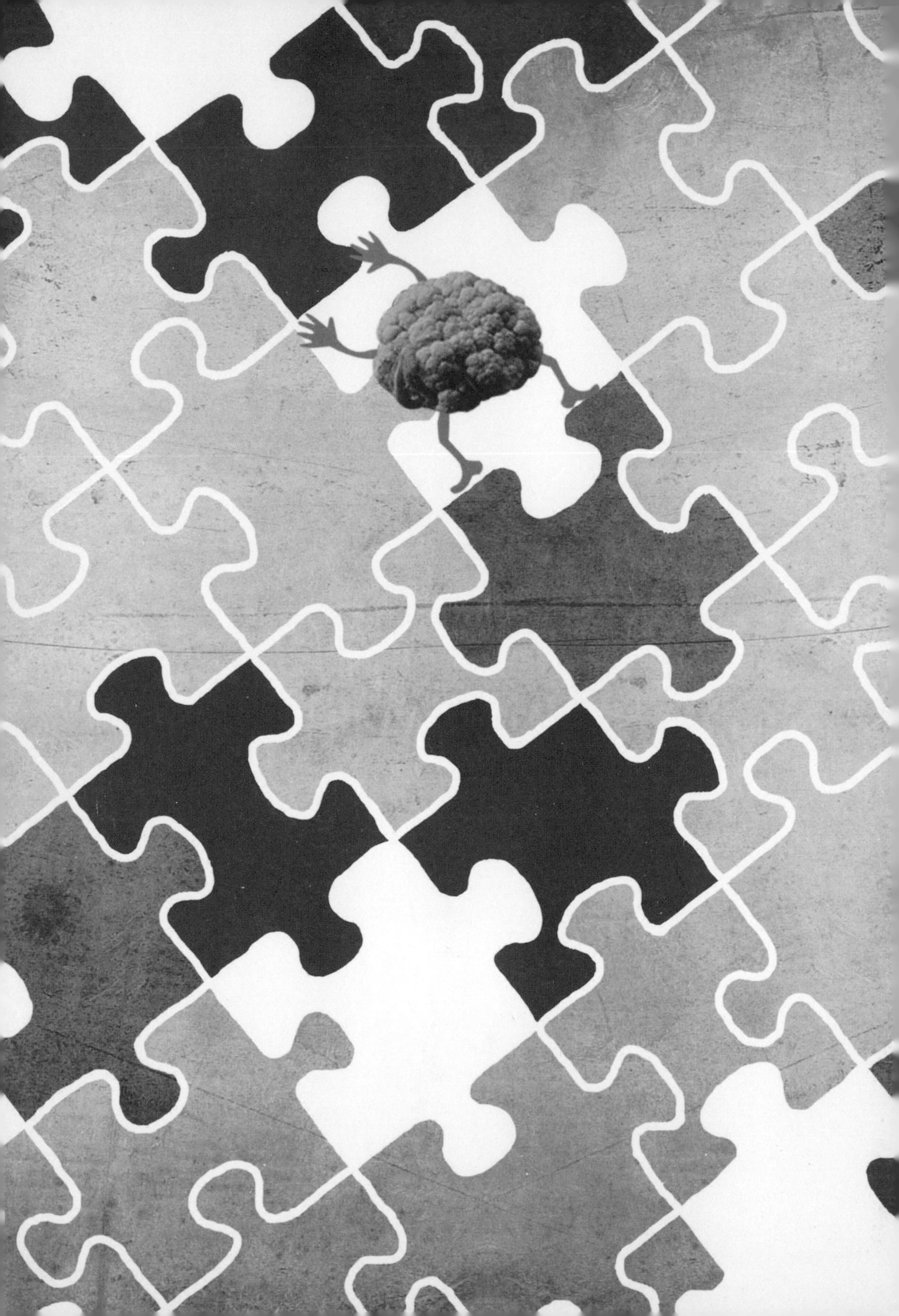

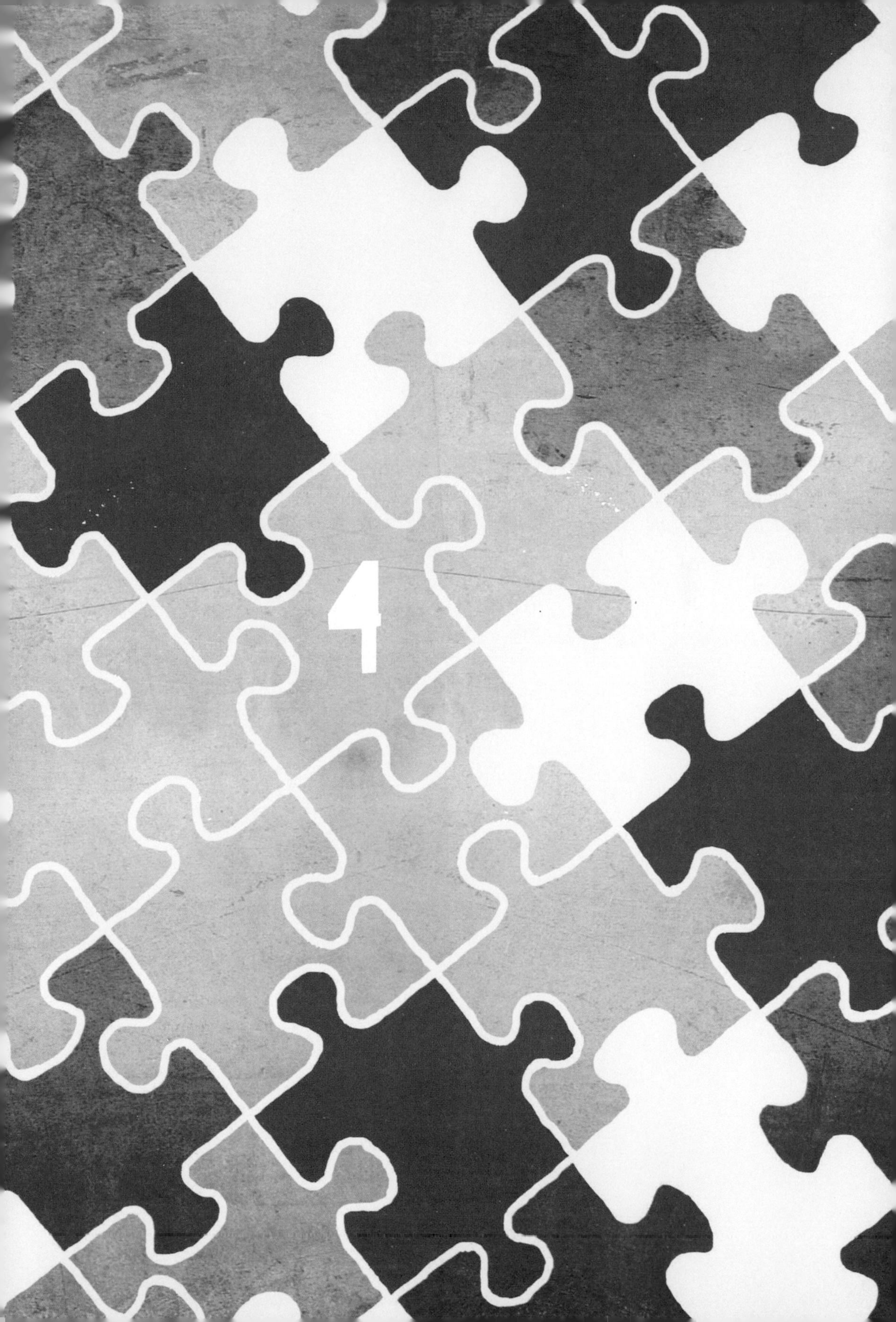
4

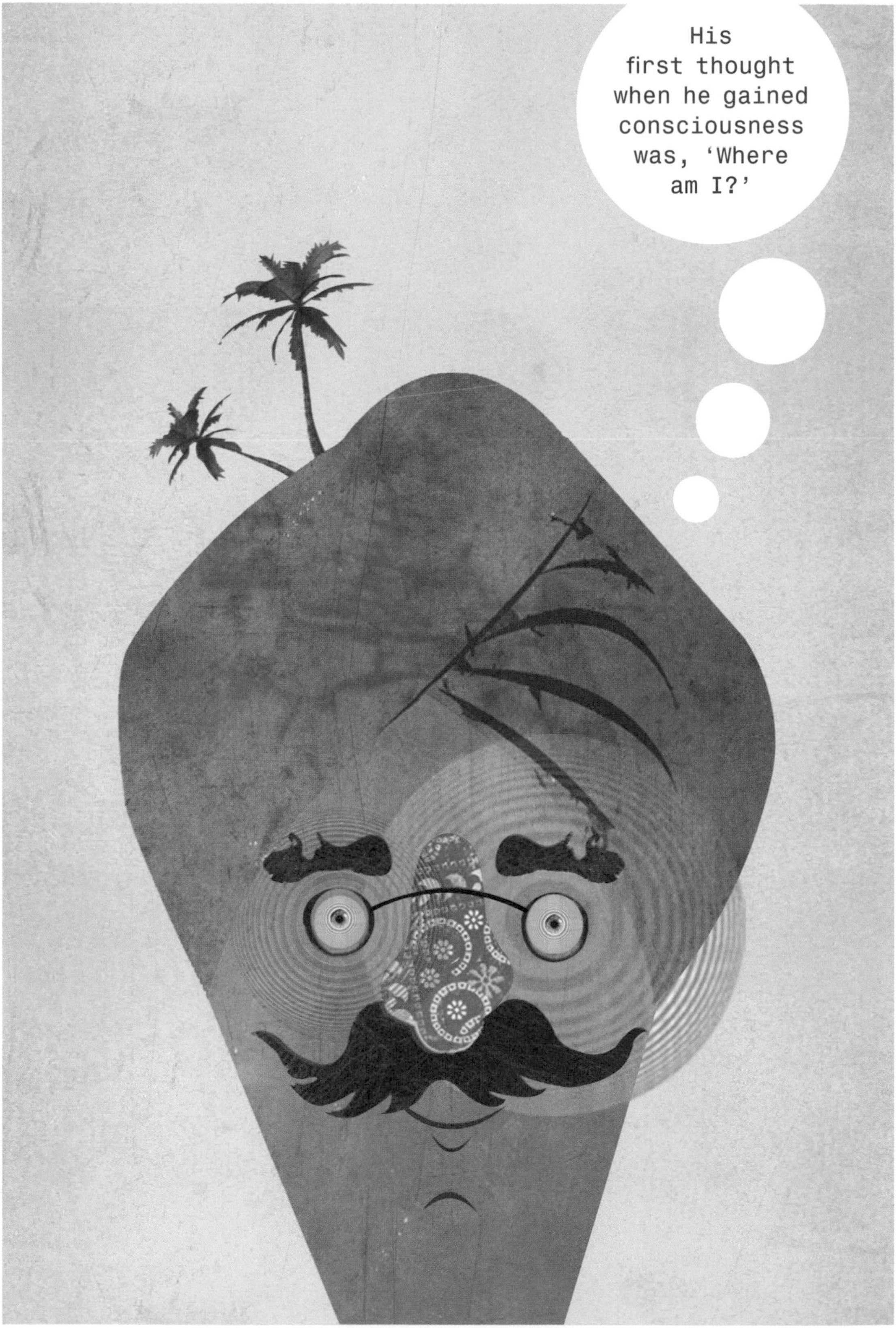
His first thought when he gained consciousness was, 'Where am I?'

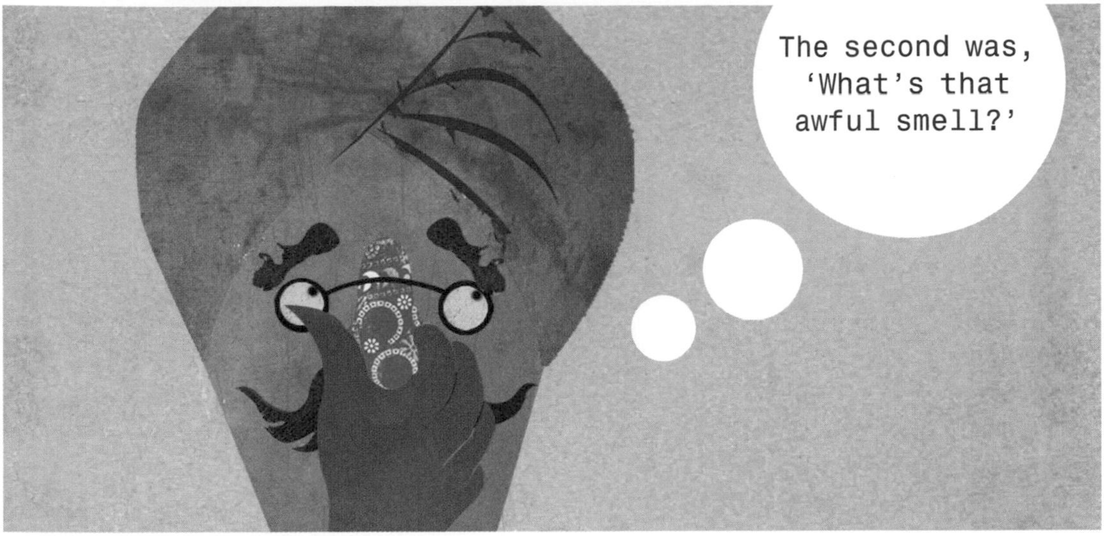
The second was, 'What's that awful smell?'

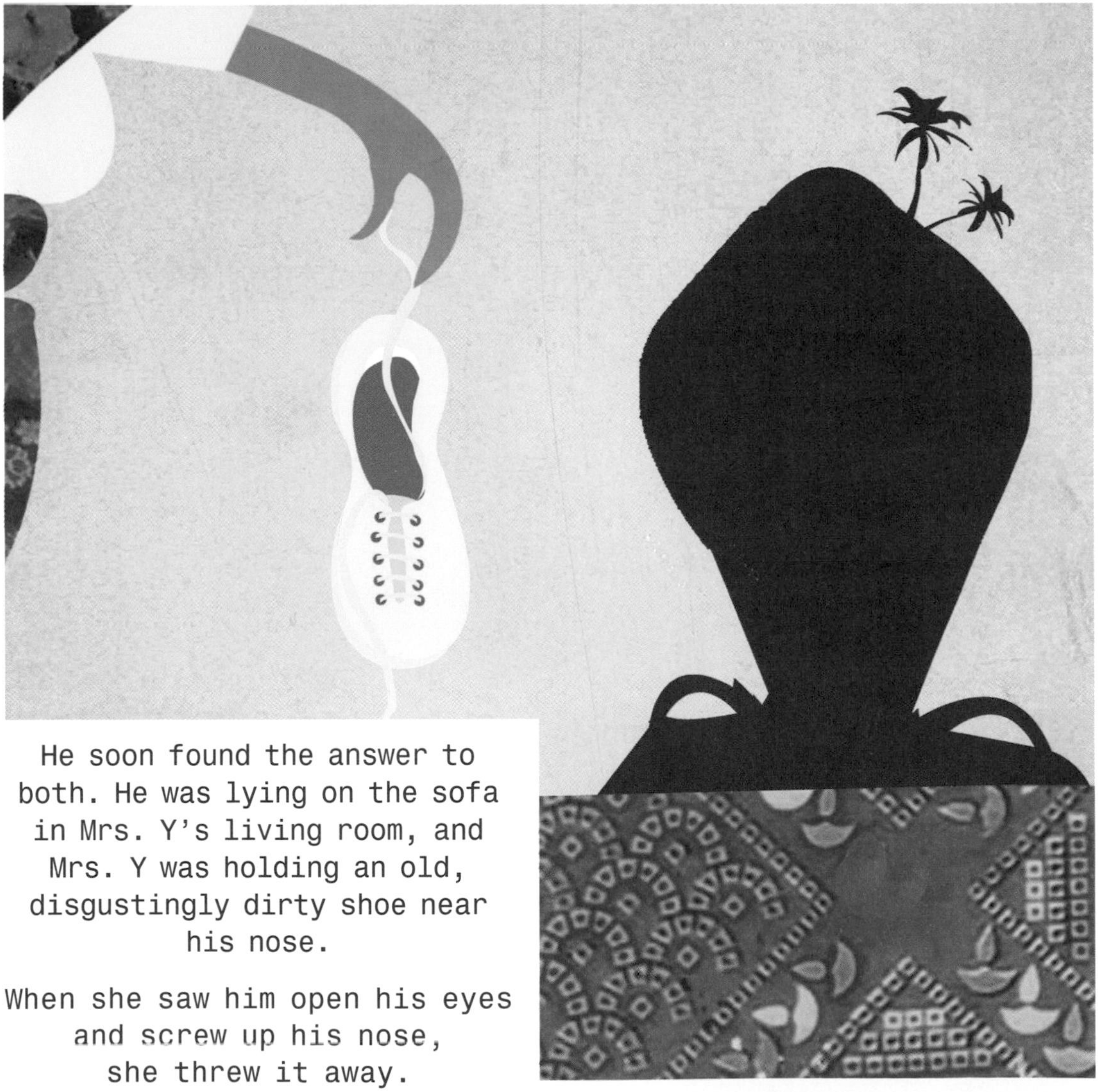
He soon found the answer to both. He was lying on the sofa in Mrs. Y's living room, and Mrs. Y was holding an old, disgustingly dirty shoe near his nose.
When she saw him open his eyes and screw up his nose, she threw it away.

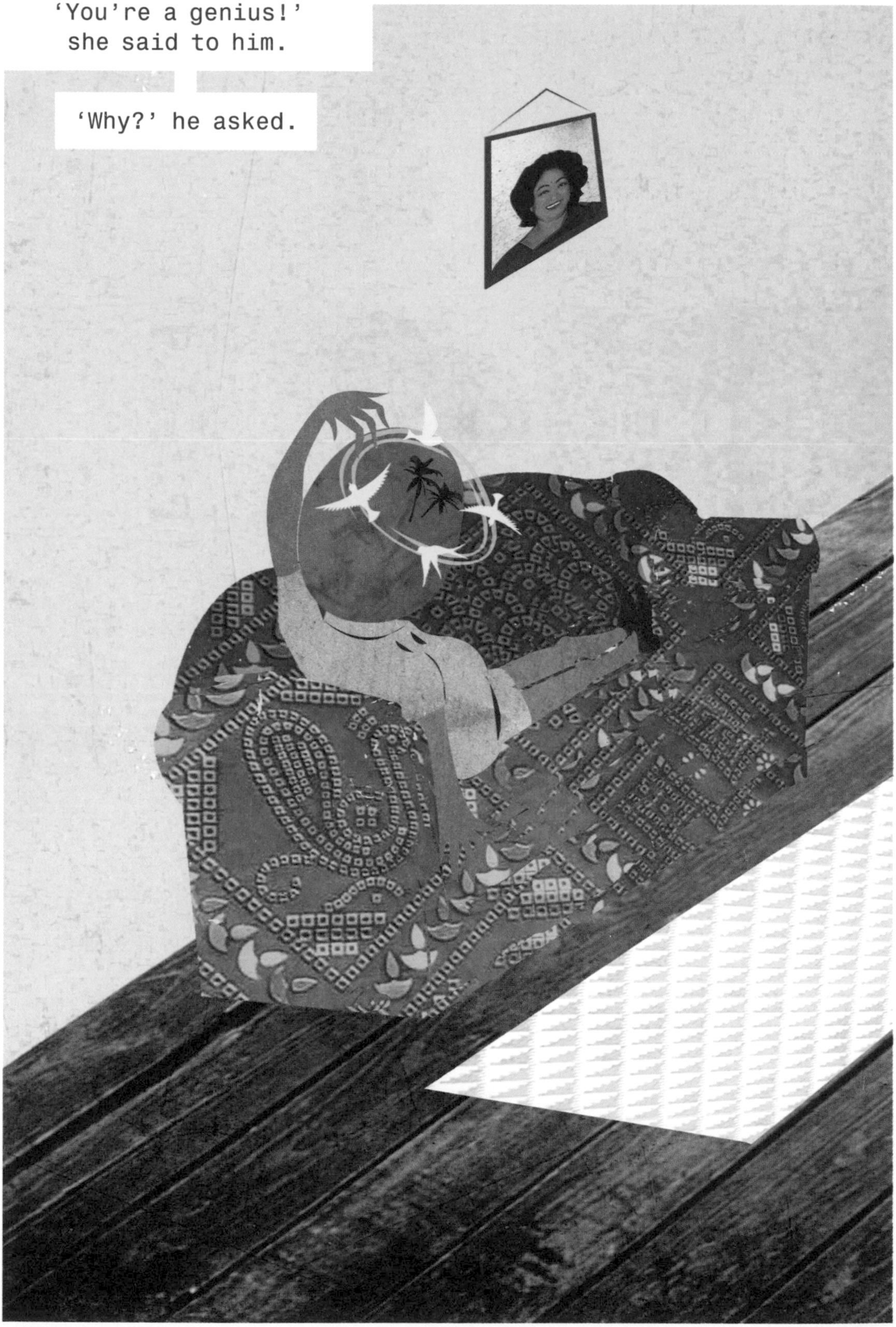
'You're a genius!' she said to him.
'Why?' he asked.

'You found the peel!' beamed Mrs. Y, holding up the banana peel on which he had slipped.

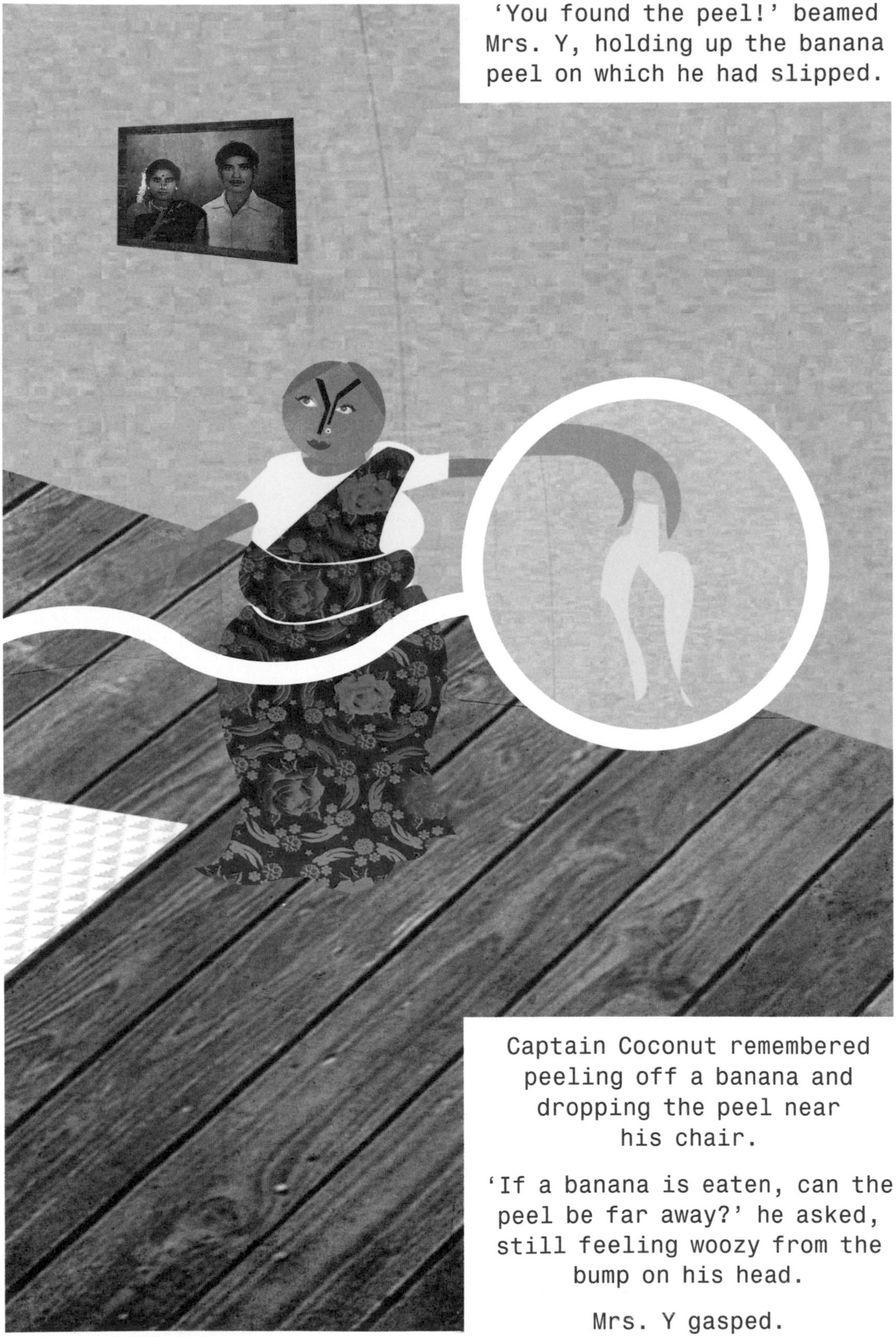

Captain Coconut remembered peeling off a banana and dropping the peel near his chair.

'If a banana is eaten, can the peel be far away?' he asked, still feeling woozy from the bump on his head.

Mrs. Y gasped.

'You're an even greater genius than I thought!' she cried. She ran off to the kitchen and came back with seven banana peels.

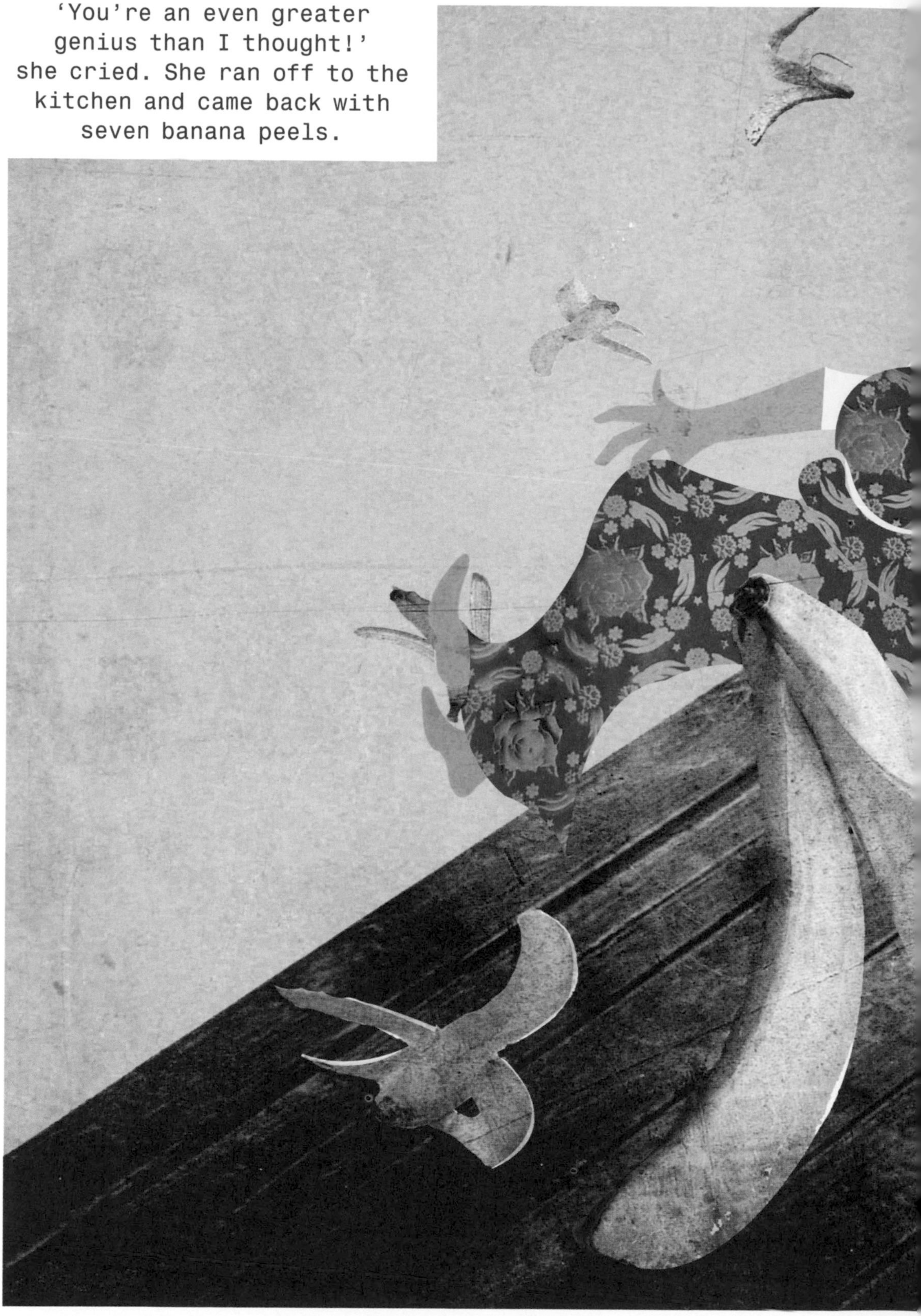

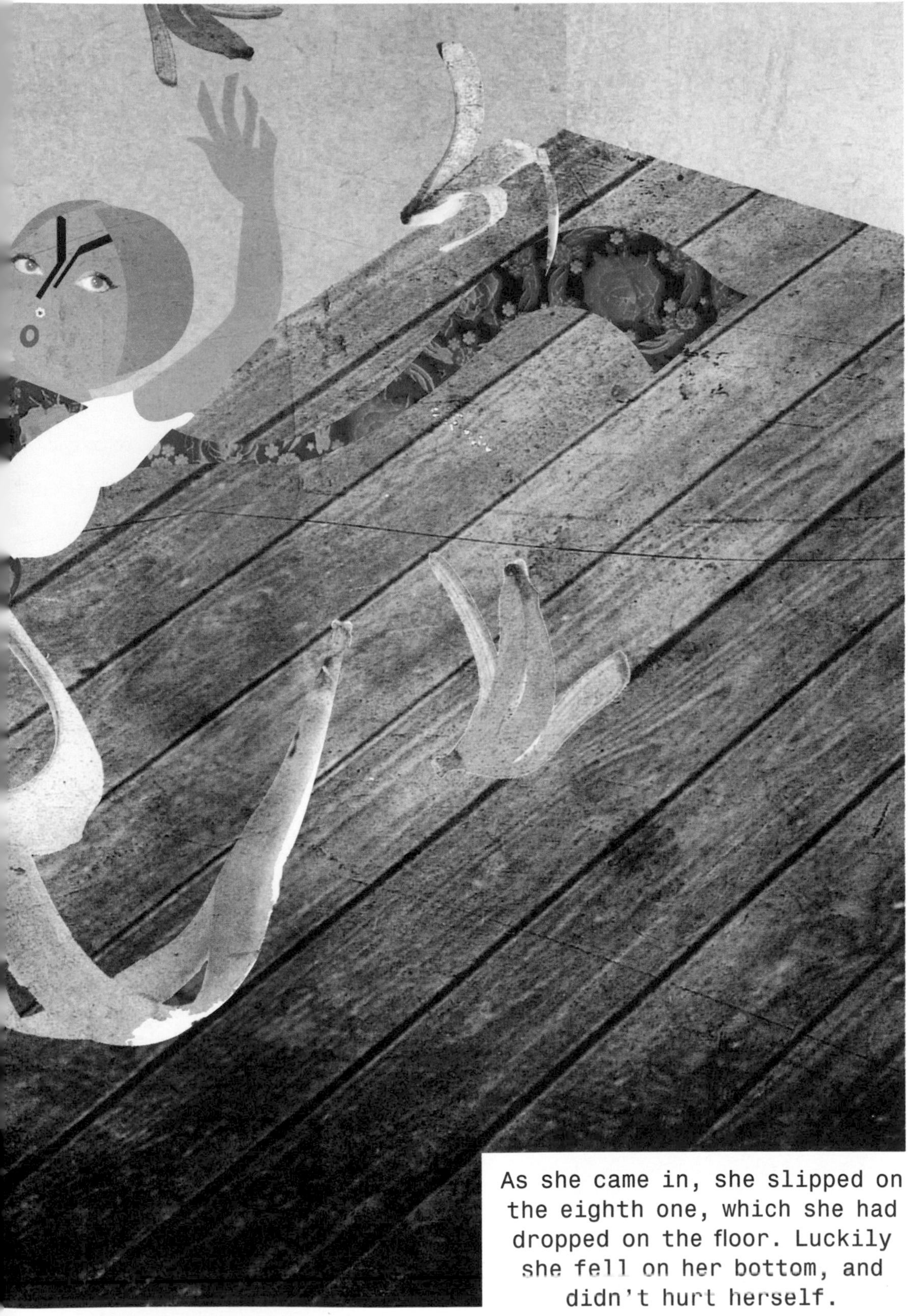

As she came in, she slipped on the eighth one, which she had dropped on the floor. Luckily she fell on her bottom, and didn't hurt herself.

'Eight peels!' said the Captain. He wrote this new fact in his notebook, along with some old facts.

Bananas gone from bunch: 8 (+ 1 = 9)

Peels found: 7 (+ 1 = 8)

Peel thrown in green garbage bin: 1

Therefore total no. of peels = total no. of bananas gone from bunch = 9

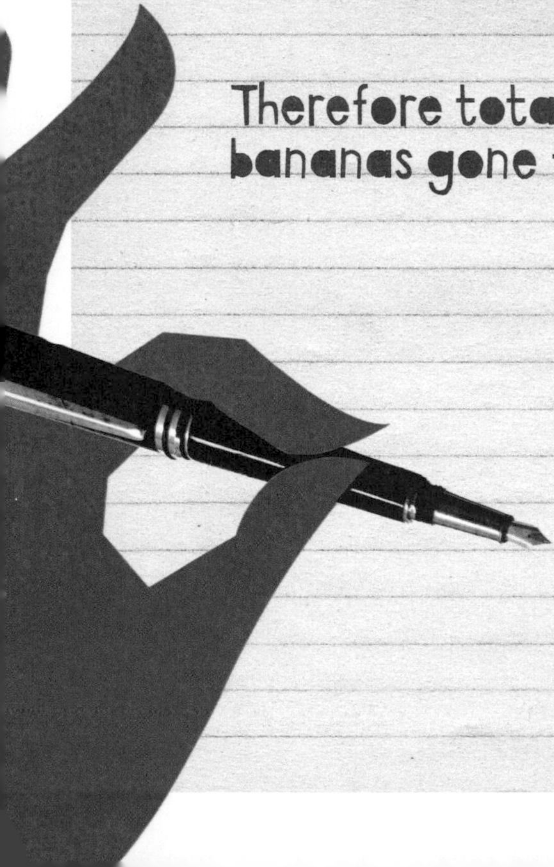

He knew that these facts should say something to him. But what? It was all very difficult and complicated, and Captain Coconut could see that even with his clever brain and his great experience it was not going to be easy. His head was aching.

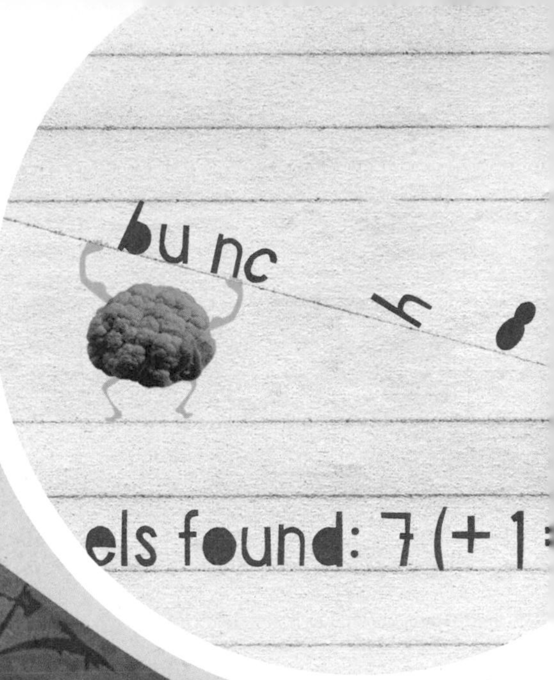
bu nc
h
8
els found: 7 (+1

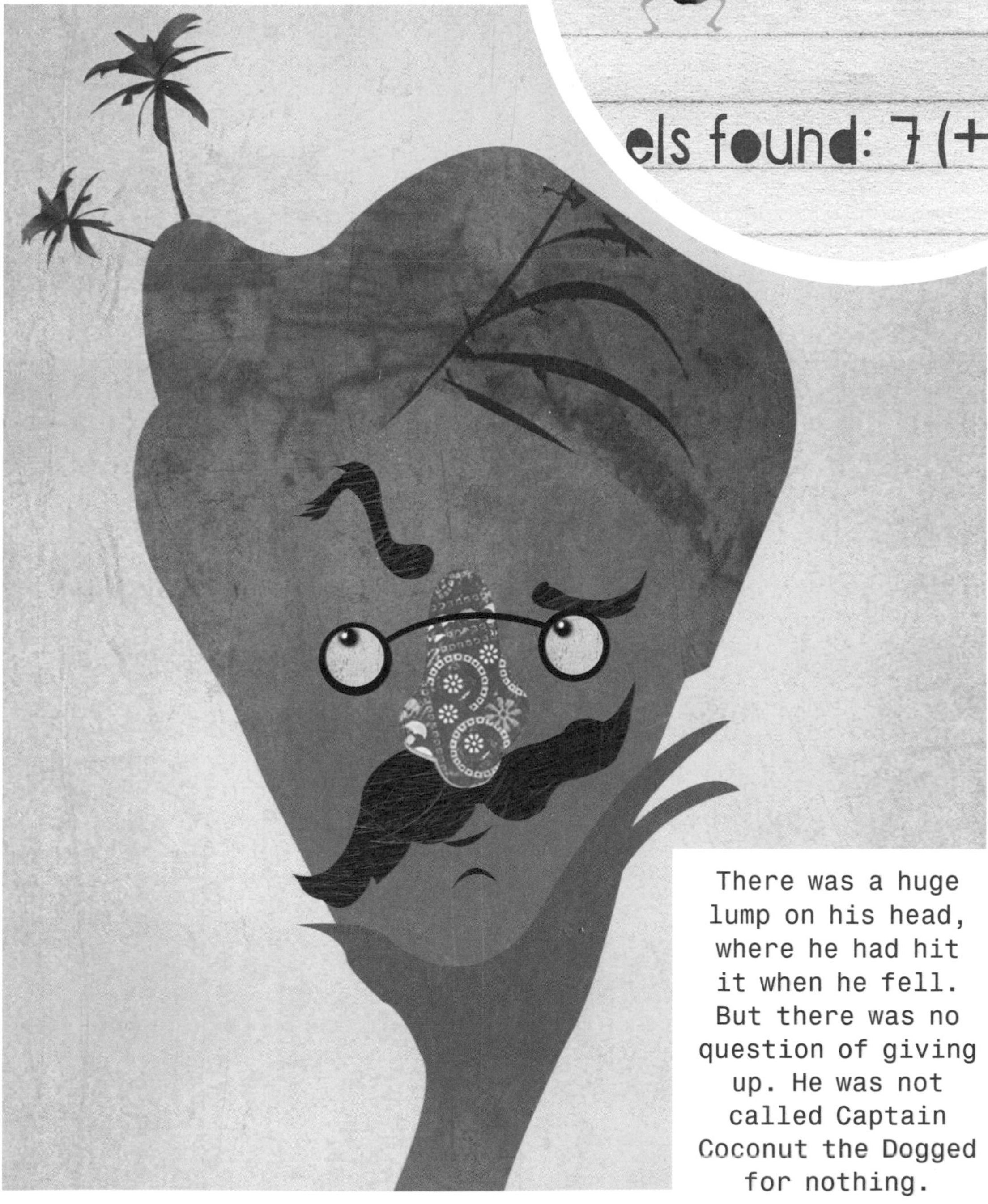

There was a huge lump on his head, where he had hit it when he fell. But there was no question of giving up. He was not called Captain Coconut the Dogged for nothing.

SONG:

HE'S A ROCK

(COCONUT THE DOGGED)

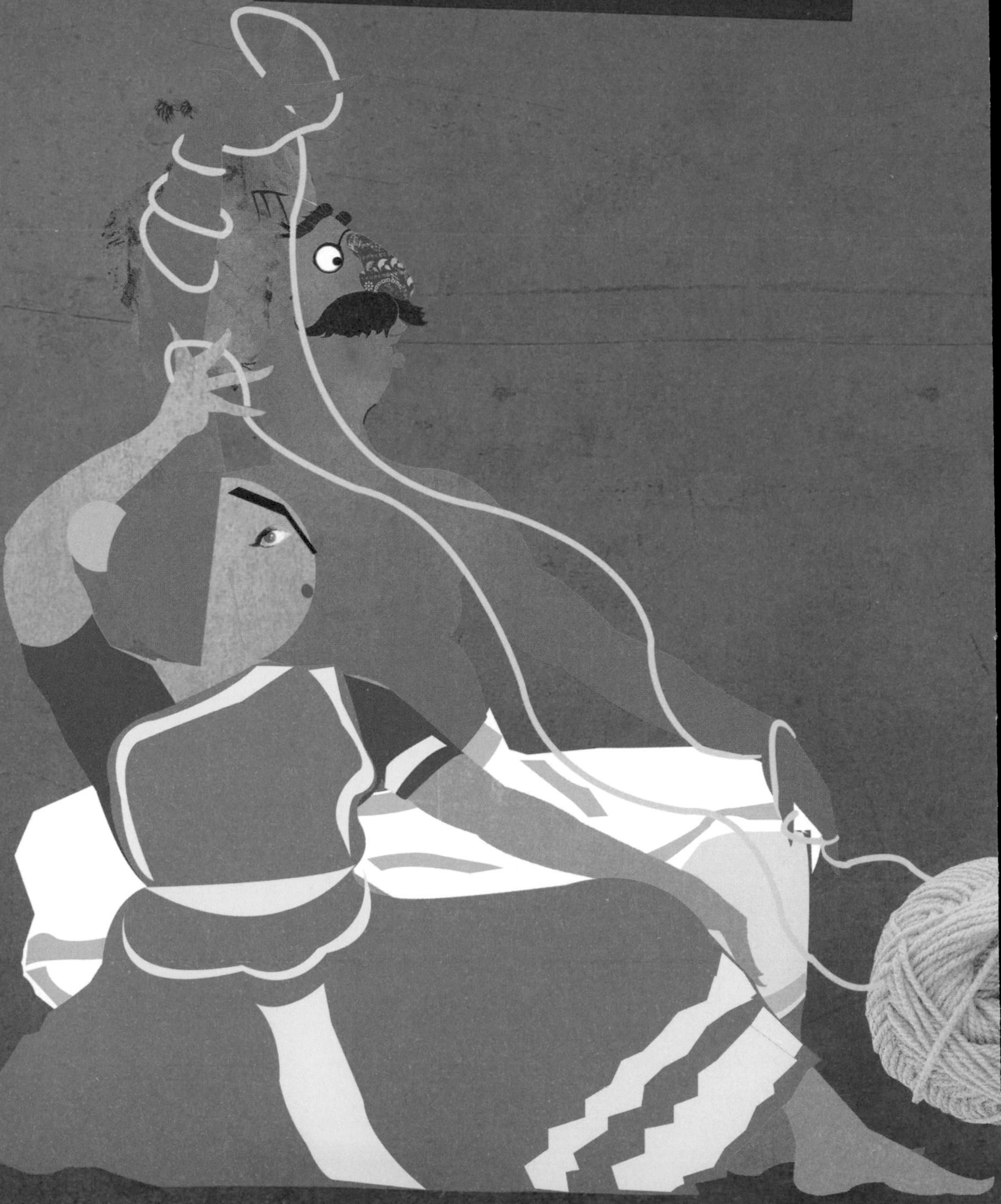

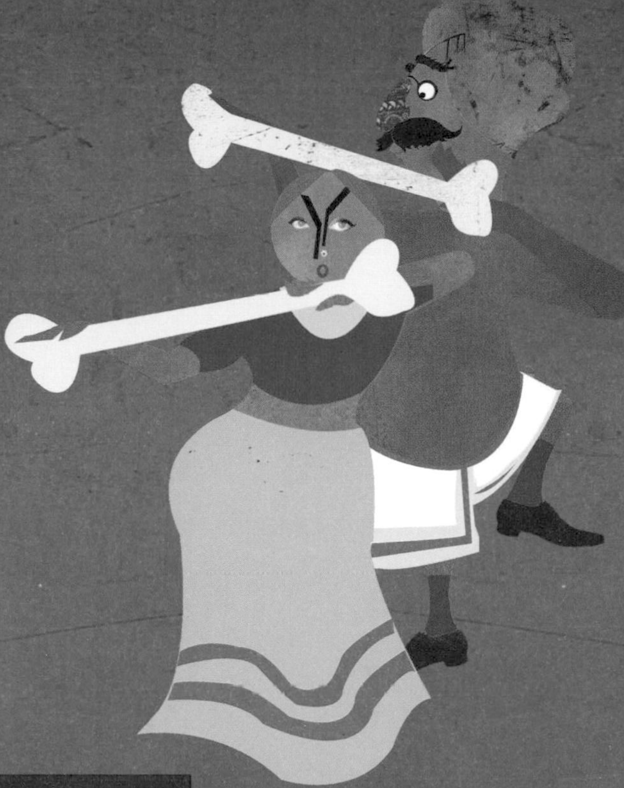

Ca-aptain Coconut!
Ca-aptain Coconut!

Coconut the Dogged
Is as stubborn as a mule
When he's in a corner
He doesn't lose his cool
He worries at the problem
Like a cat with a ball of wool

Oh yes! Captain Coconut
Is like a dog with a bone!
When he's onto something,
He won't leave it alone
Some say he's a rock
And some say he's a stone!

Yes, Coconut the Dogged is a class
of his own!!

He stared at the facts in his notebook and tried to guess what they were saying.

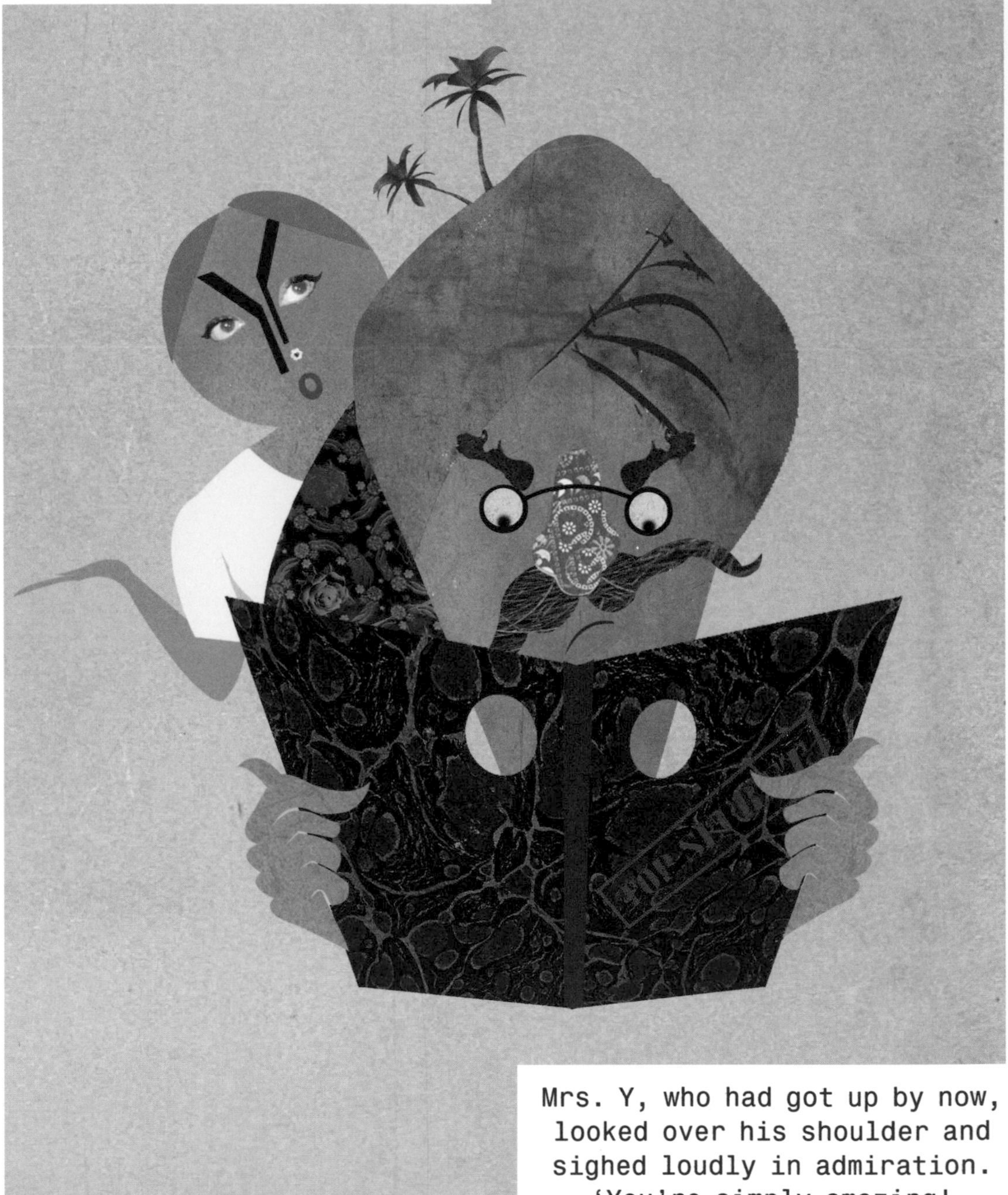

Mrs. Y, who had got up by now, looked over his shoulder and sighed loudly in admiration. 'You're simply amazing! It's quite clear from your deductions that those four missing bananas were eaten by someone in this very house! Who could it be?'

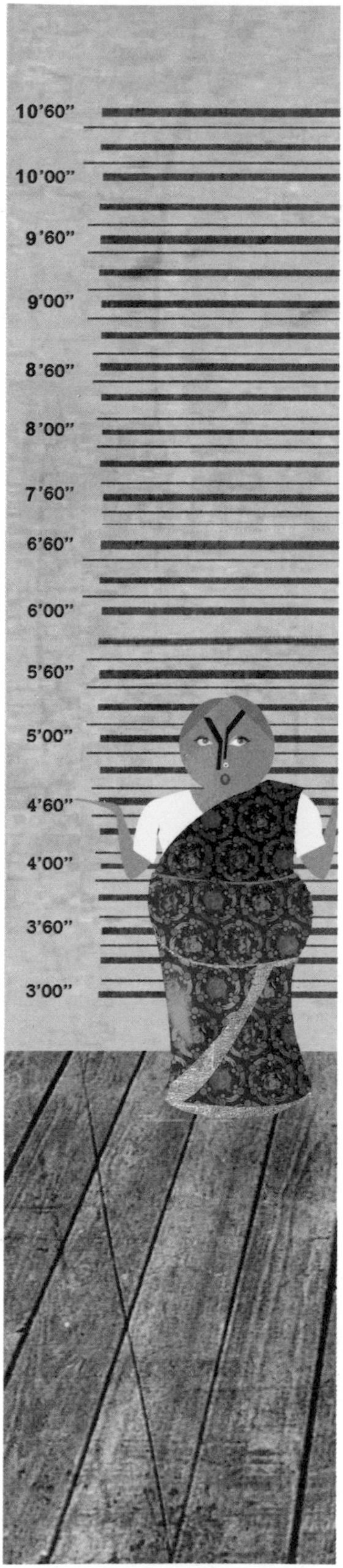
10'60"
10'00"
9'60"
9'00"
8'60"
8'00"
7'60"
6'60"
6'00"
5'60"
5'00"
4'60"
4'00"
3'60"
3'00"

Captain Coconut's
clever brain
began to work.
All the banana peels
(except for the
one that was in the
green garbage bin)
were in the house.

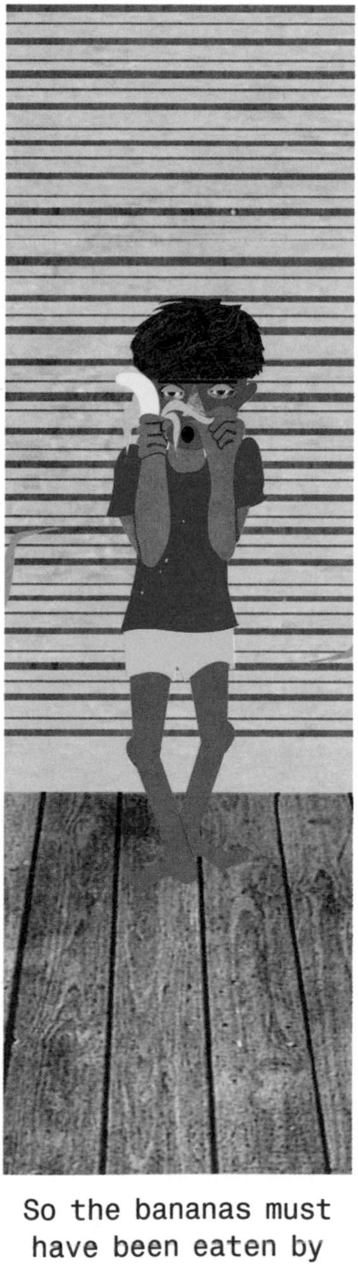

So the bananas must
have been eaten by
Mrs. Y, her sister
or her nephew Gilli.

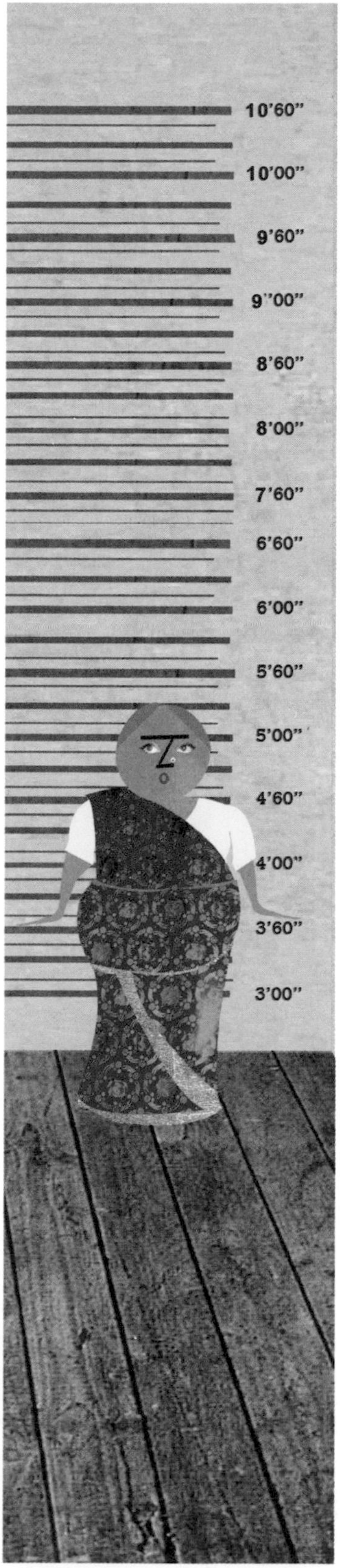
10'60"
10'00"
9'60"
9"00"
8'60"
8'00"
7'60"
6'60"
6'00"
5'60"
5'00"
4'60"
4'00"
3'60"
3'00"

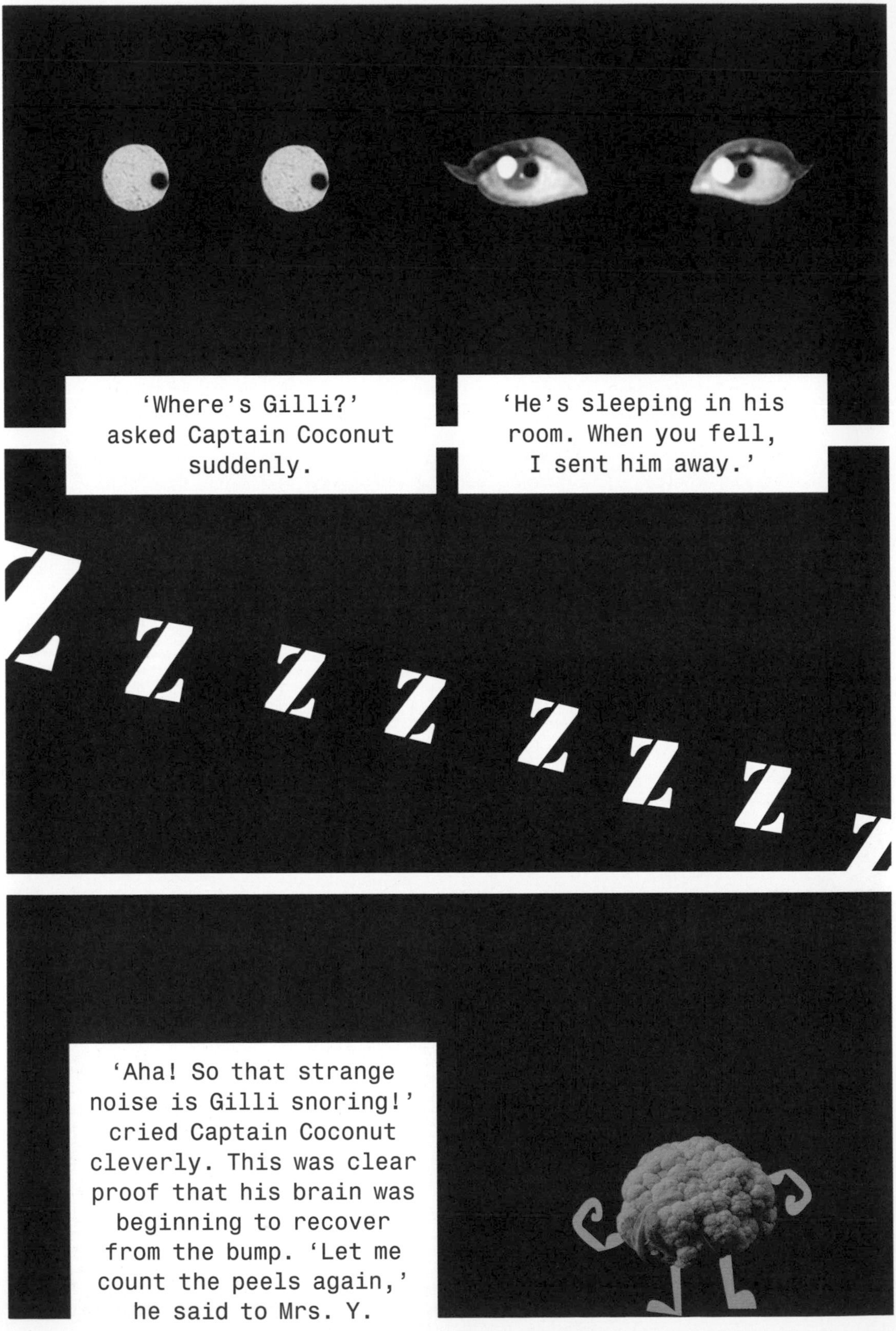
'Where's Gilli?' asked Captain Coconut suddenly.
'He's sleeping in his room. When you fell, I sent him away.'
Z Z Z Z Z Z
'Aha! So that strange noise is Gilli snoring!' cried Captain Coconut cleverly. This was clear proof that his brain was beginning to recover from the bump. 'Let me count the peels again,' he said to Mrs. Y.

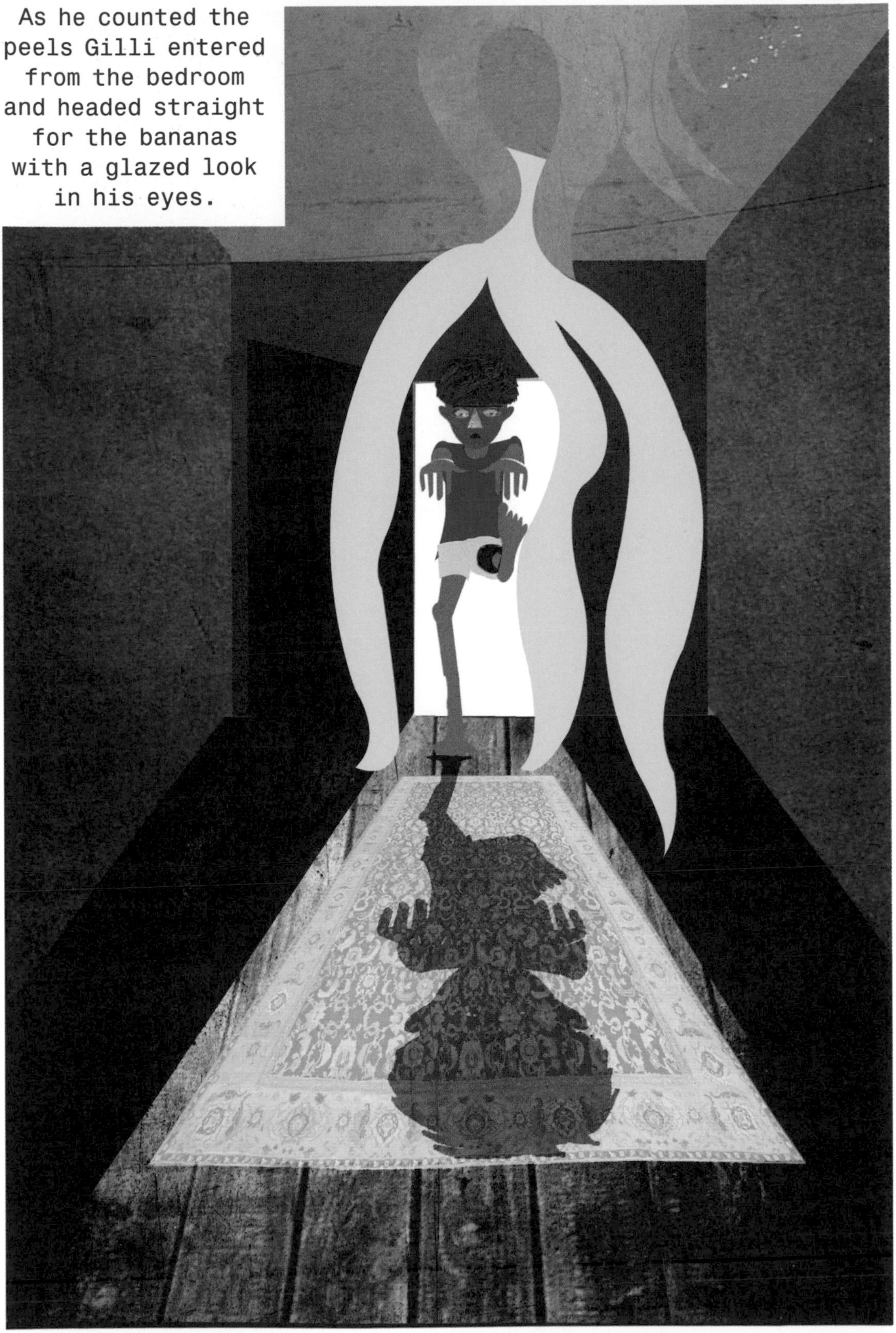
As he counted the peels Gilli entered from the bedroom and headed straight for the bananas with a glazed look in his eyes.

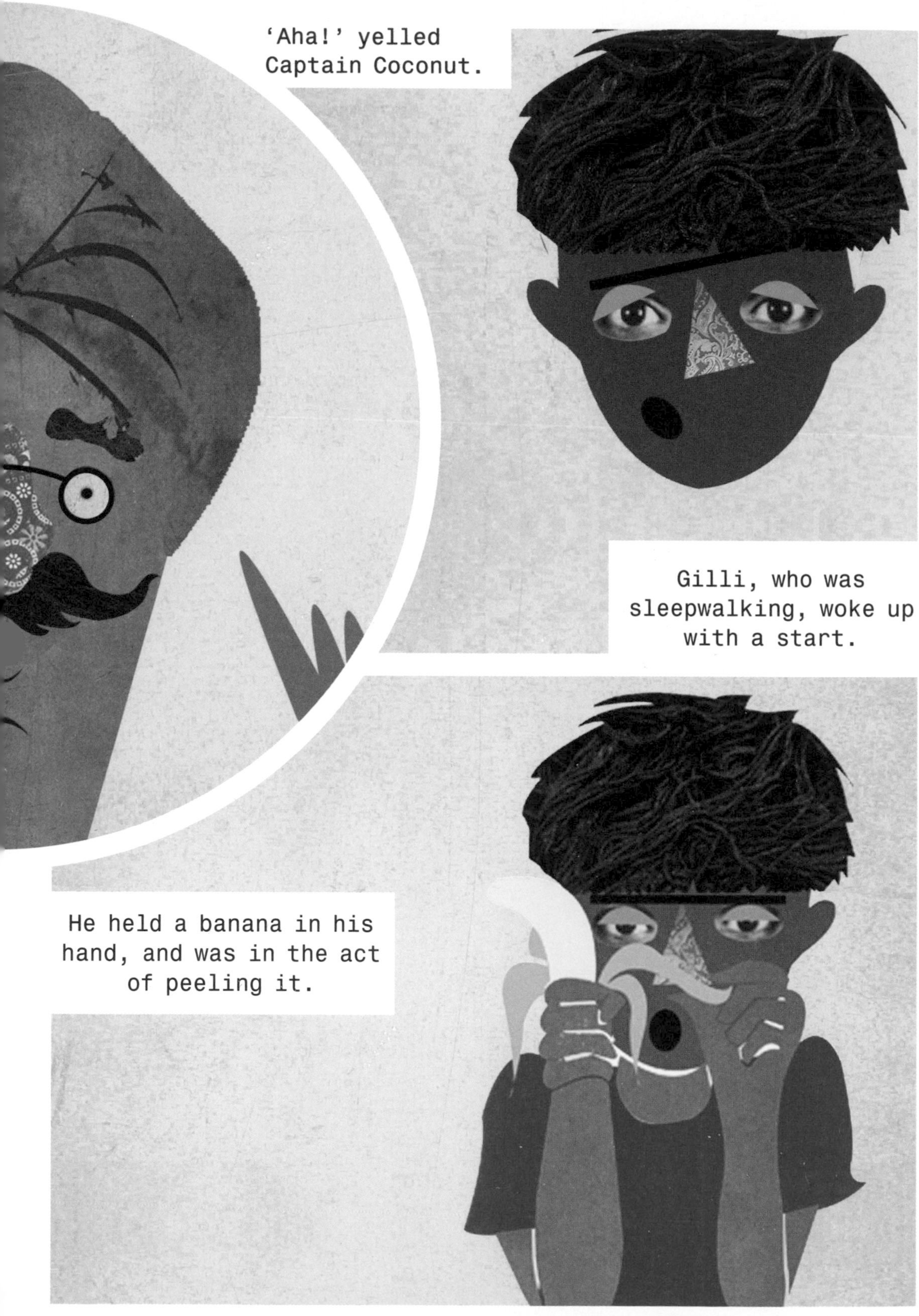
'Aha!' yelled Captain Coconut.
Gilli, who was sleepwalking, woke up with a start.
He held a banana in his hand, and was in the act of peeling it.

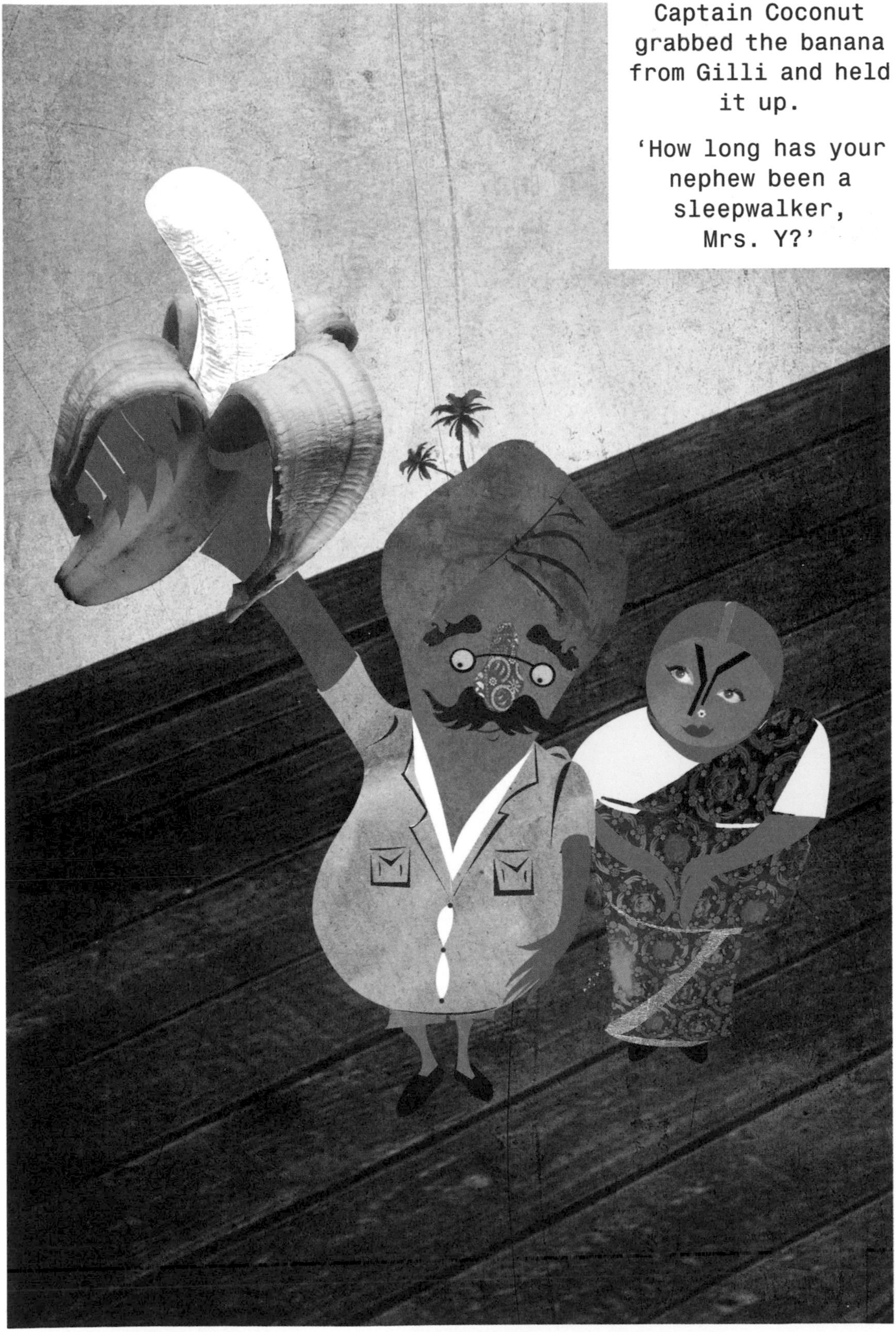

Captain Coconut grabbed the banana from Gilli and held it up.

'How long has your nephew been a sleepwalker, Mrs. Y?'

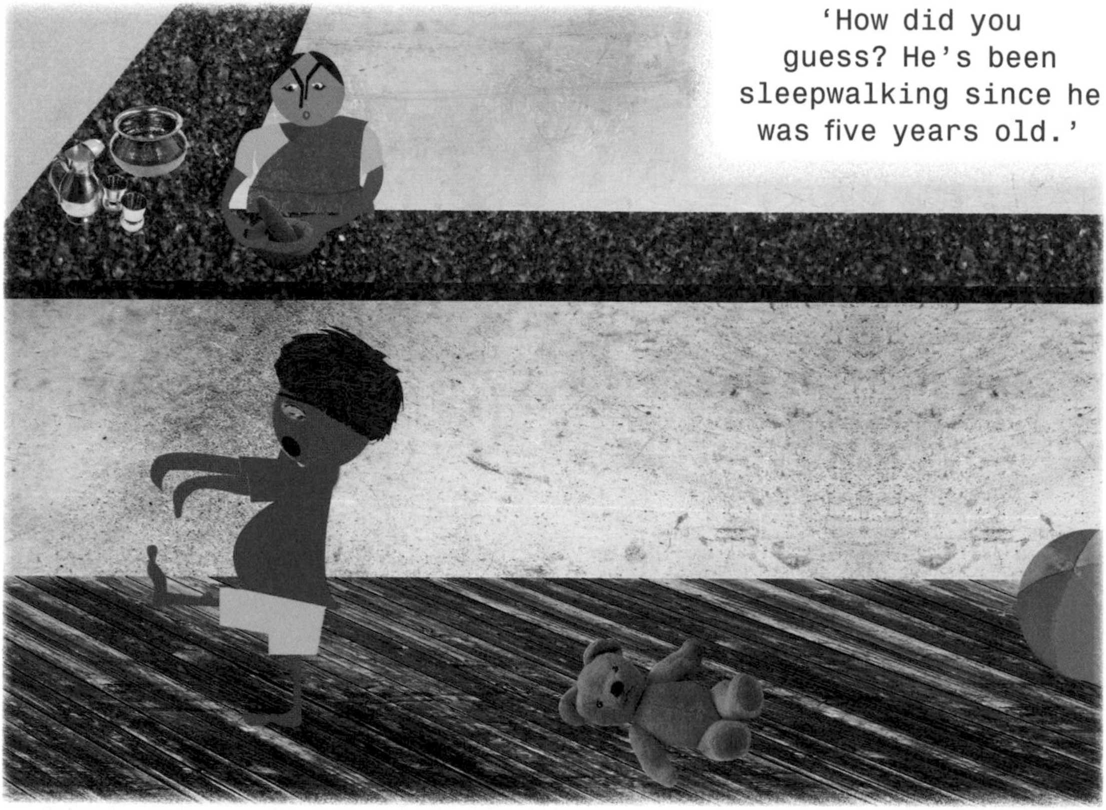

'How did you guess? He's been sleepwalking since he was five years old.'

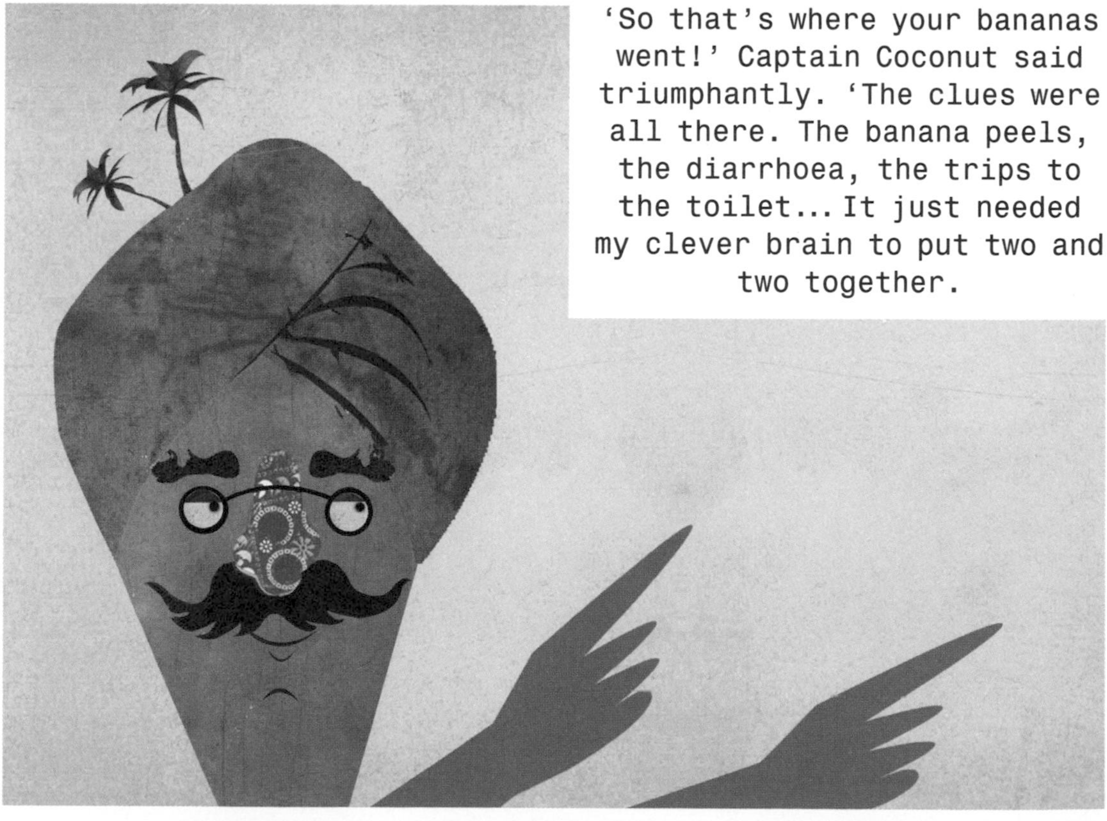

'So that's where your bananas went!' Captain Coconut said triumphantly. 'The clues were all there. The banana peels, the diarrhoea, the trips to the toilet... It just needed my clever brain to put two and two together.

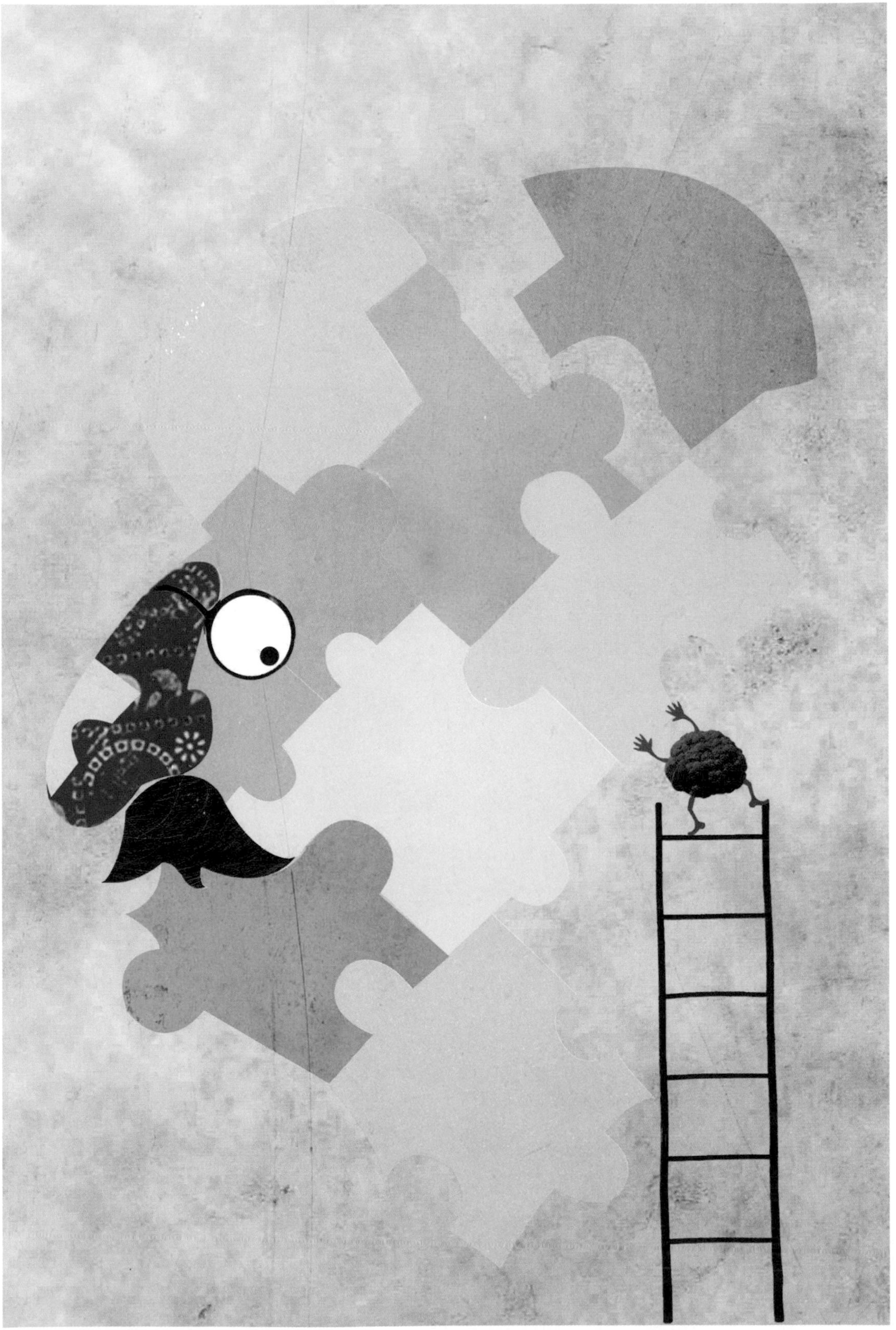

Last night after eating one banana, Gilli went to bed. There he dreamt of bananas, and walking in his sleep, he came to the dining room and ate, not one, not two, but four bananas! Making a total of....'

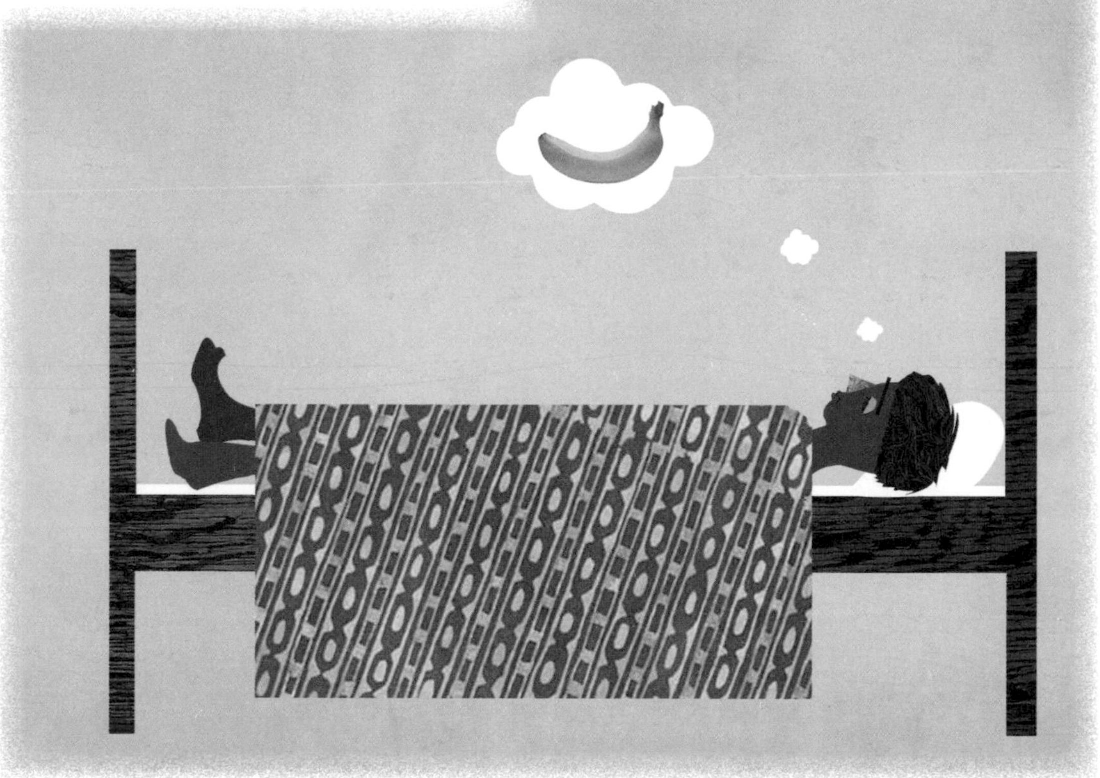

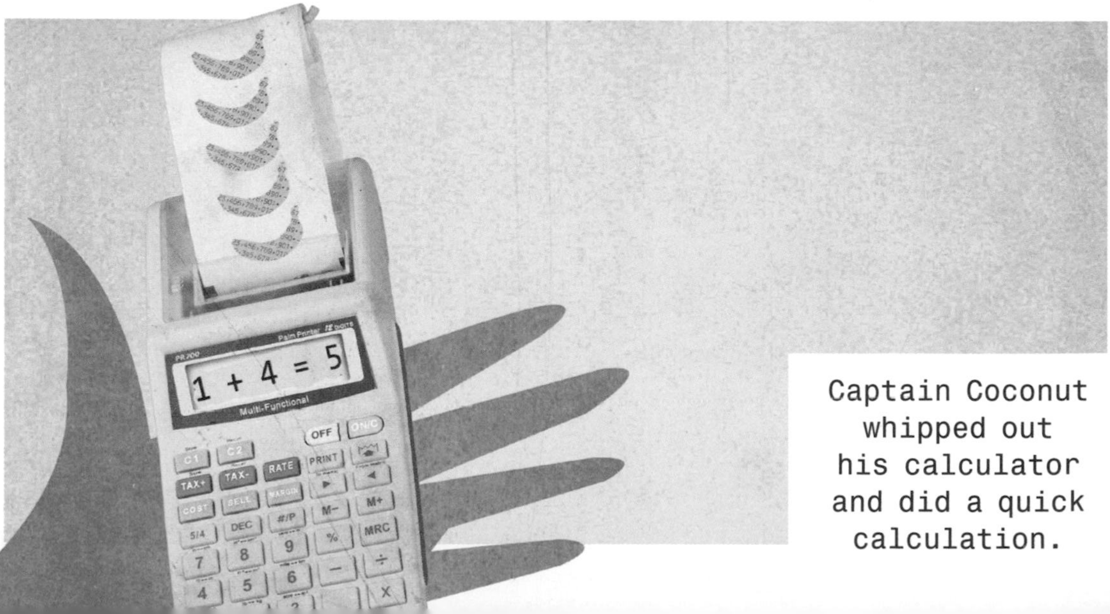
1 + 4 = 5

Captain Coconut whipped out his calculator and did a quick calculation.

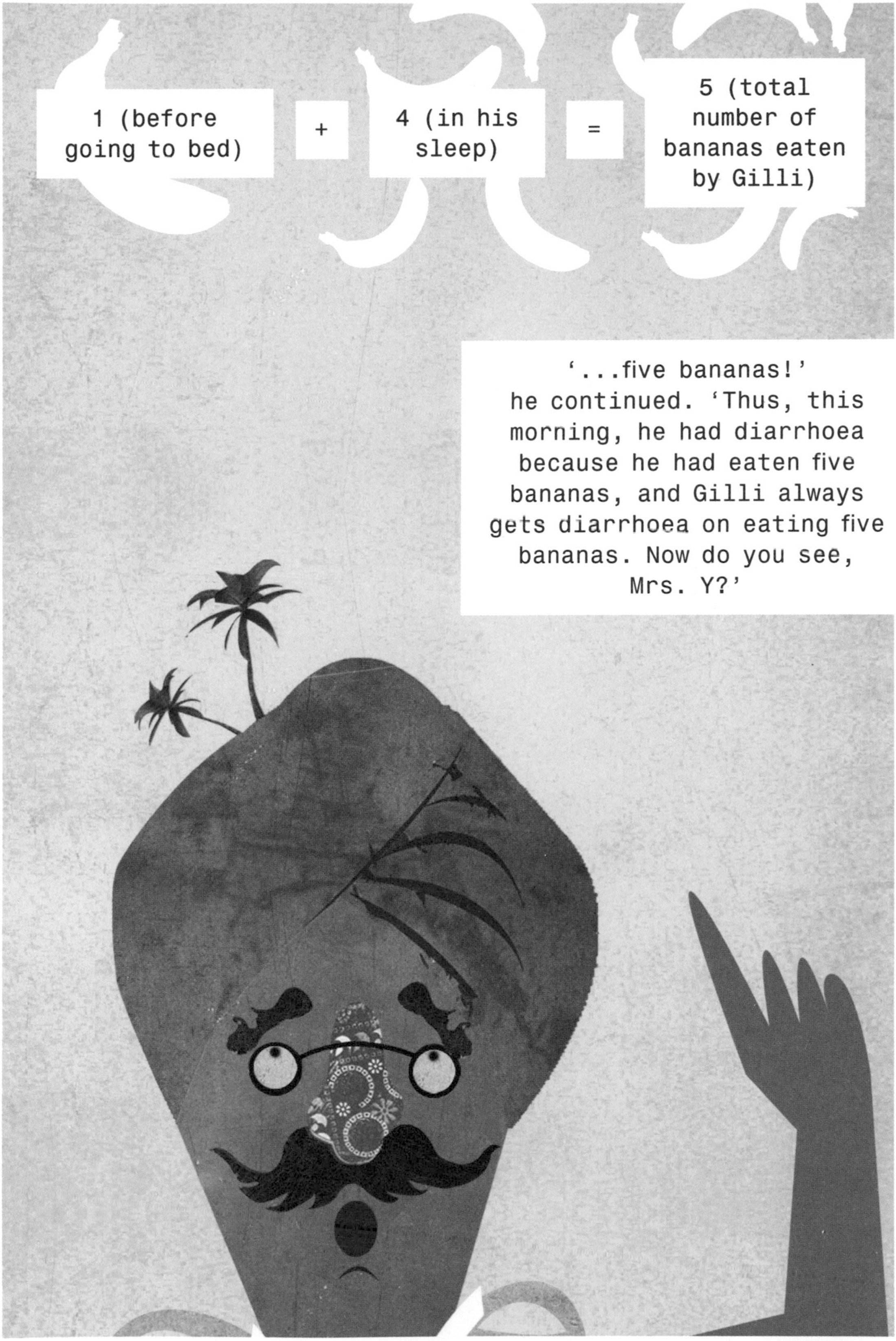
1 (before going to bed)
+
4 (in his sleep)
=
5 (total number of bananas eaten by Gilli)
'...five bananas!' he continued. 'Thus, this morning, he had diarrhoea because he had eaten five bananas, and Gilli always gets diarrhoea on eating five bananas. Now do you see, Mrs. Y?'

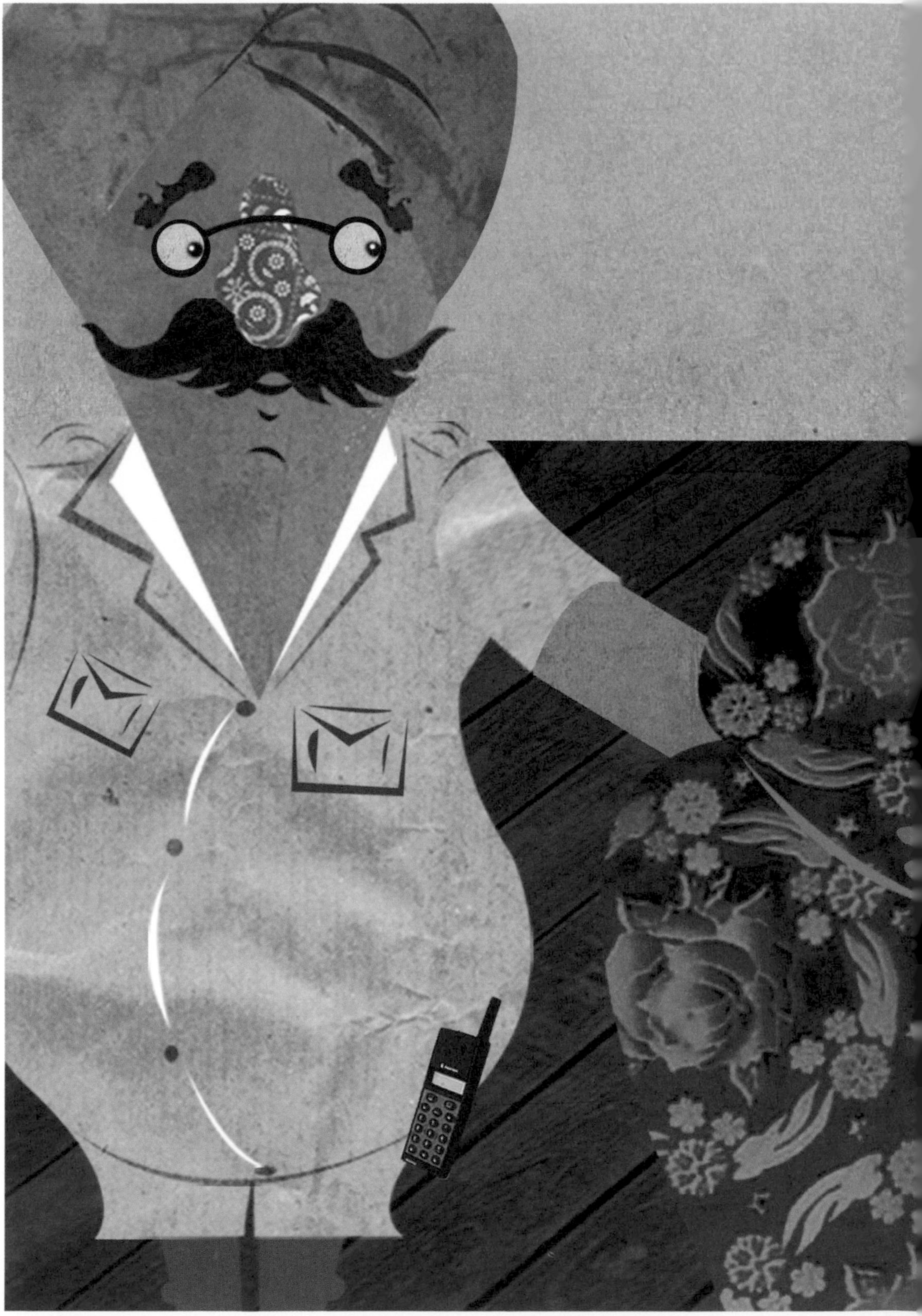

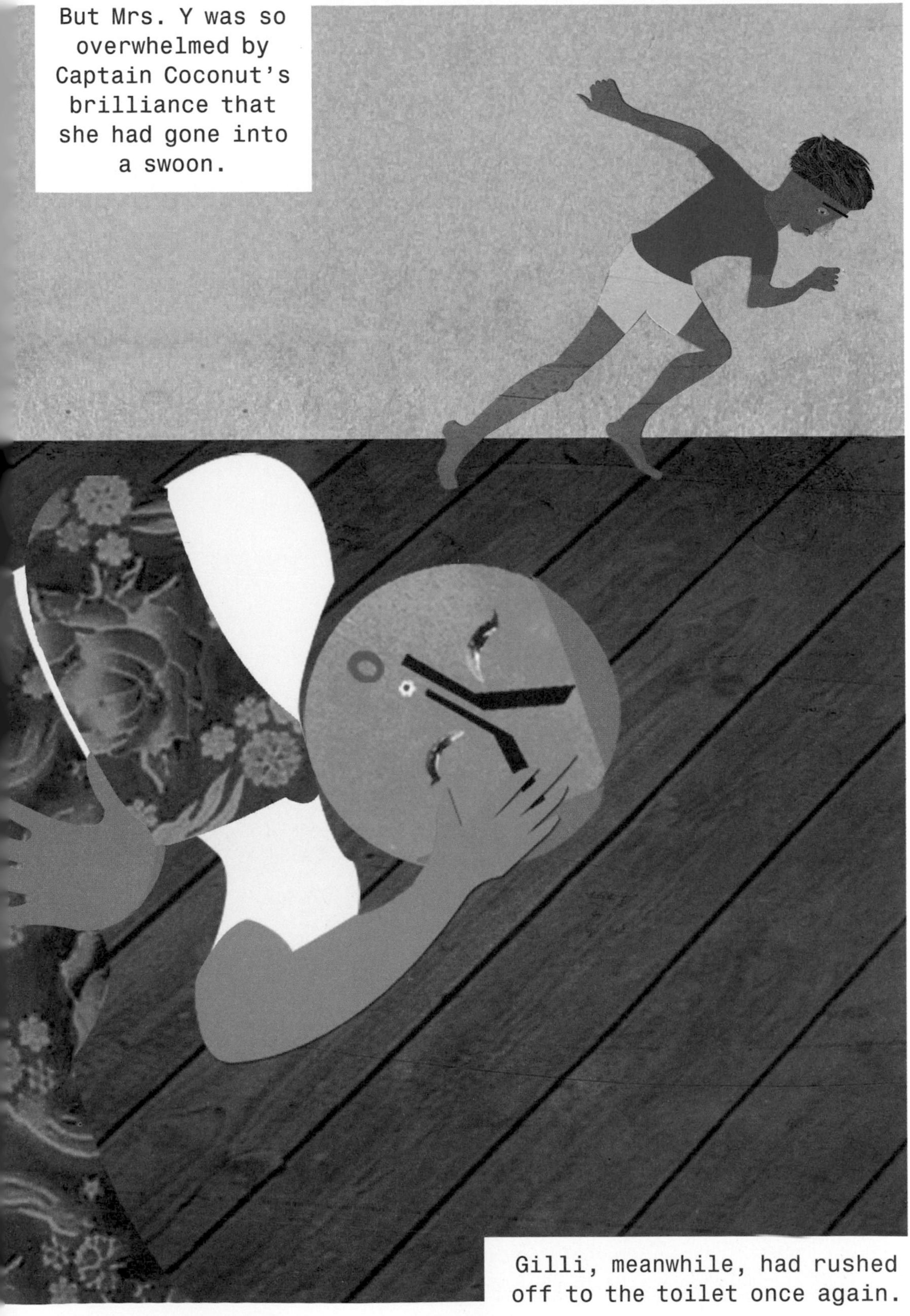
But Mrs. Y was so overwhelmed by Captain Coconut's brilliance that she had gone into a swoon.
Gilli, meanwhile, had rushed off to the toilet once again.

Captain Coconut sat on the sofa, sighed with satisfaction, and waited for Mrs. Y to gain consciousness.

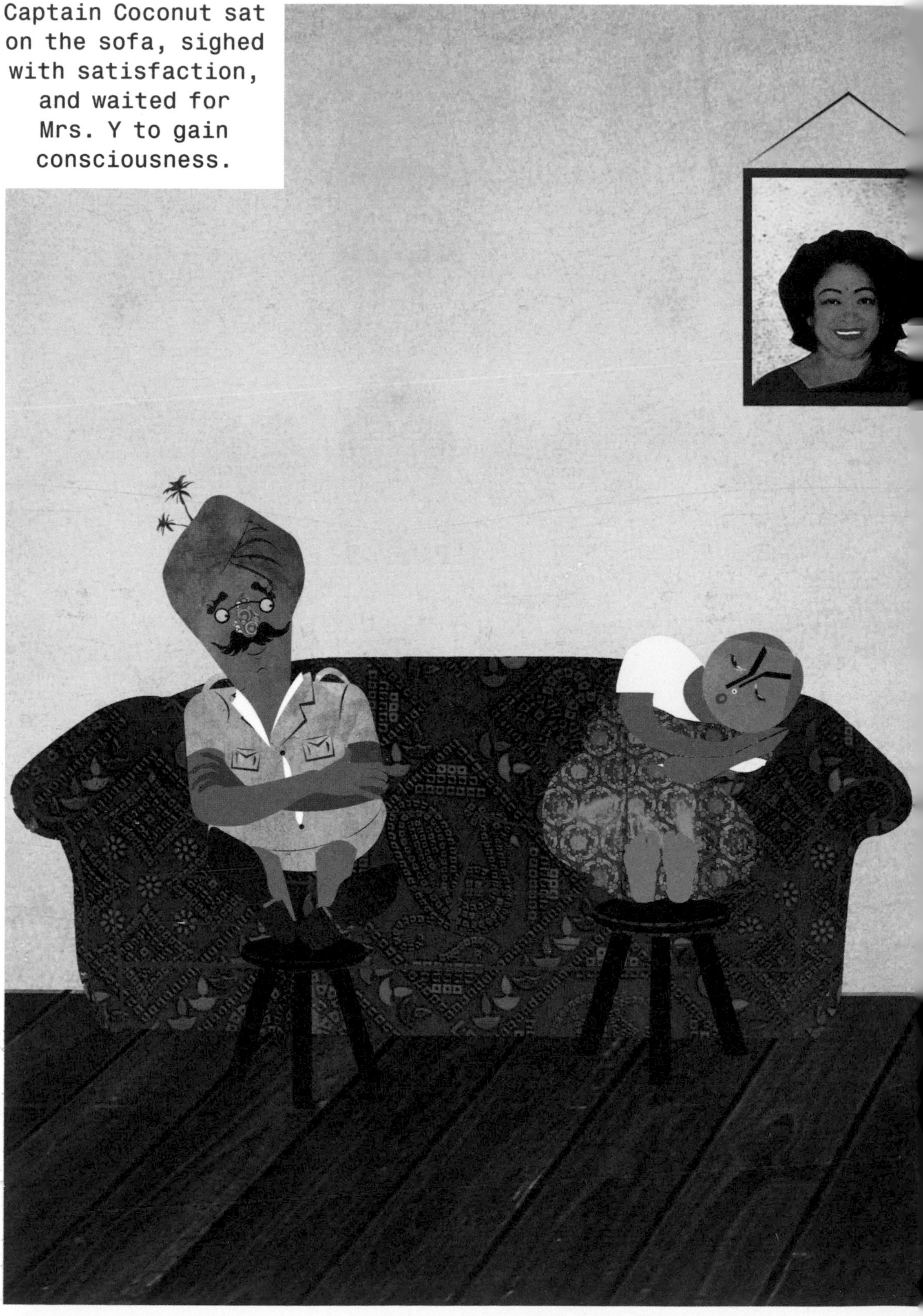

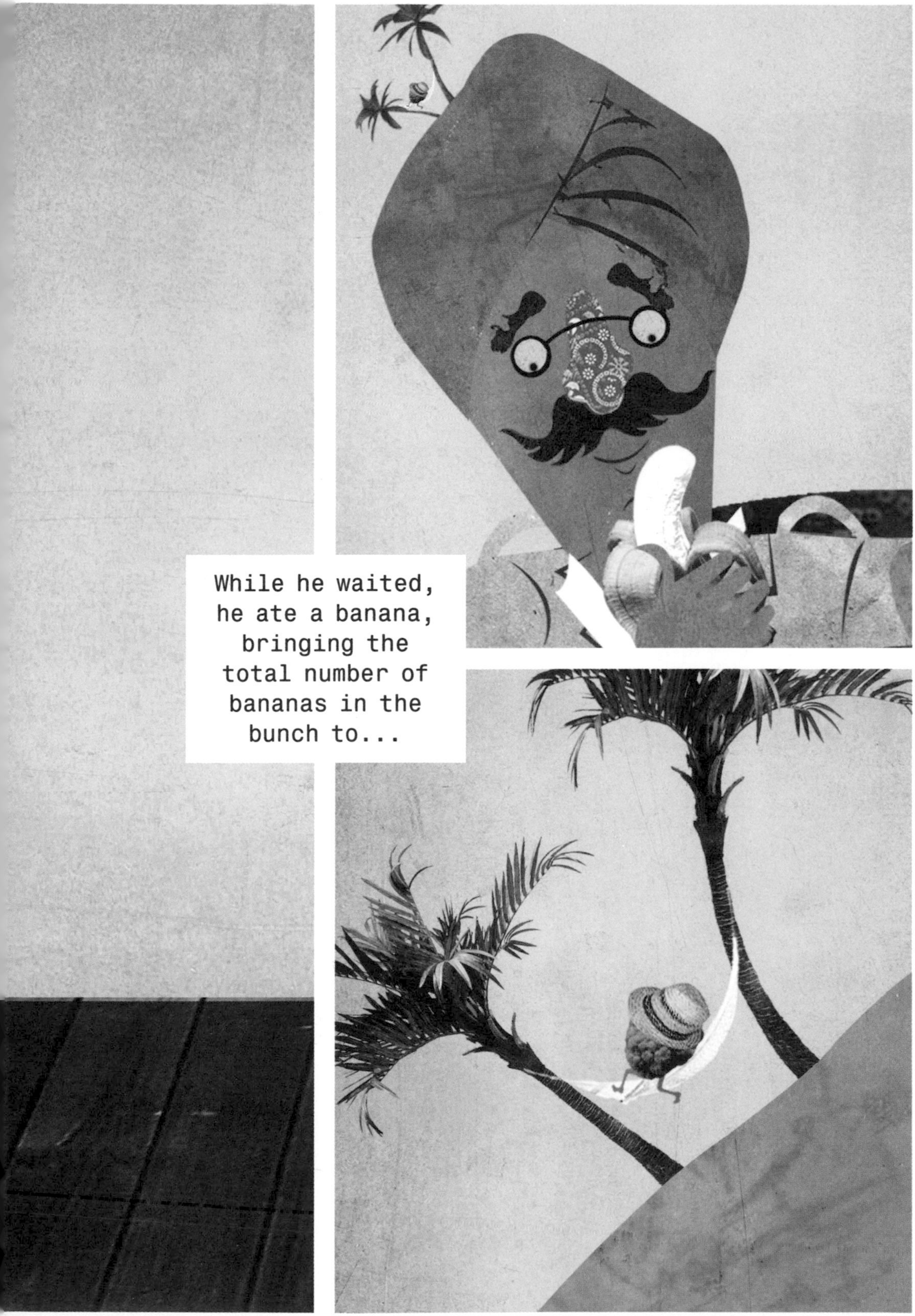
While he waited, he ate a banana, bringing the total number of bananas in the bunch to...

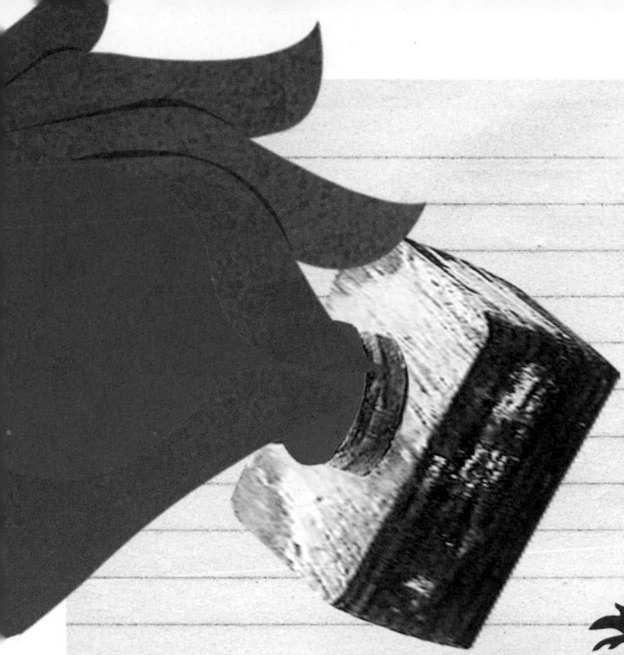

FOUR
5 -1 = 4.

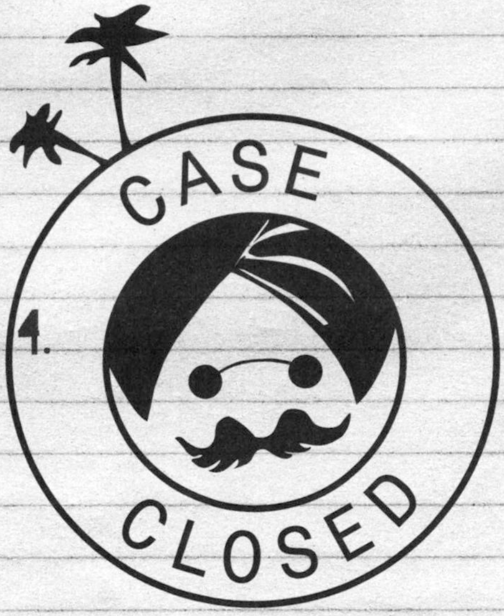
CASE
CLOSED

Captain Coconut
Copyright © 2014 Tara Books Private Limited

For the text: Anushka Ravishankar
For the illustrations: Priya Sundram

For this edition:
Tara Publishing Ltd., UK <www.tarabooks.com/uk>
and
Tara Books Pvt. Ltd., India <www.tarabooks.com>

Design: Nia Murphy
Production: C. Arumugam
Printed in China by Leo Paper Products Ltd.

ISBN: 978-93-83145-22-5

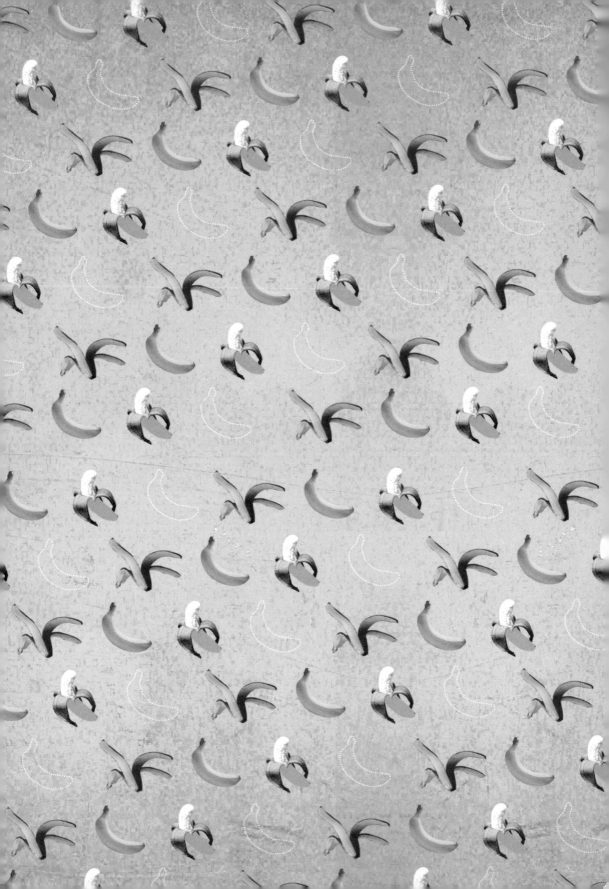